Two: Alone

Darlene Rose Busse

First printing

ISBN: 1-58851-081-6
PUBLISHED BY AMERICA HOUSE BOOK
PUBLISHERS
www.publishamerica.com
Baltimore

Printed in the United States of America

I dedicate this book to my best friend, Jesus.
May He be glorified.

Darlene

To Nerina!

You are such
a beautiful lady.
I am sure
your spirit is a
nice as you are.

ACKNOWLEDGMENT

In this information age, being computer illiterate has many disadvantages. In my case, it allowed me the privilege of seeing many of my church family and friends support me with their actions, words of encouragement, and prayers. They helped me make this book possible.

Thanks to:

Bonnie Christopher who volunteered many, many hours of typing and re-typing-until the final draft appeared. Her dedication overwhelms me and I will not forget what she did for me.

Cherry Dugan who did a terrific job on all my E-mail and computer correspondence. Although, physically unable to see, in reality has a spiritual sight of seeing what is deep in your heart.

Sharon Fonger, Cheryl Busse, Sally Schwartz, Janette Hyatt, Kathy Johnson and Amy Chilton.

To my sister, Anne Holderbein, who praised my every word.

To my Pastor, Ed Hyatt, who saw the good in me.

Special thanks to my husband, my children, sisters, brothers and friends, that let me share parts of their lives with others.

Finally, to AmErica House for taking a chance on me, an unknown author from small town Canada.

Each of you have helped me fulfill my dream.

Darlene Rose Busse

CONTENTS

Forward
Introduction

1   Reflections of a Little Girl:
            Fun and fear

2   Alone and Out of Control:
            Life without Jesus

3   Wasted Years:
            Rebellion and anger

4   A Glimpse of the Road Back:
            Are you there Lord?

5   I Hear You Lord!
            Decisions, decisions

6   I Taste the Wine; I Smell the Roses:
            The sting of the serpent

7   Two: Alone
            I speak but no one answers

8   Sink or Swim?
            Shall I drown or grow fins?

9   "Yet Shall I Trust In Him"
            "Though He slay me..." Job 13:15, KJV

10   Out of the Ashes:
            Restoration through Jesus

11   Alone With God:
          Here I am Lord, use me

12   Fill Up With Jesus:
          Empty is defeat - Full is victory

Let me introduce you to Heinrich and Irene Mueller:

Live in their story in Europe.
Travel with them as they are forced to leave their homeland.
Sail the ocean with them to Canada.
Homestead with them.
Share in Irene's pride and joy - her six children.
Cry for the children when they are physically and emotionally abused.
Rejoice with Irene as she gives her heart to Jesus.
Share in Irene's excitement when at the age of forty-one, she gives birth to her seventh child, a girl.

Susan Arlene: This Is Her Story!
Follow Susan as she changes from a happy little girl who loves Jesus into a rebellious teenager who wants God out of her life.
Feel her pain as she is sexually abused; and as a result ruins her life in "The World."
Grow up with her as she grows up with her children.
Listen with her as she hears God tugging at her heart strings.
Help her endure tragedy, betrayal and rejection.
Hurt with her through divorce.
Live in her re-marriage, "ALONE in a house of TWO."
Rejoice with her as she learns the secret to happiness.
Wrestle with her emotionally as she opposes God's will in her life.
Sense her anxiety and excitement as she becomes obedient to the Lord.
Finally, inhale the fragrance as she is restored to the beautiful sweet-smelling soul that God created.

As you read "TWO: ALONE":

I pray that if Jesus is tugging at your heart strings, you will run to Him. He will wrap His loving arms around you. He will heal your broken heart. He will restore your life and make you whole again.

I pray that you will learn how to be victorious in your Christian life.

I pray that you can live in peace and contentment in spite of your circumstances.

I pray that Jesus will become so real to you that as you walk beside Him, you will actually hear Him breathe.

Foreward

Over twenty years ago I met a devastated and broken Darlene Rose Busse. As I shared Jesus love with her I was convinced God had his hand upon her life. I also knew then that she had a story to tell. These many years later the story is ready to be told. *Two: Alone* is that story. I am deeply humbled and grateful to have played a small part in God's miracle of transformation.

Darlene is a Christian on a journey, as you will discover in her book. In no way does she pretend to have arrived or want to glorify the broken experiences of her life. In her heart she possesses a desire to see others touched by God's great love and kindness. She has a deep longing to turn the events of her life into gold for the Kingdom of God. I personally can only cheer her on for her courage, transparency and devotion to God. I can personally attest to the veracity of the story. This is her life. The miracle and the heart of the story is God's saving and transforming love. Darlene has experienced the transformational power of God. She has grown to be a woman with a heart and soul for God. She thinks deeply and cares deeply. In the Church fellowship and in the world around her she seeks to live out her faith in, and love for her Savior, Jesus Christ.

The book she has written speaks to our broken world. There are many people, especially women (possibly you), who will find her work helpful and full of hope. The practical lessons her life teaches provide direction for the seeker and the hurting. As I read the book I found myself being drawn into her life and touched by God's wonderful drawing love. If this happened to me, I believe it can happen to you. As you read may you

encounter the one she met and discover love as never before.
Thank you Darlene for sharing your story.

Dr. Ed Hyatt
Senior Pastor
East Side Church of God
Swift Current, Saskatchewan, Canada

INTRODUCTION

The year is 1922. It is summer in the village of Ramonouel, Romania.

Irene is brushing her long brown hair almost mechanically as she stares out her bedroom window. She is gazing at the beauty of her family's peaceful farm yard.

She inhales the sweet smell of flowers blooming, holds it for a second, then slowly releases the wonderful aroma from her nostrils. "I have to do this every day for the next month," she tells herself, "so that I can remember this after I'm married."

The thought of marriage brings her back to reality. She giggles a little as she thinks of Clarence. He is so handsome. Irene is only seventeen and very shy, so even the thought of a husband makes her blush. She hurriedly puts her hair in a bun at the back of her head and runs down to the kitchen to help make breakfast.

She is late and everyone is already seated. She quickly takes her seat and whispers, "Sorry Mama." Irene's stepfather John now sits at the head of the table where her father used to sit. Her real father died when she was young. John is a good man, but she misses her father sometimes.

The children are seated according to age. Irene sits next to her oldest stepsister, Ida. They are close because they do much of the heavy work together. They milk the cows, do the gardening, cooking, baking, cleaning, and wash the dishes. Next is Christina.

She is the favourite, and doesn't have to do hard work. She is a seamstress. The rest of the children at the table are from John's previous marriage. His wife Katreena died many years ago.

The family is busily chatting in German. No one in their village speaks English. Suddenly, there is a loud knock on the door. Silence falls over the kitchen. "Come quickly Irene, Clarence is very sick." It is Heinrich, Clarence's younger brother.

Clarence and Heinrich come from a wealthy family. Their family owns a flour mill that employs many people. Clarence, being the oldest, has to stay home and help run the mill. Heinrich is younger, and not allowed to help.

The two brothers are not at all alike. Clarence is kind and gentle; Heinrich is rigid and stern. He is quick tempered and has a mean streak. However, his personality enables him to survive his time in the fierce Romanian army. Irene doesn't like him much.

Irene's heart is pounding so hard she can't hear her feet hitting the ground. She is running as fast as a deer, yet it seems as if she is in slow motion. "Please be all right, please be all right," she pleads as she arrives at his house. "He's got the Consumption," she is told as she enters his room.

Irene gasps and takes a step back when she sees Clarence lying there. Except for the movement of his body when he coughs, he looks like he is dead. "I'll sit with him for a while," she tells the family. After they leave she tenderly takes his hand and strokes it. She feels such love. "This is going to be my husband," she tells herself. She whispers just loud enough for Clarence to hear, "Please get well."

The sunshine is very bright the day of the funeral, but to Irene it seems dull and cloudy. She thinks it might rain. "How can I live without Clarence? What about our wedding, all our plans?" There are so many unanswered questions. "I don't know if I can make it through this funeral," she thinks as she walks into the church. She doesn't look around, but she knows the church is full.

The flour mill is closed for the day. The employees want to pay their last respects to the family, because they loved Clarence too. He will be missed at the mill. She wants to scream: "Everybody go home! It's all a mistake! There's nobody in that coffin!" Irene doesn't hear one word that is being said. Her ears have gone numb along with the rest of her body. "Why are people looking at me?" She imagines they are wondering why she isn't crying. "Don't they know I have no tears left? I will never be happy again."

The gentle tapping on Irene's door breaks the deafening silence. "Go away!" The tapping continues. "I don't want to talk to anybody," she yells. "Irene, Heinrich is here to see you," her Mama offers. "You must see him. You know you have to marry him now that Clarence is gone. We already have the dowry, and Heinrich is the next in line for marriage." Irene leaps off her bed and throws open the door. "Please, Mama, don't make me marry him! You know I don't like him! I'm afraid of him!"

The wedding day is approaching too quickly. Irene is just starting to like Heinrich a little, but she certainly doesn't love him. She decides life isn't fair. She should already be happily married to Clarence.

Heinrich is taking her to a dance in the village tonight. She doesn't like to dance, but her parents insist she go. "It would please Heinrich."

At the dance Heinrich offers her some wine. She doesn't like the taste of it, so he drinks enough for both of them. She tries to be happy but her heart isn't in it. The hours drag on, and finally the dance is over. "Now I can go home!" she whispers to herself.

Irene enjoys the walk home. The full moon is beautiful as it reflects a soft glow over the country side. She notices Heinrich is swaying a little, but doesn't worry about it. At the end of the pathway to her house, Irene says "Good night, Heinrich," and gives him a little peck on the cheek. He forcibly grabs her and pulls her into the bushes next to the road. She tries to push him away, but he pulls her tighter and tries to kiss her. She fights hard to get away, but he is too strong, and he forces his sexual desires on her. When it is over, Heinrich sneaks away like a rat that is exposed to the light. Irene buries her face in the grass and weeps. "I feel so ashamed! I hate him!"

The wedding is only a memory now. Married life is a little better than Irene expects it to be. Heinrich doesn't show much affection, but he is a good provider.

The months pass quickly as they await the arrival of their first baby. Labor is long and hard, but the midwife waits patiently until it is over. Sophia is born in October 1925.

Unrest in neighbouring Russia has erupted and the Russians are on the move. "The army is coming. What they aren't taking, they're burning," Heinrich informs Irene. "They have taken over our family's flour mill. We have nothing left. We must leave the country. I fear for our lives!"

They quickly sell everything they own, including Irene's wedding band. They take the clothes they are wearing, the small amount of cash they have gathered together, and their eighteen month old daughter, and they flee the country.

The "Metagama" is the biggest ship Heinrich and Irene have ever seen. They aren't sea sick, even though this is their first ocean voyage. While they are sailing through the English Channel, Heinrich is frantically running around the ship looking for the captain. He can't speak English, so it is difficult trying to explain to the captain that his wife is in labor.

After much commotion, the ship's doctor delivers a bouncing baby boy. Heinrich and Irene are very thankful to the doctor, and in honour of him, they name their son after him: Adolph "Ronald." It is March 1927.

Irene is crying as they finally board the train in Halifax. "How will we ever get all the way to Alberta? We can't speak English! Nobody understands us!" When the children fuss, Heinrich becomes irritated and tells Irene, "Keep them quiet!" After a few hours, everybody settles down and they even enjoy the train ride. "This country is beautiful," Irene ponders, "but it is so far from home."

Montreal: Canada Customs

Heinrich and Irene are completely lost. They look at each other and wonder, "What do we do now?" Heinrich tells Irene, "I must find someone who speaks English and German to help us." He leaves her and the children alone on a bench. She is frightened!

It seems like an eternity until Customs understands that they aren't criminals fleeing their country. "We are immigrating to Canada," Heinrich offers. "We want to be citizens. We have sponsors, so we have a place to go. I have a letter! We are going to Alberta." Finally, at the end of the day, Customs agrees to let them enter the country.

Back on the train the next morning, they start the last part of their journey. "Today it really feels like we are starting a new life," Irene tells her children. "We are taking you to your new home."

Irene's excitement fades a little as they start across the prairies. There is little to see. Miles and miles of hills and grass with very few trees and very few people. "I wonder what Ida is doing today? I miss her." Irene shakes her head a little as if waking from a bad dream. "It will be all right," she tells herself. She wiggles around in her seat until she gets comfortable. She decides not to worry.

Heinrich and Irene are hired hands on a farm near Medicine Hat. The work is hard and the pay is poor. After about a year, an opportunity arises for Heinrich to manage a ranch in the Cypress Hills. He jumps at the chance. They will have to put up hay feed for about two hundred
head of cattle. Irene works right along side Heinrich, even though she is pregnant. In March 1929 their third child is born. Her name is Anne.

Life seems to get harder for Irene. She is baking eight loaves of bread every day because she has to make lunches for Heinrich and the workers and then carry them to the field. It is a three to four mile return trip. Sophia and Adolph have to walk along. She knows she can't carry the food and the baby. She struggles with her decision, but she knows it is the only way.

Irene speaks gently to Anne as she puts her in the rocking chair. "I am so sorry, Anne. Mama has to tie you in this chair until we get back. I can't take you along. You will be safe here. Maybe you can have a little sleep. We must hurry now, because your father will be very angry if we are late." Her stomach ties itself in knots as she closes the door behind her.

To Irene's delight, the Mueller family continues to grow.

May 1931, a boy, William Fredrick.

December 1933, a boy, Norman Heinrich.

May 1935, a girl, Alice.

"That makes six," Irene counts. "I love them more than life itself. I am so lucky!"

Heinrich is not afraid to take a financial risk. Whenever an opportunity arises for him to purchase something that will make him some money, he takes advantage of it. His English is pretty good by this time and this helps him convince the banker that he is a good investment. Besides, Heinrich is a smooth talker.

Over the next few years, he buys thirteen quarters of land and a sawmill and planer. He has a good herd of cattle, horses, pigs and sheep. His biggest problem is still his quick temper and mean streak. He argues with his workers and neighbours, and sometimes he can be heard yelling "a mile away."

Through the years Irene has become very quiet and soft-spoken. "She wouldn't hurt a fly." She is known around the country for her good cooking and baking. It isn't uncommon for company to drop in 'just at mealtime.' Irene always finds enough food for everybody. "It is good to have company," she decides. "Heinrich is much nicer when people are here."

Irene is happiest when her children are around her. They aren't afraid of her. "It is good to hear my children laugh," she tells herself. "If only Heinrich wasn't so mean!"

The girls have to work hard. They work in the bush and the sawmill, as well as on the ranch. They think that their father hates them because he is always yelling at them. He shouts at them, "You're no good! Can't you do anything right?" The girls are happy when they can go to school. They feel special there because they find out that they can do lots of things 'right.'

The boys aren't so lucky. They can only go to school when they aren't needed at home, and that isn't very often. They work very hard. In the spring, summer, and fall, they do farm work. In the winter they work in the bush, and the sawmill, with their sisters. Sometimes the snow is so deep that they sink into it up to their waists. Their father gets so angry at them that he picks up whatever is close and starts swinging. One of the boys happens to be in the way of a chain. The beating doesn't stop until one of his ears is partially torn off.

Life is hard. Irene silently cries herself to sleep many nights. She cries for her children, her precious children. Her soul is in anguish. "Why can't Heinrich love his children? Why is he so cruel?" She wonders what life would have been like with Clarence.

Heinrich and Irene are asked to go along with some neighbours to a revival meeting. The church isn't far away; besides, they haven't been to church since their wedding back in Romania. "Can we please go, Heinrich?" she pleads. "It will be so nice to go to church again."

It is a beautiful summer evening - very warm. The Cypress Hills are especially beautiful this year - rain at just the right time. Tonight a very special event takes place in Irene's life. At the age of thirty-five, she gives her heart to Jesus.

From this night forward, Irene starts a Christian journey that impacts her family for the rest of their lives. The circumstances remain the same at home, but Irene is changed. She doesn't exactly know what has taken place, she only knows she feels happy enough to burst. It doesn't even make her cry when Heinrich calls her a "whore." "He can't hurt me anymore," she tells herself. "I have Jesus in my heart."

12:01 a.m. 1945: Irene wakes up abruptly, as if a gun has been shot. Her heart pounds hard for a few minutes, then quickly settles down to its normal rhythm. "A brand new year," she tells herself. "I wonder what this year has in store for us?" Her thoughts wander for a few minutes, then she drifts off to sleep again. She dreams of happy times, and soon it is morning.

The winter passes by quickly. It is already early spring. The white birch trees are bursting with buds, and the evergreens are changing from their almost black winter color. Some are a bright green, some are a beautiful blue-green. The crocuses are blooming everywhere, dotting the pastures with their purple colored petals. The Cypress Hills are coming alive. "Maybe this will be a good year," Irene hopes, as she breathes in the clean crisp air.

Years of watching her children being beaten and verbally attacked, years of being told she is "no good," have changed Irene into a very private person. She isn't able to share her feelings with anyone. There are two exceptions, however. One is her Lord and Saviour. The other is her best friend Hilda.

Gus and Hilda Schlenker are the closest neighbours. The two families spend many hours together. Gus and Heinrich are total opposites, in size as well as in personality. Heinrich is a big, strong, muscular man. He is hot tempered and considers himself to be quite a charmer. He has been told that he has beautiful eyes. Gus has a small build, but isn't a 'sissy.' He stands up to Heinrich when he thinks he is doing wrong. He has a strong body and a quiet spirit. These two men are an odd couple, but they are good friends. Heinrich seems to admire Gus for standing up to him.

Irene and Hilda are a perfect match. They both have gentle spirits and big hearts. Irene still wears her hair in a bun at the back of her head, even though it is graying a little, and she has put on a few pounds over the years. Hilda is short like Irene, but slimmer. She has very straight, dark auburn hair, cut one length to the shoulders. Her long bangs are pulled to one side with a barrette. She has the Post Office in her home and is the Post Mistress for the community. Irene and Hilda have a special bond between them.

Shirley is their only child. She loves to be with the 'Mueller' kids. They always have lots of fun together, because there is always something to do. Besides, Alice is her best friend. They are inseparable. They are 'sisters.'

By the end of April, Irene suspects that she is pregnant. Sophia suspects it, too, and asks her mom about it several times. Irene doesn't answer, so the question is finally dropped. She can hardly think about it herself yet. She is almost forty-one. Ten years without a baby; how is she going to tell Heinrich? She wonders if he will be angry. She wonders if she will be able to carry the baby at her age. She confides in her friend Hilda. Hilda assures her that it will be all right, and presses her to tell Heinrich. Finally, using all the courage she can find in her soul, she tells him the news. To her amazement, he is happy. Irene sighs with relief. Now she can be happy too. None of the children find out about the baby until late in the pregnancy. The ones that are away at school don't find out until the baby is born. It is a big surprise to them, but they are happy for their mother.

Over the years, Irene has developed some very large veins on her legs. The doctor says it is from being on her feet too many hours, and working too hard. Surgery is booked and some veins are removed. It is a painful surgery and she has to have complete bed rest for many weeks. Bed rest isn't as bad as Irene expects it to be. She is able to spend a lot of time with her friend, Jesus. She talks with Him often. She reads her German Bible and falls more in love with Him every day. She can tell Jesus her deepest desires and He will hear her, and He will comfort and love her. Irene does feel bad for Sophia, though. She will have to do all the work at home now, as well as nurse her back to health.

Summer is over. Anne has gone back to Camrose to finish high school. Alice and Norman are in school, and the rest are in the field every day. Sophia should also be going back to Bible School at Camrose. It is her second year, and she will graduate at the end of the year. She is looking forward to graduating, as both she and Anne are offered jobs as supervisors in two of the community schools.

Sophia is small in stature. She has dark shoulder length hair that falls into nice soft curls. She, like her father, has beautiful eyes. She is the oldest and feels she needs to be the family protector. Because she wants to stay home and help with the work, she will go back to Bible School after the harvest is over. It will not be a problem for her to catch up with her classes, as school isn't hard for her. She tells Irene, "Mother, I will stay home for a while after the baby is born and do the work. I want you to get your strength back." She knows it will be hard on her because she will have to do all the cooking and baking for the threshing crew, but somehow she will manage.

Dr. Kruger tells Irene she needs to deliver her baby in the hospital. He explains that the hospital in Medicine Hat has all the latest equipment. "There could be complications in the delivery because of your age," he informs her. Heinrich agrees, and it is settled.

Irene is happy about the decision. Other than Adolph, this will be their only baby born in a hospital. Twelve days is the usual hospital stay after having a baby. With the other five babies, she was allowed to rest the day she gave birth, but the next day she returned to her full work load.

Finally the day arrives. October 11, 1945. A girl. Everybody who sees her says she is a beautiful baby. Sophia can hardly wait to hold her. "What shall we call her?" Heinrich asks. After some discussion they come up with the name, "Jean." Sophia is horrified! She says, "She is too beautiful to be just plain Jean. Let's call her Susan Arlene."

Irene loves it when the nurses bring her baby 'Susie' to her at feeding time. She kisses her little fingers and toes. She feels such love for this precious little girl the Lord has given to her. She marvels at her blonde hair. It seems strange to have such a "blondie," when all the
other children have dark hair. She prays that this little one will have a better life than her other six children. As Susan sleeps beside her on the bed, Irene's thoughts drift back in time.

She remembers the time Sophia is thirteen and beaten with a horse bridle until she passes out. No reason! She just happens to be the closest person to Heinrich when he loses his temper.

She remembers the time Adolph has to get the cows home to milk. He can't find them and Heinrich beats him "black and blue" with a tree branch.

She remembers the beatings Anne and William got.

Norman: Beat with a chain.

And Alice, my precious little girl. Spanked so hard as a baby, she passes out. The reason: Her eczema is very itchy.

She scratches until it is bleeding. It hurts. She cries and keeps Heinrich awake. She gets a good "licken."

Irene shakes her head, as if to clear out the bad memories. "I must remember the good things," she reminds herself.

She knows the children have lots of fun when their father isn't around. She can hear them laughing. They ride horses, play softball and pick berries in the bush. The boys "rough house" with each other. The girls watch and cheer. She knows they love to have friends over, because life is better with other people around. Shirley is their favorite friend. It seems they are always posing for pictures taken with the new "Brownie" camera.

Sometimes Irene has to laugh too:

She laughs whenever William hitches two small calves to a wagon and flips the reins like the adults do with the horses. "Giddy up, giddy up!" he yells, but they don't move. They only bellow for their mothers.

She loves to watch Norman ride William's horse, Dynamite. He rides like the wind! She marvels at his wonderful sense of humor. Norman loves to laugh and clown around.

She is thankful for Adolph, the protector. He is always trying to keep Norman out of trouble. That is a full time job.

She is thankful for Sophia, who watches over everybody.

She remembers how Alice loves coffee. Alice thinks sugar will cool her coffee. There is always more sugar in her coffee than milk ... or the home-made butter she eats by the spoonfuls when she thinks nobody is watching her.

She laughs when she hears one of the boys' friends ask Anne to go out with him, and her reply is, "Go stick your head in the slop pail."

She chuckles to herself when something happens that 'nobody' is going to take the blame for. They tell their father, "The wind must'a done it!"

Irene is starting to feel a little drowsy so she decides to have a nap while Susie is sleeping. The memories will wait.

CHAPTER ONE

Reflections of a Little Girl:

Fun and fear

Today, I, Susan Arlene, am going to my new home for the very first time. I can't see anybody yet, but I can feel that I am loved. I have brothers and sisters waiting to hold me and spoil me. I hope my daddy will love me too. My Auntie Hilda and Uncle Gus love me, and so does my "other sister" Shirley. All I am going to do for a while is drink, burp, sleep, and get my diapers changed. I can hardly wait to see everybody, and walk and talk.

When it finally happens, I know my life will really begin! I feel happy and secure. Why shouldn't I? Everybody loves me.

When I am older I am going to be like Christopher Columbus, who "sailed the ocean blue." He wanted to discover what was just over the horizon. There will be so much for me to explore in these Cypress Hills. Besides, there isn't much else to do. All my brothers and sisters are at school, or away at Bible School, or working in the field all the time. I am a little lonely, but I have my rag doll Snuggles with me. We go everywhere together. She is soft and cuddly, with short, white fur for hair. She has pretty blue eyes, a cute little pug nose and pink lips. My mom says she is pretty like me. I think if she looks like me, then she can be my little sister. Snuggles and I talk to each other all the time. She is my best friend, and we really love each other. I'm not lonely when she is with me.

Snuggles and I do lots of stuff together. When I put my rubber boots on to play in the mud, she asks, "Can I come too?" So I take her along. When I have a tea party, she lets me serve her tea and cookies. We make mud pies too. We put the mud dough into my little cake tins and let the dough bake in the sun. When they are cooked, we ask our pretend friends over for dinner. But our most favorite thing to do is tear the catalogue pages into nice little strips, put them in a big pot, sneak some salt and pepper from the kitchen, mix it all up with lots of water, pretend-cook it and then pretend-eat it. Snuggles has to sneeze a lot, though.

Saturday night is my favorite night of the whole week, because it is bath night. My mom pulls out the old, grey, tin bathtub. She puts it in front of the warm wood- and coal-burning stove; then she pours some hot water in it. I am lucky; I can bathe first because I am the youngest. I want Snuggles to bathe with me because she got dirty playing in the mud, but my mom says she can't because she will shrink if she gets wet. I hope I'm not going to shrink, because I want to get big like my sisters.

Next to bathe is my sister Alice, then my brother Norm. My mom keeps adding hot water. Next is my brother Bill. By the time it is my dad's turn to bathe, the water is pretty dirty. He doesn't seem to care, because he takes his turn too. I wonder how such a big man can fit into such a little tub. Afterward, my mom cuts a white tea towel into long narrow strips and wraps small strands of my hair into the strips and ties them up. In the morning I will have beautiful ringlets and curls. I love to get my hair curled. It makes me feel pretty.

After we all finish our baths, my mom gives us a cup of warm milk with sugar in it. We can have a piece of cake, or pie, or a cookie or two. Then off to bed we go.

I love our ranch house. My dad and my brothers built it. My dad is a good carpenter. Our house has two floors and lots of windows. It is painted white with blue trim. I like it because it looks like the sky.

The dining room is my favorite room in the whole house. It has a big, long wooden table with lots of chairs around it. In this room my family is together. After we pray in the morning, my dad turns the big battery radio on. We listen to the news. The words come all the way from another country. "Great Falls, Montana." Every morning there is a man on the battery radio who has a real deep voice. He booms out the words, "DON'T SAY COFFEE - SAY FOLGERS." I like the sound of his voice, and I like coffee too.

My brothers and sisters aren't allowed a long time to eat. Sometimes I think they don't even chew their food - they just swallow it whole. They 'gobble' everything down fast, so that when my dad says, "Let's go," they are full and ready to go back to work.

It is really fun when my mom and dad go to Medicine Hat for supplies and we have to stay home. We kids can fool around and have fun at the table. Today Bill is sitting at the head of the table where my dad always sits. He puts his hands on the arms of the chair, sits up straight and says, "Let's pray - Amen - Hitch up, boys." Everybody laughs and laughs, but nobody has to hurry. Today we can take as much time as we want.

The kitchen is a good room too. There is always the really good smell of fresh bread baking, and something is always cooking on the stove. We have lots of homemade soup and sausage. Each of my brothers and sisters has a different kind of favorite soup. I don't know how she does it, but sometimes my mom makes six different kinds of soup at once. That makes us feel really special. We really love our mom.

Just next to the dining room is the one room in the house I don't like. It is the living room, and my bed is in it. The room is very big and it always looks dark inside. I am afraid in there. I hate to have my afternoon nap because I am afraid that if I shut my eyes something will get me. At night, after all the coal oil lamps are blown out, it is so dark in there that I can't see my fingers when I wiggle them in front of my eyes. My mom and dad are just in the next room, so sometimes when I am really afraid I whisper, "Mom!" She is sleeping and doesn't hear me. So I whisper a little louder, "Mom!" She still doesn't hear me. I can't whisper any louder and I can't talk out loud because then my dad will wake up and be angry at me. Snuggles is afraid too. We swallow real hard, close our eyes real tight, and think about happy things. Finally we fall asleep.

The living room is where the adults visit, so I am always real happy when we have company. I can't go to sleep while they are visiting, so that means I can go upstairs and sleep in one of the two bedrooms with my sisters. I feel safe with them and I'm not afraid anymore. I am really protected up there. All three of my brothers sleep upstairs, too, in one big room across the hall from us.

In the summer we don't cook or eat in the big house unless we have company. My dad and my brothers built a little square building that they call the 'summer house.' It is white with blue trim, like the big house. In front, there is a white fence that I love to climb on. I can see the whole inside of the house at once and there isn't one place in it that is scary. It is like a big playhouse. There is a huge table in the middle of the room where the whole family sits to eat. Against one wall, there are some softer chairs where my dad and my brothers sit while the food is being dished up. The cupboards and the wash basin are along another wall. Another wall has a huge black and silver coal and wood burning stove in front of it. The coal pail sits beside it.

This stove is bigger than the one in the main house. My mom needs more room on this stove because she has to make jam and can fresh berries that my brothers and sisters pick. She cans lots of other stuff too, but the raspberry jam and peaches are my favorites.

Auntie Hilda gave me a new set of little dishes for my tea parties. I am happy because the little tea kettle has a whistle in it. When the water starts to boil, it whistles to tell me the water is just right for tea. It doesn't take very long to whistle, because there is only enough water in it for one cup of tea for Snuggles and me. My mom always has the water boiled so that we can have tea for dinner.

One day my mom forgets to put the tea kettle on the stove, so she puts it on just as we are sitting down to eat. Mealtime is serious business at our house; no fooling around, just eat as fast as you can and get back to work. While we are praying, the little tea kettle starts to whistle. It is whistling really loud. I am thinking, "Oh, oh, I'm going to get it now." I look up at my brothers and sisters. They are trying hard not to laugh. I look at my dad. He just keeps his eyes closed and his head forward. We are all surprised when all my dad says is, "The water's boiling." This is my lucky day! No 'licken' today!

Spring time on the ranch means there is lots of work to do and everybody has to work real hard. After the crop is seeded it's haying time. We have lots of cattle and horses, so they need lots to eat. Haying time is fun for me though, because I'm too little to work. My dad always cuts the hay, and after it dries, Anne and Bill rake it into straight rows with two big rakes and two teams of horses. Norm and Alice each have a hay wagon and a team of horses to haul the hay back to the yard. I love to watch them unload the hay wagons. They drive up to a big derrick that is shaped like a pyramid with a square top. It is so high that I have to put my head way back to see the top. The hay on the wagon is fastened with some ropes and steel things that my mom calls cables. Then the horses slowly pull the load 'way to the top of the derrick. The cables make a big 'snapping' sound, the ropes fall off and the hay falls all the way to the ground in a pile. The pile gets so high that it almost touches the sky. It is so much fun to watch. When everybody goes back out to the field, I roll around in the hay. I love the smell of it.

Haying is almost over. My mom and I are watching Alice bring the last load of hay to the yard. She is hurrying because a big storm is brewing close by. Just when she gets to the edge of the yard, lightning strikes the tree in front of her. There is a very bright flash of light, and right away there is a big, big bang. The team of horses gets spooked and starts running. Alice can't hold them back and they start running toward me. I am really scared! I start to run across the creek that flows down the middle of the yard, beside the road. My little legs are going as fast as they can, but the horses and wagon keep coming toward me. I just about make it across the creek when I slip and fall. One of the horses kicks my head with its hoof. I can't remember what happens next, but when I wake up, Alice is sitting beside me crying. She says, "I'm sorry, Susie." I know it's not her fault, but my dad beat her anyway. He told her she was no good and if she wasn't so dumb, she could have held the horses back. I don't like thunder and lightning anymore. Now I always hide under the bed when it is thundering and lightning. I am really afraid!

One day I overhear my mom and dad talking about her stepsister, Ida. They are saying that now that the war is over, Ida, her husband Otto, and her stepfather, John, want to come to Canada. They don't have the money to come, so they want my mom and dad to help them. My mom and dad have enough money to sponsor them, so my mom will write them and tell them to come to our place and stay with us until they can find work. My mom is very excited because she hasn't seen her sister for almost twenty years.

Summer is the best time of the whole year. There is so much to see and do. The yard has so many places to explore. My brothers and sisters are home too. I love to be with them and just watch them do all kinds of stuff.

I love it when my brothers have to milk the cows, because then I know they are going to feed the kittens. They try to squirt milk into their little mouths from a long way away. The kittens get milk in their eyes, their ears, their noses: everywhere! When some milk does go into their mouths, they swallow real fast so that they can get more to drink.

I love to play with my dogs, Skippy and Shippy. Skippy is the young, black and white dog. Shippy is yellow and white. He is older and is a little grumpy. One day when I pulled his tail, he bit my nose. It hurt and I cried. My mom kissed it better.

I love to lie on the little wooden walk bridge that goes across the creek by the summer house. I like the sound of the 'plop' when I throw a little rock in the water. The splash makes ripples in the water that get bigger and bigger until they are gone.

I love to watch the leaves on the trees as they flutter in the wind. The tips of the leaves shine like silver when they move. I can even hear the leaves flutter; it sounds the same as dry leaves crushing under my feet when I jump on them in the fall.

I love to ride my horse, Moonshine. It really isn't my horse. It belongs to Alice, but she lets me say it's mine because she is nice. Moonshine is nice too. He walks slow and doesn't buck me off.

I love it when my dad brings home some dry ice from Medicine Hat. That means we are going to have homemade ice cream. My mom makes two kinds - vanilla and chocolate. My dad turns the handle on the ice cream maker, 'round and 'round, for a long time until finally the ice cream is frozen. It seems like it takes a hundred years. I can hardly wait to taste it! The whole family loves my mom's ice cream. It is a special treat.

I don't like to go close to the chicken coop or the turkey house. I don't like to step in the mess they make all over the yard. There is a big turkey gobbler that doesn't like me. He always chases me and I run to my mom, crying. She says,

"Well, don't go there anymore," but I just have to go back there again.

I don't like it when I sit on an anthill while I'm playing with my pet lamb, and I really don't like it when I find out I'm eating lamb chops. I think I ate my lamb. Then I feel sick to my tummy.

One day while I am outside playing, I hear my dad and Uncle Gus yelling at each other. I get as close as I can without them seeing me. My mom is there too, and she is crying. Uncle Gus is yelling at my dad, "Why are you cheating on Irene? Mueller, are you crazy?" My dad is yelling back, "It's none of your business, you old goat!" Uncle Gus says to my dad, "You better look out or I'll whop you!" They yell lots more, then finally quit. I am so scared! I don't know what cheating is, but I know it's bad. I don't say a word to anyone but Snuggles.

I get scared easy now when I hear yelling. One day I hear some yelling coming from outside. As I jump up on the cupboard to see what's going on, I can see my dad is hitting one of my brothers with something he has in his hand. I don't know what it is, but my brother is crying out loud, "I won't do it again I promise! I won't do it again!" I am really scared and I start to shake. My mom comes over to me, takes me down from the cupboard, and holds me close. She says, "Susie, you shouldn't be watching." I can see she is crying.

My heart says, "I don't like my dad for always making my mom cry." My heart says, "I don't like my dad for always hurting my brothers and sisters!" I'm too little to be so afraid of my dad. I hope it will get better soon. I don't want to be like my dad, because he makes everybody cry. I just want to have fun and be happy.

One day late in summer, I hear my mom say to Alice, "Today is a very happy day for me. I finally get to see my sister, Ida, after so many years!" My mom and dad are going to

Medicine Hat to pick them up, and while they are gone I am busy practicing how to say "Hello," in German. I think I'm supposed to say, "Gooten Daug," or something. Mom says my aunt and uncle can only speak a little English. I don't understand how a 'Good Dog' can mean hello, but I'm going to keep practicing.

I watch the road all day for the car to come home. I am happy to have another aunt and uncle. I hope they are as nice as Uncle Gus and Auntie Hilda. I wonder what they will look like? Will my aunt look like my mom? Will my dad and uncle be friends? Will they like me? I hope they like me because I'm going to like them. I look down the road a hundred times to see if they are coming. Finally they are here.

When my Uncle Otto gets out of the car and stands up, I can't believe my eyes. He is so tall and has big, big muscles on his arms, and a big smile on his big, round face. When he laughs, his whole body shakes like jelly. He comes right over to me, gives me a hug and kiss and says something to me in German that I don't understand. "I forget what I'm supposed to say to you," I tell him. He laughs, but I don't think he understands me. Then he picks me up, puts me way up on his shoulders and he and my dad walk all around the yard, looking things over. I like him. I think he likes me too.

After a while Uncle Otto puts me down from his shoulders so that I can go in the house and be with my mom and Aunt Ida. "I have to look her over too," I tell myself. When I walk in they are laughing and talking. I can't understand them, but I know they are happy. I'm happy too. It's nice to see my mom laughing.

At supper time, I watch my new aunt and uncle really close. I see that Uncle Otto has really big hands. I wonder if he ever hits anybody with them? I don't think so, because he is smiling all the time. Aunt Ida is a little taller than my mom and slimmer. They really don't look like sisters, except their noses look the same. I like to listen to them talking and laughing. "I think this is going to be good," I tell myself.

As I am coming down the stairs one morning for breakfast, I miss one step and start to fall. I roll and roll, until I finally hit the bottom. I try, but I can't get up. I start to cry, "I can't get up! I can't get up!" By this time, everybody is here to see what has happened. Uncle Otto picks me up in his big arms, and gently carries me to my bed. I can't walk for a whole week. It isn't a bad thing for me to be in bed all week because everybody comes to check on me, and brings me stuff. This is more fun than being sick with tonsils. When I get sick with tonsils I don't feel good, and my throat hurts, and I have a fever.

By the time the week is over, Uncle Otto and I are really good friends. I think Snuggles feels left out, though. I'm all better now, so I can play again. Aunt Ida says I can play dress up with some of her clothes and jewelry. She has pretty things for me to wear. I feel all grown up in her dresses and shoes.

One night while we are eating supper, Uncle Otto tells us he was in the Nazi army. He said, "It was very hard for me there. I didn't want to join the Nazis, but some soldiers came to my parents' house and told them their boys had to join the army or everybody in the house would be shot." He said he had to do some bad things, but he was afraid the soldiers would shoot his mom and dad if he didn't do what he was told. I don't understand what all these words mean, but I'm glad he is here on our ranch, and not shot dead.

My dad and Uncle Otto are not real good friends. I think my dad is a little bit afraid of him. He is so big and strong, and he tells my dad he doesn't like the way he treats his wife and children. Uncle Otto protects me from getting a licken from my dad. When I do something wrong and I think I'm going to get it, I run to my uncle. He puts me up on his shoulders and says to my dad, "If you want her, you have to go through me first!" My dad turns and walks away, but I know he is angry. I sure like it when my uncle protects me.

Summer is almost over, and I am sad. Uncle Otto is leaving me. He is going to be an engineer for the Canadian Pacific Railway. He is going to drive a big train. They are moving to Medicine Hat. I will miss him very much. Who will protect me from my dad? Maybe Uncle Gus will?

My dad says he is going to buy a bunch of baby calves. He says he's going to let them grow big, sell them, and make a profit. The banker will give my dad the money to buy them. I think it is called a loan, because he has to pay the money back. The calves are kind of on loan. My mom says that we shouldn't buy calves right now because the prices are too high. My dad says to her, "You have to spend money to make money!" My dad doesn't listen to my mom and he buys fifty calves. Then one day at breakfast time, the man on the battery radio says, "Hoof and Mouth Disease causes prices to drop to an all-time low." My dad says, "Oh! Oh! We could lose our shirts!"

There are so many things I don't understand, but I know this is a bad thing. I keep watching to see if my dad loses his shirt, but he wears one every day so I guess he didn't lose it. Maybe he is just trying to scare us.

My dad doesn't let my mom have very much money. I know, because after my brothers milk the cows, they bring the milk to the house and take it to a little room by the kitchen. My mom puts the milk in some kind of a machine and turns the handle 'round and 'round. Something happens to the milk because it comes out of two different holes. Milk comes out of one and cream comes out of the other. My mom says it separates. When that is done, she makes some white stuff with the milk and sells it: cottage something. She sells the cream too. That's all the money she gets. My dad always has money, though, because sometimes when he opens his wallet, I see it.

Some of my brothers and sisters are going to Medicine Hat today. I want to go with them. My mom says I can't go. So I tell her, "I don't want to stay home with you! You are an Old Fogie!" She puts her head down and I know she feels bad, but I don't care, because I'm spoiled and I want my way. Then I start to cry, but I still can't go along. Snuggles and I are going upstairs and we are going to stomp all the way up because I am pouting. I feel really sorry for myself! After a while, my heart starts to feel sad for saying that to my mom, so Snuggles and I go downstairs and tell my mom we are sorry. She gives us both a big hug and kiss and tells us she loves us.

My mom and some of my brothers and sisters are going to dig up the vegetables from the garden today and I have to help. I like potatoes the best and onions too. When we get back to the house, we have to take all the vegetables down to the root cellar under the house. It's a real scary place! My mom always makes me carry some carrots down there. It smells like mouldy dirt, and it's real dark. I drop the carrots and run for my life! My mom laughs and says, "Susie, you are being silly." "I don't care! I'm getting out of here!"

Autumn in the Cypress Hills is so pretty. There are so many trees and they look like they are all changing clothes. They must be tired of wearing green clothes all the time. Some trees change into yellow clothes, some into gold clothes, and some into different shades of brown clothes. I like Autumn because it will soon be harvest time and everybody is happy at harvest time, even my dad.

My dad and Al cut the barley, wheat, and oats into bundles with the binder. Then the rest of my family stands the bundles into piles to dry. My mom says we are 'stooking.' All of a sudden the threshing crew is here. There are lots of people around and everybody is talking and laughing. Anne and Bill load a bunch of 'sheaves' onto a wagon and bring them to the threshing machine. Anne says, "This work is too hard for a girl," but she has to do it anyway.

The threshing machine has a big mouth at the back end of it. Some men feed it the bundles. The threshing machine must be really hungry because it eats up all the sheaves and spits out the seeds at the front end. Nobody is getting angry, so it must be all right.

I can see my mom coming with dinner for everybody. She walked all the way from the house. The threshing crew loves my mom's cooking and baking, and they tell her she is the best cook in the whole Cypress Hills. I think so too. She is happy to hear nice things.

My dad must be happy too, because after dinner, before the men go to work again, they take turns wrestling with my dad. My dad loves to wrestle. When they are wrestling, some men make grunting noises like the little pigs do, and some get angry when they lose, because my dad wins lots of times. After a few days all the stooks are gone, and so are the men. Harvest is over and it's quiet again.

One day while Snuggles and I are playing with the kittens in the hayloft of the barn, my mom and dad come in to start milking the cows. We lie real quiet so they can't hear us, because we're not supposed to be up here. My mom says we can fall and break our necks. I hear my dad tell my mom about a lot in Medicine Hat. I whisper to Snuggles, "A lot of what?" She doesn't know either. Then my dad says, "I think it's time for the boys to take over." I don't understand this either. There is so much stuff that grown-ups talk about that I don't understand. I hope I grow up real soon so I can be smart like my mom and dad. As soon as my brothers come in to help milk, they don't talk about it anymore.

Every December, my dad and my brothers butcher a pig and a cow. It is fun because everybody has to help, even me. We cut and wrap some of the meat and put it into the summer house to freeze. We grind up the rest of the meat and make hamburger and sausage. After the sausage is made, my mom fries some up for supper. I make a sandwich with a bun, raspberry jam and sausage. Snuggles doesn't want any of my sandwich. She says it tastes funny, so I eat it all.

Pretty soon it starts to snow. We get lots of snow in the Cypress Hills. I love the snow because I can go and lie in it and make angels all over the yard. It's really easy to make angels. All I have to do is move both arms up and down in the snow to make the wings, and move my legs from side to side to make the skirt to cover their legs. They lie there until it snows again and then I have to go and make some more angels.

The big house is cold in the winter, so I don't like to get up early. My mom gets up really early, though, to start a fire in the stove. Then she puts a bunch of wood and coal in the stove and when it is nice and warm in the kitchen, she comes to my bed and says, "You can get up now, Susie. It's nice and warm." My mom is so nice to me.

After breakfast I ask my dad if I can go with him and my brothers to feed the cattle. He says, "Yes, you can, but you have to bundle up good because it's cold out." As soon as I'm all bundled up, we go out to the barn and hitch up the horses to the wagon. My dad says "giddy up," and away we go down to the big stack of hay under the big, tall derrick. They load a bunch of hay on the wagon with pitchforks and away we go to the corrals. My dad yells, "Come Bossie! Come Bossie!" and the cows come running because they are hungry. I go with my dad every day, unless I am sick with tonsils again.

In the spring, my mom and dad tell us that we are going to build a house in Medicine Hat and we should be moved in by the fall. My brothers will stay on the ranch, and Alice and I will go to Medicine Hat with them. I can hardly believe my ears! I don't want to leave here! I start to cry really hard. In between big sobs I tell my Mom, "I don't want to leave my dogs and my kittens, or my horse and my lambs! I'll even miss the turkey gobbler that chases me. Who will feed my pets? Please, Mom, can't I stay with my brothers? They won't care if I stay! I'm almost five, so I can look after myself." My mom cradles me in her arms and says, "I'm sorry, Susie, but it's all settled."

I am going to cry until I have no more tears in my eyes. I am going to stomp my feet and stick my bottom lip out and pout. My mom says we are going to move to Medicine Hat and that's that. "Why don't you just have lots of fun on the ranch for the rest of the summer and we'll worry about moving later?" I know my mom is trying to cheer me up and I think she has a good idea. I AM going to have fun this summer!

My dad and my brothers go to Medicine Hat every day to build our new house. Today Snuggles and I are going along with my mom to watch because my dad says, "We're going to 'rough it in' today." I'm a little bit scared because I think that my dad is going to be rough with my brothers. I am happy when I find out they are just going to put the walls up.

On the way back to the ranch I whisper in Snuggles' ear, "As soon as we get home, we're going to go down to the gas house and hide where nobody can find us." Snuggles and I hide in the gas house lots of times because there are lots of barrels of gas with pumps on them, and lots of big pails of oil and grease. We pretend the barrels are big mountains and the pumps are the snow on top. The pails are our horses. I am riding Moonshine, and Snuggles is riding Dynamite, my brother's horse. He wants to buck her off, but she hangs on real tight. We are running away, because if we run away we won't have to move. Snuggles and I don't know how to drive a car, and besides, it makes too much noise. My mom will hear us when we leave and try to bring us back. Snuggles is getting sleepy now, so we decide to leave the mountains and go home to bed. We both wave good-bye to the horses and tell them we'll be back soon.

Snuggles and I like to sit on the front steps of the big house and watch Norm ride Dynamite. Dynamite is a big, shiny black horse, with a white diamond on his forehead. Norm likes him because he runs fast and bucks lots. Bill likes to try and make him buck. I think he wants to see Norm get bucked off, because he makes a loud clicking noise with his tongue and Dynamite bucks real high. Norm always comes over to Bill and says, "He can't buck me off - I'm the best rider in the whole world!" They both laugh real hard and then they do it all over again. I tell Snuggles that I think boys are silly.

Snuggles and I are playing really hard and having lots of fun. We are doing all our favorite things because we know we won't be playing here again next summer. We are making extra mud pies to take along to Medicine Hat because we are afraid there might not be good tasting dirt there. I'm not letting my dogs out of my sight for one minute, either, because if I play with them lots they won't forget me when I'm gone.

All of a sudden summer is over, harvest is over, and all the fall work is done. The house in town is finished and we are starting to pack. Snuggles and I are helping my mom pack the kitchen stuff. She needs help because we have to leave some dishes for my brothers. My mom says they are going to 'batch.' I think that means that there aren't going to be any girls living here. I hope somebody knows how to cook, or they'll get awful hungry.

I am trying to sleep a long time this morning because I know today is moving day. I still don't want to move, but at least now I don't cry all the time when I think about it. I won't be alone, though, because Alice and Shirl are coming along. My two sisters are going to finish school in Medicine Hat. Everybody but me is busy loading stuff on the big truck. I can't help because they say I'll get in the way, so Snuggles and I watch to see that everything gets put on the truck the right way. My mom says we are the inspectors. After lots of lifting and pushing, the truck is packed. This is it! Snuggles and I are getting into the car with my mom and dad and my sisters. My brothers are in the big truck. The motors start. We're moving. Snuggles and I hug each other. We can't look back or we'll start to cry. "Good-bye, everybody and everything. We'll miss you a lot!"

When we get to our new house in Medicine Hat, Snuggles and I are the last ones to get out of the car. Slowly we walk in the front door. We are really surprised how nice it is. There are so many windows, and it smells so clean. We decide it might be all right to live in this nice new house. We have to investigate!

Just inside the front door of the veranda is a treadle sewing machine, a big soft chair, and a bed that's just big enough for Snuggles and me.

The living room has a couch, two big soft chairs and "Yippee!" A piano! Snuggles and I can learn to play it!

The dining room has a brand new china hutch for my mom's good dishes, and a big table and chairs. There is a long mirror on the wall that is low enough for Snuggles and me to look at ourselves. We think we look nice. The floor is so shiny. My mom says it's hardwood and that I will have to help keep it clean.

The kitchen is long and narrow. The outside wall is all cupboards with a nice big sink in the middle. The sink has hot and cold running water; all we have to do is turn the handles and out it comes! We don't have to prime the pump, and pump and pump until finally some cold water comes out. Way at the end are three nice big windows. It is so bright with the sun shining in them. On the other side of the long kitchen is a door to the back entrance. That door has a lock on it. My mom says it has to stay locked so that nobody can come in. Next to the door is a brand new electric refrigerator and a gas stove. I have never seen a refrigerator before. It is really nice and white. My mom says it will keep the milk cold and the ice cream frozen. I don't understand about the cord. It is plugged into a square thing on the wall that's got electricity in it. The electricity makes the refrigerator get cold. The white gas stove has four things on it that my mom calls burners. All we have to do is turn the knobs, and 'Poof', the fire comes on. It has a really big oven so I know my mom will bake all my favorite stuff. No more wood to chop or coal to haul. I am happy! On the other side of the house are two bedrooms, one for my mom and dad and one for Alice and Shirl. Each room has a big bed and a chest of drawers for some socks and stuff. Both rooms have dressers with mirrors on them, and fancy chairs to push under the dressers. Now Snuggles and I can sit to curl our hair and still see ourselves. The closets aren't very big because we don't have many clothes.

In between the bedrooms is the bathroom. Snuggles and I can't believe what we are seeing! There is a big, white bathtub that has hot and cold water coming out of the same tap. In the corner is a nice white sink that I can wash my hands in after I make mud pies. I think everybody can have their own bath water now too! Snuggles and I think the toilet is the best, though. All we have to do is push a handle and all the water flushes away. We don't have to go outside anymore, and it won't be stinky all the time. I am really happy now! I like my new house.

As soon as we're all settled in our new house, my mom says we're going to have a wedding. My sister Sophia is getting married to a man named Ken. I like him because he tells funny stories and makes me laugh. After the wedding they are going to move to Northern Alberta, to a farm. All my brothers and sisters will be home for the wedding. I can hardly wait to see them!

Today is the wedding and Snuggles and I get to watch Sophia put on her wedding dress. She looks so beautiful! I look in the mirror and all of a sudden the bride is me, and my best friend Snuggles is helping me get dressed. We are beautiful too! I don't know who my groom is, but I know he is tall, dark and handsome. "Susie, Susie," my mom is calling, "it's time to go to the church."

Snuggles and I have never been to a wedding, so we are very excited. We are going to sit with my mom because my dad is going to walk in with my sister, and we all have to stand up when they walk by. She is so pretty! I love brides! I love weddings!

A few days after the wedding my mom and dad and Anne are going on a holiday to California. My other sisters and I have to stay home because my dad says it costs too much money for everybody to go. Snuggles and I don't like it one bit. My heart really feels sad and I start to cry. My mom feels sad too, so she holds me on her knee and rocks me like I'm her little baby. That makes me feel a little better because I know my mom loves me. My mom says my sisters will take good care of me and Snuggles, and my brothers will come and see us too. My mom says, "It won't be long and we'll be home again." I believe her, but I still want to go along.

It seems like they are gone a hundred years until one day we get a post card from the United States of America. On it is a picture of a big, big tree that has a big hole in the bottom of it, and there's a car sitting in the hole. The post card says it's a Redwood tree. Anne wrote on the card, "We'll be home soon." I tell Snuggles that I hope it's tomorrow because I miss my mom.

The first Sunday after my mom and dad get home from their holiday, my dad gets up and tells us we are all going to church today. He decided we are going to the German Church of God. My sisters and I really don't want to go because we can't speak or understand German, but my dad says we have to go. When we get there we sit at the back because it's our first time there. I like the music. There is lots of singing and a lady is playing the piano. There are some guitars too. It sounds really nice. A man starts to talk and I know he is praying, because when I look over at my mom, she has her head bent forward and her eyes are closed. I see my mom pray lots of times. I think she must be lonely because she talks to God a lot. Sometimes Snuggles and I are lonely too. Another man talks for a long time and then it's over. My family stands outside on the steps and people come over to shake our hands and welcome us. On the way home, my mom and dad decide we will go again. My mom says, "It is so good to be in God's house." My sisters just look at each other because they want to go to a church where they can understand the words.

It is so nice to be in our new house this winter. The house has a furnace in the basement that makes the warm come upstairs. I don't have to wait in bed in the morning for my mom to heat the kitchen. I can wear my summer nighty all winter. There is lots to do here in the winter too. When my sisters go skating on the outdoor rink, I go and watch them. I decide I'm going to skate, too, when I'm bigger. Some days, when it's not too cold, we go to a big hill and slide down it on a thing they call a toboggan. It's fun to come down, but my little legs have to work real hard to get back up to the top.

It's finally spring and the snow is all gone. Today Snuggles and I are going to help my mom plant the garden and we are going to put in lots of flowers too. I love flowers. Pink roses are my favorite. I hope my mom plants lots of roses. We are going to plant some grass and some trees too. We will have to put lots of water on all the stuff we plant. It will be easy because there is a long hose that has water in it. All we have to do is turn a knob and water sprays out.

By summer time the garden stuff is real big, and we are eating the radishes and onions. I like to eat a bun with lots of butter on it, and then I dip little green onions in lots of salt and eat them. Snuggles doesn't like it when I eat onion sandwiches - she says my breath stinks. I tell her she should try it too, but she doesn't.

After Alice cuts the new grass with the lawn mower, I go and get a blanket and lie on my back and look at the clouds. Sometimes I see little lambs, and sometimes I see horses - even butterflies. After I watch them for a while they go away, or they change into something else. I lie there for a long time and sometimes I even fall asleep.

One hot summer night we left all the windows open in the house when we went to bed. I am having a really nice dream, when all of a sudden there is a loud banging on the door. Everybody in the house is awake. There is a man at the back door and he is yelling, "Let me in you So and So! Let me in." Snuggles and I are scared. My dad gets up, opens the door, and starts yelling at the man. I think my dad is going to beat him up. Then my dad says, "Get out of here!" and he pushes him down the steps. He falls down. The man says some bad words, gets up and stumbles away. When my dad comes back into the house, he tells everybody to get back to sleep. "It's just a drunk from the hotel." I know there is a hotel behind our house, but I don't know what it is or what a drunk is. I tell Snuggles, "We will ask my mom in the morning."

In the morning after I talk to my mom, I tell Snuggles to sit down and I will tell her the whole story. "A hotel is a big building with lots of bedrooms in it. People have to pay money to sleep in the bedrooms. The hotel has a big room in it that they call a 'Bar.' This room has a lot of tables and chairs in it and some men, and a few women, sit and drink beer. When they drink this beer, it makes their brains go fuzzy and they get drunk. When they get drunk, they don't know where they are or what they are doing. That's why that man was here last night." Snuggles says she is afraid that a man will come and bang on the door again. I tell her we have to keep the door locked.

One day my mom says to me, "Susie, in a few weeks you have to start school. You will be in grade one. The name of your school is Montreal Street School and it's only a few blocks away. I'll walk with you for a few days until I know you won't get lost." I am really happy and I tell Snuggles that when I go to school I'll be all grown up, like my sisters. She tells me to ask my mom if she can go to school too. "Mom, can Snuggles go to school with me?" My mom says, "No, she can't." I ask her, "Why can't she?" My mom says, "Because she's only a doll and dolls can't talk." I get angry at my mom and tell her, "Yes, she can talk; she talks to me all the time!" My mom still says, "No," so I start to cry. "Cry all you want, Susie, but those are the rules." I don't like the rules and I don't even know what rules are.

The first day of school I put on my new dress and my mom walks me to school. I only know one person there - a little boy that lives by my house. His name is Rocky. I am very shy, but I see a little blonde girl sitting alone in the corner of the room. I go over and say "Hi" to her. She has pretty blue eyes like Snuggles. She says "Hi" to me too, and I sit beside her. Her name is Helen and she has a doll too. Her doll's name is 'Trudy.' I like Helen. When I get home from school, I tell Snuggles about my new friend. Snuggles is sad, but I tell her she is still my best friend.

School is lots of fun. Sometimes my teacher lets us play marbles in class. Helen and I play together. Sometimes we let Rocky play with us, but we really don't like boys very much. They are silly. I am learning how to read and write my name. We are reading about a dog named Spot. He looks like my dog Skippy, so I like to read about him. We are learning how to spell words too, and sometimes we have a spelling contest. Half of the kids stand on one side of the classroom and the other half stand on the other side. We take turns spelling a word and if we get it right, we can stay standing. I am a pretty good speller, so sometimes I get to stand a long time. Today I am the only one standing, so my teacher gives me a chocolate bar for being the best speller in her whole class. It is a Five Star chocolate bar and it is my very favorite.

There is a store on the corner by my school. I don't have any money, but sometimes my friend Helen gets some money from her mom, and we go buy bubble gum and blow big bubbles. Sometimes when Uncle Gus and Auntie Hilda come to visit us, I ask my mom for some money. She tells me she doesn't have any so Uncle Gus gives me a whole quarter. A quarter buys lots of candy. Pretty soon I ask my mom for money every time Uncle Gus comes to visit because I know he will give me a quarter. He always laughs and gives me a big hug. I think I'm pretty smart to always get a quarter.

I am going to another school too. It is called Sunday School. I like my Sunday School teacher because she talks to me in English. She tells us stories about Noah and the Ark, and we sing a song about Jonah and the Whale. "*A way down in, a way down in, a way down in, the middle of the ocea*n." Sometimes she tells us about Jesus. She says we can talk to Him when we pray. She says He loves us so much. I love Him too! He is a nice man.

My mom kneels beside me by my bed, every night, and helps me talk to Jesus. I am learning a prayer. "*Now I lay me down to sleep. I pray the Lord my soul to keep. If I should die before I wake, I pray the Lord my soul to take.*" Then I ask Jesus to "Bless my mom and my dad and my sisters and my brothers and Snuggles and Skippy and Shippy and my new friend Helen. Amen." Then I hop into bed.

One day Anne brings her boyfriend home with her. His name is Harry. She met him at Bible School in Camrose. He says he has to talk to my dad about something. He tells my dad he loves my sister and wants to marry her. My dad says yes. My sister is so happy, she gives me a big hug and kiss.

Harry comes from far away in Saskatchewan. They will be moving there after the wedding. I love Harry too! I love to 'smooch' with him. If I stand on a chair and stand on my tiptoes, I am almost tall enough to put my arms around his neck. Sometimes we have a contest. We look into each other's eyes a long time and try not to blink. Sometimes he makes me blink when he laughs or tickles me. Harry laughs a lot. Sometimes I can make him blink when I tickle him. Sometimes he lets me comb his wavy brown hair, and play with his ears. Harry has lots of brothers and sisters and I like them too.

My mom said I can sit on the bed and watch my sisters get dressed for the wedding. But first I have to clean between my toes. Anne comes over to me and asks me if I'm digging for gold. I say, "No-o silly, toe jam." She laughs at me and then she and my other sisters tickle me and make me laugh real hard. Then they tell me they love me.

I get to sit at the front of the church with my mom. My seat is at the end of the bench next to the aisle, so I can see everybody really good. I sit really quiet and listen to the music. I like the music. All of a sudden my mom says, "Susie, they're going to start." The preacher, Harry, Norm, and a man I don't know come out from a door beside the piano. They are all wearing nice brown suits. They stand in front of the platform and then they all turn around and look down the aisle. I turn around and look down the aisle too. There are all my sisters! They are starting to walk down the aisle. I am so excited I can't sit still anymore!

Shirl is first. She's not very tall so she is wearing some high heeled shoes. They make her look taller. I'm going to wear high heeled shoes, too, when I grow up. She has pretty blondish hair with waves in it. It is all fluffy today. Everybody says she looks like Auntie Hilda, but I think she looks like a princess. Her green eyes are sparkling. She winks at me when she walks by. She is a bridesmaid. Her dress is long and it is pink.

Next is Alice. She is the tallest of all my sisters, so she doesn't need to wear high heeled shoes. She is the maid of honor, and gets to help the bride and hold her flowers. She is so pretty in her long blue dress. She is carrying my favorite flowers in the whole world - pink roses! Alice has long, dark, and really curly hair that she combs back off her forehead. She has beautiful eyes like my dad. She doesn't see me when she walks by because she is daydreaming again. She is probably dreaming about her wedding and her perfect husband.

All of a sudden the preacher says, "All rise," and the music gets really loud. My dad and Anne are walking down the aisle together. My sister is so beautiful! Her dress is so white it looks like fresh snow in the winter. Her long, golden brown hair is so shiny, it looks like the sun is dancing on it. Her red roses are really shaking when she walks by me. I think she's scared.

It is really quiet in the church now and I can hear every word. I am hardly breathing. It is so exciting! The preacher reads some verses from the Bible and then he starts talking to my sister and Harry. He tells them stuff like they are supposed to always love each other and be nice to each other. Then the preacher asks the bride and groom to face each other. They make a promise to love each other. When they are all done promising, they both say,"I do." After Harry puts a ring on my sister's finger, the preacher says to Harry, "You may kiss the bride." Harry is really shy but he gives her a kiss anyway. They go into a room and when they come out they are husband and wife. I know that when I get married, my wedding will be beautiful, just like my sister's.

A few days after Anne's wedding, my mom tells me there is going to be another wedding in a month. My brother, Al, is getting married. After the wedding they are going to live on a farm right next to our ranch in the Cypress Hills. Maybe my mom will let me stay with them sometime?

I am going to be a flower girl in the wedding. I will be wearing a pretty long blue dress, and guess what? I am going to carry some pink roses. My very favorites! I feel really pretty as I walk down the aisle. My mom blows me a kiss when I walk by her. I wish this day would last forever - but I know it won't.

Our house is only a block away from the train tracks. Around the corner and up the street from our house is the train station. One day my mom and I have to walk my dad to the train station. My mom says he is going on the train to pick up a brand new car from the factory in Ontario. He will drive the new car home as soon as he gets it. My dad is happy today.

My dad is gone a long time. Then one day while I am playing outside, my dad comes home. He sees me and honks the horn. The new car is nice and shiny clean. It is a 1951, two-tone green Ford. It has four doors and is really big inside. I ask my dad if he will teach me to drive when I grow up. He says he will.

People really must like to get married, because now Bill is going to get married too. We are going all the way to Vernon, British Columbia, for the wedding. He will be living there after the wedding and I won't be able to see him very much. I will miss him. We are driving in our new car, but my mom says it's going to be a long drive on a narrow road. I am happy anyway, because this is my first holiday ever.

We are all very excited when we get to Vernon because it is so pretty, and it is nice and warm. There are fruit trees everywhere. They even have peach trees, but my mom says we can't take any peaches home - they aren't ripe yet. She says the cherries are ready, though, and we will take some home when we go, and then I can help her can them. My mom says canned cherries are very good, but I don't think so because peaches are the best.

Alice made me a pretty dress to wear for the wedding because I am a flower girl. My dress is white like the bride's dress. I love it so much! It is soft and shiny like satin, and it has some pretty lace around the neck and all around the bottom. It is really long to the floor, so my sister says I have to be careful not to step on it when I walk. I am so lucky because my mom bought me a new pair of white shoes and a locket to wear around my neck. I don't have any pictures in my locket yet, but I'm going to put a picture of Snuggles in it because my mom says she is getting pretty old and won't be around much longer. I don't think Snuggles is going away or she would have told me.

I am the first to walk down the aisle this time. I feel really beautiful because my mom told me I am. I am carrying a little white basket with a whole bunch of daisies in it. I have three pretty flowers in my hair too. They are white like my dress. Alice curled my hair and she put some nice smelling perfume on me. I have to walk slowly and take little steps because of my long dress. I am pretending to be the bride, because I just know some day I will be a bride for real.

Quite a while after we get home from the wedding my mom asks me if I want to take piano lessons, because she says I'm old enough now - Oh boy! I say yes right away! "Well," she says, "then you can start next week, but you have to practice lots." I promise her I will.

My first lesson I am a little bit afraid because I have to go into my teacher's house all by myself. She is nice, though, so I am not afraid very long. I like her husband too, but I don't think he can talk very good because he always says to me, "So you're going to learn how to play the pi-an-er, are ya?" I will learn how to touch the key on the piano that the book tells me to. I think it will be hard to learn, but I will practice lots because I want to play good like the lady at our church.

One morning, my mom wakes us up real early and tells us we're going to the ranch to see Norm. He is all alone there now because my other brothers are married. I think he is lonely. We are going to stay on the ranch for a few days to help him. Alice doesn't want to come along but my dad says she has to.

When we get there Norm asks my dad if we can hire a man and wife to come help him on the ranch. It is too much work for one man. Al comes over from his farm to help sometimes, but he is busy too. My dad says he'll look for someone.

After dinner Al comes over to help do some work on the big truck. I tell my mom I'm going to go down to the gas house where they're working and say hi to my brother. On the way down I hear some awful yelling. I stop real quick and listen. My heart is pounding really hard and I am scared! It's my dad. He's yelling at Al and hitting him and hitting him. I run back to the house as fast as I can so my dad won't see me. My mom says, "What's the matter, Susie?" I tell her my dad is hitting Al. Alice says, "How can he be hitting him? He's a married man. He must be crazy!" My mom says, " I don't know, but you better stay out of it or you'll get it too." The rest of the day we are all sad but nobody talks about it again. I don't like my dad when he is mean.

I am seven years old and I think I'm pretty smart. Alice and I fight all the time because she always wants me to help her do something around the house. She says, "Help with the dishes, or help wax the floor, or make your bed!" I tell her, "No! You can't make me - you're not my mom!" She goes to my mom and tells on me. My mom says, "Susie gets sick with tonsillitis so often we have to go easy on her." My sister says, "You're a spoiled brat!" I tell her she is too!

Alice loves me, though, even if I am a brat. I know that for sure because my dad is getting ready to give me a licken and Alice tells me it will be all right because she and Shirl will have a treat for me after. I am very scared of my dad! I do get a real good licken, but I am brave! I am not going to let him see me cry! My heart gets all hurt and angry at him because I think he is mean and I don't like him. I wish he would go away and never come back. After the licken, I march to my sisters' bedroom and I really, really cry, because my dad hit me very hard with a big belt.

Alice and Shirl come in and give me hugs and kisses, and wipe my tears away with a nice clean white hankie. Then they give me my treat. Oh boy! A whole brick of Neapolitan ice cream and I can eat as much as I want. My sisters love me!

My dad is sick quite a bit, and sometimes he goes to the doctor. My mom says it's some "male problem." I don't know what that means. Finally the doctor tells him he has to go to Winnipeg to see a specialist. My dad is going by himself and we are all happy that he is going. Nobody will be afraid while he's gone. He will be gone two weeks.

I am afraid lots of times - especially at night when I am trying to sleep and I hear noises from outside. I think a drunk man is going to try to get in the door again. I cover my head with the blankets so I can't hear anything. Then my heart starts to beat real fast and I start to sweat all over. I have to take the blankets off my head for a second because I can't breathe anymore. I am still afraid, so I jump out of bed and run to my mom and dad's bedroom door. Sometimes I just stand there and cry real soft. Sometimes I whisper, "Mom," but she doesn't hear me. Then I say, "Mom," a little louder. If she still doesn't hear me, then I just lay down on the floor by the door and curl up in a ball. Sometimes my mom hears me and says, "Susie, go back to bed. There's nothing to be afraid of." But I don't go.

Sometimes I even fall asleep there because I feel safe with my mom only a few steps away.

I am really afraid of thunder and lightning but I just stay in bed and cover my head with my blankets, because I know lightning catches you when you run. Sometimes my blankets are soaking wet by the time the storm is over. But I don't care because I'm safe in my bed when I'm covered up.

One Sunday morning after church, my dad goes over to talk to the preacher. They are talking when all of a sudden my dad gets real angry at him. He yells at him and his hands and arms are flying all over the place. Everybody is looking at them so I go and hide behind my mom. We finally go to the car to wait for him. By the time he comes to the car he is calmer, but I know he's not happy.

I am surprised when it's night time and my dad says we're going to church tonight. I don't want to go because I'm afraid he will yell at the preacher again, but we all have to go along. I like the music tonight. It's fast and lively and it makes me feel happy inside. After the preacher is done talking my dad goes up to the altar. He is crying and asking forgiveness, so I say to my mom, "Why is dad crying?" She says, "They're only crocodile tears, Susie. Nothing will change." I hope she is wrong.

The next morning my dad tells Alice and Shirl that they can look for another church. "If you find one you like and they speak English, we will start going there." My sisters are very happy about that.

A little while later they tell my dad they found a church they would like to go to. They call it Assembly of God. They have good music and the pastor preaches a good sermon. We are all going to try it out this Sunday, my dad says.

Today is Sunday and we are going to our new church. Inside it is very big, and there are lots of people there. People clap their hands when they sing and put their arms up in the air when they pray. It is really different from our old church, but we all like it. They sing some new songs we've never heard before, but they sound so nice. A big man gets up to sing a solo. His name is Al Matson and he is a Medicine Hat policeman. There is a beautiful girl playing the organ, and an older lady playing the piano. The music sounds so nice I get "goose bumps" all over my body. I love this church! I think my dad likes it too, because he is smiling.

I like to sing. My mom and dad say I can sing like a bird. The pastor says the church is going to start a junior choir and asks me if I want to join it. I really want to and my mom says I can. I get to wear a special blouse and skirt when we sing. The blouse is a pretty yellow and it has a pretty green bow tie around the neck. I must sound pretty good because sometimes my choir leader asks me to sing a solo. She says I should take voice lessons. My mom talks to a music teacher but she says I'm too young and my voice will change too much. I am sad that I can't take lessons, but I still want to sing in church.

My new church has lots of fun things to do - especially in the summer. I went to Daily Vacation Bible School yesterday and I am going back today. We will be doing some crafts today. We are going to make something out of popsicle sticks. We are learning about some people in the Bible. Yesterday my teacher asked us if we wanted to ask Jesus to come into our hearts and I said, "Yes." She prayed with me and I asked Jesus to forgive my sins and asked Him to help me to be a good girl. My mom is happy for me.

My dad is going to Winnipeg again today. Even though I'm happy when he's gone I know something is wrong, because my mom is sad and cries a lot. She prays a lot too. She always used to be happy when my dad went away for a while.

I think my dad must be really sick because he goes to the hospital in Winnipeg so often. He doesn't look sick, though, because he always combs some kind of brown color in his hair to cover up the gray, and he always wears lots of nice clothes. He must be okay because he always comes home. In my heart I know there is something wrong.

Alice finished high school in June, and she wants to be a nurse. One morning she asks my dad if he will pay for her training and he says, "No, I haven't got any money." She gets really upset and starts to raise her voice to my dad. I think she better not say any more or she'll get a beating. But she keeps on. She says, "You've always got money for your girlfriend in Winnipeg! Why don't you have any money for me? You never give Mom any money either. She only has two dresses to her name! Why do you have money for your girlfriend and not for us? How could you do that to Mom after all she's done for you?" Finally when she stops yelling, my dad says to her, "I have no girlfriend!" She yells at him, "You're a liar!" I think, "Oh, oh, she's going to get it." But she doesn't, and my dad tells her again, "I have no girlfriend." Alice yells, "Yes, you have, and she's a nurse in the Winnipeg hospital! I saw a picture of her, so you can't deny it. I have proof." My dad says, "I won't give you any money for school," and he turns around and walks away.

Alice is so upset she is shaking like a leaf that's blowing in the wind. Shirl has to calm her down and says she will get the money from her dad to pay for Alice's training. My sister is crying now and she thanks Shirl over and over. She says somehow she'll find a way to pay them back.

My mom goes into her bedroom and my dad follows her. They shut the door, but Snuggles and I are going to get as close to the door as we can so that we can listen. I hear my dad say he wants a divorce. My mom says, "No, I won't give you one!" Then my dad says, "I don't want you anymore - I love Mildred and we want to be together." My mom starts to cry. She says "No," again. My dad's voice is getting a little louder and I'm afraid for my mom so I hold Snuggles real tight. My mom says, "Why have you done this Heinrich? Why do you want another woman? What have I ever done to you to make you do this?" My dad is angry now and he is yelling. "You never loved me like you loved Clarence. You never wanted to marry me; Clarence was always first in your heart! How do you think that makes me feel?" My mom quietly said, "Clarence has been dead for a lifetime, and you changed the way I felt about you when you forced yourself on me and then called me a whore." It gets real quiet, so Snuggles and I figure we better get out of here before my dad sees us.

After my dad leaves the bedroom he walks out of the house, slams the door, gets into our car and drives away. It is real quiet in the house. My mom is still in her room and my sisters are in their room with the door closed. Snuggles and I are going to sit outside on the steps. We are happier out there and we can't hear anybody crying. I ask Snuggles if she thinks my dad doesn't want me anymore either.

Auntie Hilda and Uncle Gus are here to visit Shirl but they go into my mom's room first and close the door. They talk for a long time. Finally all three of them come out, and my mom says she is going to make some lunch for everybody. Her eyes are all red and puffy from crying and I feel sad for her.

My mom is in the kitchen cooking supper when my dad finally comes home. She calls, "Heinrich, I want to talk to you. Please come and sit down." My dad listens to her and sits down. "I have decided that you can have a divorce on one condition. You have to sign everything over to me; the ranch, the livestock, the house and your money. You can keep the car." He yells, "You can't do that! You can't take everything!" She says, "Oh, yes, I can and I will, because I still have a family to look after."

I watch my dad as he leaves again. This time he walks. He doesn't come home until supper is over, and my mom is outside working in the garden. He says to her, "She doesn't want me if I lose everything. I guess she only wanted me for my money. I called it off because I don't want to lose everything I own." My mom is quiet as a mouse and just keeps pulling weeds. I make a promise to myself that I will never let anybody hurt me like my dad hurts my mom. I am very angry at my dad!

Everything is quiet at our house for a while - no arguing, no crying, no 'lickens.' I think everything is all right again except for my dad. Sometimes at night I hear him walking around the house. My mom says that he can't sleep. She says the sleeping pills he has been taking for a long time don't help him anymore. He is going to get some stronger ones from the doctor. My mom wants my dad to quit taking them, but he says that he needs them or he will never sleep.

My dad is trying to be nicer to my mom now. It must be because of the divorce talk. They are going on a holiday to Montana and Idaho. My mom is very surprised when my dad says she can have half of the travellers cheques in her name. This is the first holiday my mom will have since they went to California. While they are gone Norm is going to take my sisters and me to Saskatchewan to visit Anne and Harry. We go to their farm every summer. I love to go there because everybody laughs and has lots of fun. My brother and Harry play their guitars and sing, and on Sundays we go to a little white church beside their farm. There are lots of nice kids at church too! I love it at their house.

When we get back to Medicine Hat my mom and dad are already home from their holiday. Alice wants to hear all about it. My mom says that the scenery is very beautiful in the mountains and it was nice to see so many trees again. The weather was nice and she had a good rest. My sister wants to know how much money she has left and what she's going to

buy with it. My mom says she doesn't have any left. "Heinrich made me use all my travellers
cheques first. The only money left is in his name." My sister is upset and says that he's a monster.

Norm is here today. He and my dad are standing on the front lawn talking about the ranch. My brother is quite a bit taller than my dad. His brown hair is cut in a brush cut. His eyes are a beautiful blue color. He has big strong muscles from doing lots of hard work on the ranch. His voice is soft and he is as gentle as my pet lamb.

My brother tells my dad that we need to sell the ranch. "The couple you hired to help me are not doing a very good job. The woman smokes all the time and I found ashes in the bread she baked." He tells my dad the man is lazy and doesn't want to work. My dad says that he will look for a buyer and that my brother should start looking for a job in Medicine Hat.

It doesn't take very long and the ranch is sold and Norm has a job driving a truck for a wholesale grocery chain. We have to move all his stuff off the ranch and he will sleep in the bedroom in the basement for a while.

I am worried about my dogs, though, so I ask my dad where they will live. He says to me, "We put them to sleep." I ask him, "What do you mean, put them to sleep?" He says, "We had to shoot them." I feel like I've been punched in the stomach! Skippy and Shippy dead? "Why didn't he give them to Uncle Gus to watch?" I decide I am not going to let him see me cry, but I am very hurt and angry at my dad.

A few weeks after the ranch is sold my dad tells us he's going to buy a chicken ranch in Redcliff. There is a house there and he will be living there. My mom will stay in Medicine Hat some of the time, but she will need to go there and help him too. There are one thousand chickens, so there will be lots of eggs to gather every day. The eggs all need to be washed and graded by their size. I think it's a good idea, because when my dad isn't home everybody is happier!

CHAPTER TWO

Alone and Out of Control:

Life without Jesus

September - time to go back to school. Life is going to be different in our house. Alice is taking nurses' training and will only come home once in a while, because she will live at the nurses' residence. Shirl has a job in Moose Jaw and will be moving there and will only come home on holidays. Norm is gone most of the time. He works lots and when he's off he goes out, or he goes away for the weekend. I know I will be lonely sometimes, but my mom says that I have to get used to it because that's the way it's going to be from now on. She doesn't admit it, but I know she will miss the girls too.

There is an outdoor skating rink in my schoolyard so I can spend a lot of time skating this winter. My mom bought me a new pair of white figure skates. She says if I practice lots I will be able to skate like Barbara Ann Scott. Every spare minute I have after I practice my piano, I go skating. When I put my skates on I am as free as a bird. I love the feel of the wind on my face as I glide from one foot to the other, faster and faster. I skate until my legs get tired and can't carry me anymore. I rest for a while and then skate some more. I try to twirl around and around. Sometimes I can do it and sometimes I fall hard on my hind end. It really hurts, but I won't cry. I'm tough!

It is one week until Christmas. My mom says my dad is coming home tonight and he will be bringing a Christmas tree with him. I am so excited I can hardly stand it! We have never had a Christmas tree before! My mom even bought some decorations to put on it. "After supper," she says, "we'll decorate it."

My dad saws a little off the bottom of the tree and then we put it in a special stand. We mix up some sugar water and give it a good drink. My mom says that we need to give it lots of water so it won't dry out. I think that all the decorations are on the tree when she says, "There's one more decoration that I saved until last, and, Susie, you can put it on the tree."

She hands me the most beautiful angel I have ever seen! Her hair shines like pure gold and her halo sparkles like diamonds. Her long white gown is covered with lace and pearls; each pearl looks like a tiny snowball. She is smiling and I know why! She has seen the baby Jesus. I feel like I am touching a piece of Heaven. "Oh, thank you, Mom. I love her!"

Today is the last day of school before the Christmas holidays. I can hardly wait! Alice will be home for a few days and Shirl will be home too. Shirl and Auntie Hilda and Uncle Gus will be at our house for Christmas Eve. Norm will be there too. We are all going to open presents together and have some Christmas treats. There are some presents under the tree with my name on them, but I don't know what's in them. I shake them and feel them, but I can't tell what they are. It's real hard to wait, but I only have to wait one more day.

Christmas Eve is finally here. Supper is over and dishes are done. After everybody finds a place to sit, my mom tells us the Christmas story. I have heard it before, but tonight it seems like magic. Maybe it's because of the tree and the angel. We all sing '*Silent night, Holy night, all is calm, all is bright.*' When the song is over my mom tells me to pass out all the presents. We all take turns opening them.

I have four gifts - a little blue bottle of perfume from my sisters called 'Evening in Paris,' two pairs of white socks with pink trim from my brother, and five dollars from Auntie Hilda and Uncle Gus. The last present is from my mom and dad. It is my very own Bible! It is black leather and has a zipper all the way around it. At the end of the zipper is a chain with a beautiful gold cross on it. This is the best present ever!

While my mom and Auntie Hilda are getting the Christmas treats on the table, my sisters and I go into my room. Alice says, "Shut the door. I want to tell you a secret." The secret is: After my dad is asleep tonight, she is going to empty all his sleeping pill capsules and put sugar in them. She says that he will never know the difference. It says in one of her nursing books that after a person takes sleeping pills for a long time they work about as good as eating sugar. That's how she got the idea. I hope she doesn't get caught or she'll get a good licken.

The first day back to school after the holidays we have a new girl in our class. Her name is Jodie. She is short and quite thin. She has curly short black hair, brown eyes, and freckles. She's very friendly - not shy like Helen and me. She asks us if she can walk home with us after school. We tell her she can.

It doesn't take long until we are good friends. I like her a lot, even though I know she lives different than we do. Her clothes always smell like smoke and I think she smokes too. My mom doesn't want me to spend too much time with her. She says she's a bad influence and I'm not supposed to forget about my friend Helen. I promise I won't, but Jodie is so much fun and she makes me laugh, and she's always happy.

Jodie wants me to come to her house after school. She says nobody is home so we can listen to music and dance. My mom and dad are both at the chicken ranch today so I decide to go. Her mom and dad are divorced, and her mom has to work to make ends meet. Her older brother and sister work too. I can smell smoke as soon as we open the door. I ask her if she smokes. She says she doesn't, but her mom and sister do. She says she is going to try it sometime, though. She puts a record on the record player and turns it up real loud. We sneak into her sister's room and put her lipstick on. I love the smell of lipstick. Jodie says, "Let's dance." I tell her that I don't know how to dance. She says, "Come on, I'll teach you." Dancing is really easy and it's a lot of fun too. The music has a good beat. I love music!

On the way home I feel a little guilty. I know I shouldn't have been dancing and wearing lipstick. I decide I'm not going to tell my mom I went to Jodie's, and I decide I'm not going to go back there again. When I go there I do things I shouldn't be doing.

The next day at school I spend most of my time with my friend Helen. I think I hurt Jodie's feelings but I don't want to do things I'm not supposed to do. I should ask Jodie to come to church with me, but I don't think she will come anyway.

School isn't much fun when I'm not with Jodie, so I decide I'll spend more time with her again. I won't tell my mom - besides, she's been at Redcliff lots and Norm is gone a lot too. Who will know?

I go to Jodie's every day after school when my mom isn't home. We dance and laugh; we wear lipstick and talk about boys! I even put a cigarette in my mouth. It isn't lit, but I like the smell of fresh tobacco.

Every time I go home I feel guilty, and promise God I won't go there again, and every time she asks me to come over, I go. I want to go to church and be good but I want to dance too. I don't understand why this is happening to me. I know I should stay away from Jodie.

My mom and dad are still on the chicken ranch and my brother is going away for the weekend. I will be all alone in the house and I know I'm going to be afraid. I want to ask Jodie to stay with me, but I know my mom doesn't want her to. I decide I'm going to stay up real late and I'm going to leave the bathroom light on all night. By midnight I am real sleepy, so I decide to go to bed. "I'll be able to sleep now," I tell myself.

All of a sudden I hear someone banging on the door. I am wide awake and I am scared! "What am I going to do? Is he going to break the door down? Please God, don't let him get in! I promise I'll be good." I'm really sweating because the covers are up over my head! I don't move a muscle! Finally the man goes away, but I don't close my eyes anymore until the sun comes up.

About ten o'clock my mom and dad come home from Redcliff. I'm still sleeping, so my mom comes into the bedroom and whispers, "Susie, why is the bathroom light on, and why are you still in bed?" I explain about the drunk and she says it will be okay now because she'll be able to stay home for a while. I am glad I don't have to be alone again tonight.

Now that my mom is home I can't go over to Jodie's anymore. That's all right, though, because our Junior Choir at church is going to do a concert on Sunday and we have to practice every night this week. Helen comes along with me and listens while we practice.

For the rest of the winter I don't spend much time with Jodie at school. She has another friend; her name is Mary Ann. She goes over to Jodie's after school now. That's okay. I still have Helen, but I kind of miss Jodie.

One Saturday morning after I get up, I am getting dressed when I see some red on my panties. I can't believe my eyes! "What's the matter with me? Am I going to bleed to death and die?" "I bet it's because I danced; God is going to punish me." I don't want mom to know because she'll know that I've been bad.

Finally I get up enough nerve to call Alice at the nurses' residence. I tell her she needs to come home right away because there's something terribly wrong with me. She says she'll come home as soon as she can. By the time she gets here I'm really scared. It seems to be getting worse. I tell her that I think I'm bleeding to death. She says, "Is that all?" "What do you mean, is that all? I'm going to die!" She laughs and tells me it's just a part of growing up. She didn't realize how grown up I am. She says to me, "We need to go to the store and buy you a brassiere too. You should have been wearing one long ago."

When we get home, Alice tells me to look in the mirror. The girl looking back at me in the mirror is not little Susie Mueller - she is Susan Arlene and she looks very grown up.

I can't believe it's me in the mirror! "When did I grow up?" For the first time I see how I really look. My very long, brown hair is so shiny and soft looking. It flips up on the ends and soft bangs fall over my forehead. My eyes are a blue-grey color: 'Mueller eyes.' My sister says, "You look like you're eighteen, not eleven." What a day this has been!

It's summer time again and school is over. I am really looking forward to going to Anne and Harry's again this summer. Norm is taking me there. He likes to go there, too, because all the girls there think he's handsome, and they want to go out with him.

After we come back from Saskatchewan, my mom and dad tell me that I have to stay with them at the chicken ranch for a while. I really don't want to, but I don't want to stay alone in Medicine Hat if I don't have to. My mom says that the time will pass quickly. She says that I can help her clean the eggs and she'll pay me a little bit. I like that idea!

After a week, my mom tells me that I have to go back to Medicine Hat. She says that Norm will be back by now and he will stay with me. I tell her that he'd better be there because I don't want to stay alone anymore. She says to keep the doors locked and I'll be fine. I have no choice, I have to go back.

One hot day Jodie phones me and asks me if I want to go swimming with her. I tell her I can't swim, but I'll go in the pool and stay in the shallow end. She tells me that she can't swim either, but we can get wet and then suntan beside the pool.

I haven't put my bathing suit on for a long time, and this time I feel a little embarrassed, because it is filled out in places it wasn't filled out before. Jodie says that I look fine and we jump in the pool. The water is cool and it feels good. "Jodie, who's your friend?" A guy is swimming over to us. I lean over to Jodie and ask her who he is. She says, "That's my brother." He is very good looking! He has curly brown hair and big muscles.

When Jodie and I get out of the pool to go suntanning, I know he is watching me. I don't like it when he watches me; it makes me feel self-conscious. Before he leaves the pool he whispers something to Jodie. Later, she tells me that her brother thinks I'm a 'honey.'

After we leave the pool, we go to the park. I have a blanket so that we can lay on the grass. Jodie says she has a surprise for me. I love surprises! She pulls out a package of cigarettes and some matches. She says she started smoking and she wants me to try it too. I tell her I don't want to. She asks me if I'm a chicken. I say, "No." "Well then try it!" I keep saying, "No," but she doesn't give up. Finally I say, "Okay!" She will show me how to do it. She lights one up, puts it in my mouth and says, "Take a drag." I do, and quickly blow it out. It tastes terrible and I give it back to her. She hands it back to me and tells me I have to inhale. "Okay, okay!" I take a puff, take a deep breath and blow it out. I have to cough and boy - do I get dizzy! The sky and the trees are spinning so I lie down on the blanket. I tell her that I think I'm going to be sick. She laughs and tells me that I'll live. After we finish the cigarette she says, "Why don't you come over to my house and we'll have a Coke?"

When we get to her house there is nobody home but her brother. He is in his room playing his record player. Jodie goes to the fridge while I get the glasses. She says, "There's no pop left. My brother must have drank it all." He tells her he did and gives her some money. "Go buy some more."

Jodie tells me to wait here and she'll be right back. I am feeling uneasy in her house without her. I quietly go into the living room and sit on the couch. If I am very quiet, he won't know I'm here and I'll be all right! I have no reason to be afraid of him; I just met him. He is Jodie's brother and Jodie is really nice, so he will be nice too. I wish I had gone along with Jodie. I'd rather be anywhere than here! I should have gone home after swimming! My mom doesn't even want me to come here! I say a silent prayer hoping to calm my pounding heart. "Please God, please God!" I don't know what I'm afraid of, but I am afraid.

Just then, Jodie's brother comes out of his room. He is surprised to see me. I tell him Jodie went for Coke. "Ya, right ... Do you like Elvis?" he asks. "I love him." He tells me he just bought a record of his and asks me if I want to hear it. I say, "Sure." He tells me to come to his room and he'll play it for me. I walk behind him down the hall, and I stop short at the door of his room. My heart starts to pound real hard and I can feel it throbbing on my face. He turns around and tells me it's only a record. He's right, it's only a record. After all, this is Jodie's brother!

I am standing by the door, not wanting to take another step. This is the first time I've ever been in a man's room, other than my brothers'. Elvis starts to sing, "*Love me tender, love me sweet; never let me go.*" It is a beautiful song, so I start to relax a little and listen to the words. He keeps singing, "*You have made my life complete, and I love you so.*" I have 'goose bumps' all over. "*Love me tender, love me true ...*" "Come here, girl. Let's dance!" I shake my head, "No." He says, "It's only a waltz." "No, thank you, I'll just listen." Before I can move he grabs me, puts his muscular arms around me and pulls me close

68

to him. He puts his cheek up against my hair, "*all my dreams fulfill, for my darling, I love you, and I always will.*" I want to pull away from him but I feel safe in his arms, and I do love to dance. "You are so beautiful," he whispers in my ear, and you smell so nice."

Instantly I think about the perfume I got for Christmas, and the tree, and the Bible. The Bible! I start to panic! What am I doing here? Where is Jodie? Why isn't she back yet? I need to get out of here! I try to pull away but he grabs me tighter and kisses me hard on the mouth. I don't like it. The more I try to push away, the tighter he holds me. I try to pound his chest but he grabs my wrists and throws me on the bed. I try to get off the bed and run but he catches me.

I am begging, "Please let me go! Please, I want to go home!" He says, "I want you!" My whole body is shaking and I can't quit crying. "Please don't hurt me!" I fight but he pins me down! I try to kick him! He's too strong! I try to scratch him! He grabs my wrists and holds them above my head.

All the time he's hurting me, I am pretending I'm not here. I can see myself sitting on my mom's knee. She's rocking me back and forth and telling me she loves me, and Jesus loves me too. I cry. "Please, Mama, help me!"

He's shaking me. "Snap out of it!" I don't know where I am for a minute, then I remember and cry, "Oh God, let me out of here!I just want to get out of here!I've got to get home!" He's saying, "I'm sorry I lost control. Please don't tell anybody, I could get in a lot of trouble."

My life was over. My innocence was gone. I was forever changed!

I knew I was running, but I didn't know who I was or where I was running to! My mind raced."I hate Jodie for leaving me! I hate men! I wish they would all die! Oh dear God, what if I'm pregnant? Dad will kill me! I wish I'd never been born! And my mom; oh Mom, I'm so sorry I didn't listen to you! I can't tell anybody! What am I going to do?"

I ran so hard that my lungs hurt and I couldn't get my breath. I had to slow my pace or pass out. It seemed like everything around me was out of focus. People looked like they were walking in slow motion and the street noise sounded hollow, yet it echoed in my ears. I couldn't think clearly; in fact, I didn't want to think. I just wanted to die!

When I got to the end of my street I stopped and stood motionless for a minute. So many thoughts raced through my mind. I needed to think clearly. Think, Susan, think! "Where am I going to tell Mom I was? I'll have to lie, but she'll know I'm lying when she looks at me!" Think! Think! "Maybe she won't be home! Please God, don't let her be home!"

After what seemed like a lifetime, I got to my yard. I walked by the garage and looked in the window to see if the car was home. It wasn't. I was relieved because I wouldn't have to make up a story. I snuck into the house even though I knew nobody was home.

The first thing I did when I got into my room was fall to my knees beside by bed and sob. I pleaded with God to forgive me and I begged Him not to let me be pregnant. I was on my knees for a long time. I just didn't feel forgiven. I didn't feel clean. I thought, "I have to bathe. I need to wash this day out of my life!" I made the water as hot as I could stand it and I scrubbed and scrubbed, and I cried and cried. Finally I quit crying. It was as if the well suddenly went dry.

I dried myself off, went into the bedroom, dug Snuggles out of the corner, and started punching her with my fists. I punched her in the face. I punched her in the stomach. I pounded and pounded until I had no more strength in my arms. I yelled at her, "I'm not a little girl anymore! I hate you! I hate you! I don't need you anymore!" I threw her in my waste paper basket, walked out of my room and shut the door!

The phone rang but I didn't answer it, because I knew it would be Jodie. She would be home by now and wondering what happened to me. I knew her brother wouldn't say anything. I let it ring and ring. It sounded as loud as the fire alarm bell at school, deafening, yet I could hardly hear it. Finally it stopped.

I pleaded with God every day not to let me be pregnant. I bargained: if I'm not pregnant then I won't have to tell anybody. Nobody will ever know. I would pretend everything was normal. I would never go to Jodie's house again and I promised never to smoke or dance again. I would forget this day and never think about it again. God did answer my prayer and I thought the whole thing was over.

The rest of the summer I avoided Jodie and spent my time with my church friends. We went to Daily Vacation Bible School, and we went to Sunday School camp at Sylvan Lake. I did all the right church things, but I still didn't feel clean. Some days I hated myself and convinced myself that I was no good, and deserved what happened to me. Some days I was okay, and I could even laugh a little.

I started to hate practicing the piano - I could never play in church now, anyway. I told Mom I wanted to quit piano lessons. She tried to talk me out of it, but I said I wasn't going and that was it. Finally she gave up and said, "Whatever you want, Susie!" I screamed at her, "Don't call me Susie anymore! I'm Susan!" She looked a little hurt and I know she didn't understand why I yelled at her, but I didn't care.

The longest summer of my life was finally over. I would be attending Junior High this fall. It was bigger than my old school. I was happy about that because there would be more kids around, and maybe I wouldn't have to see Jodie. I still blamed her for leaving me alone at her house. I knew I couldn't face her without telling her the whole story and I couldn't do that, so it was easier to just avoid her.

It wasn't long after school started that I began to hate it there. I hated myself more. I felt like hiding inside myself. I was sure everybody in the whole school knew what had happened to me. In my heart I knew that only God and I knew, but that didn't help the way I felt.

Most of the time I didn't want to go to school so I'd tell Mom I didn't feel good. "Could I please stay home today?" She usually let me. I was glad when she had to go the chicken ranch because then I didn't have to ask her. I just stayed home. The school would phone to ask why I wasn't there and I would tell them that I was sick. I just couldn't forget.

I knew one day I would run into Jodie, but when it happened I wasn't prepared for it. As if by magic, there she was, standing in front of my locker. We just stared at each other for a minute. I thought, "I miss her." She must have read my mind because she said, "I miss you too! Why won't you talk to me? Whatever I did to you, please forgive me. I don't want to lose you as a friend, just tell me what I did."

I lied, "You didn't do anything. I just can't come to your house anymore." She said, "Is that all? We don't have to go there if you don't want, only please, let's be friends again." I stared at her for a minute, not even blinking. I wanted to say no, but I heard myself say, "Okay." I told myself it wasn't really her fault, it was mine. We hugged and vowed never to stop being friends.

In May, Alice graduated. She was a Registered Nurse. She was offered a job in the Lethbridge Hospital and she was also offered a job as a Missionary Nurse at Hay River, in Northern Alberta. Two weeks later she moved to Lethbridge.

My life seemed to be getting a little better. I started to enjoy going to youth activities with my church friends, but I quit singing in the choir. Jodie and I walked home from school together every day. We talked and laughed, but I never went to her house. When she offered me a cigarette, it was easier to say no than it was before.

Norm took me to Harry and Anne's as soon as school was out. He was going to leave me there for two weeks. He had to get back because he had lots to do before he got married in August. He rented a suite and would be moving right away. He and Sharon would live there after the wedding. I still loved to go to my sister's. I loved to go to their little white country church, and I loved to see Harry. He was like a father to me, and he was my friend. I always gave him hugs and kisses. I felt like somebody cared about me.

That summer Harry's brother, Pete, was helping out on the farm. When he came, he brought his friend Douglas with him. They were in the youth group at church, and we were all about the same age. They were both shy so they were quiet around me.

The two weeks flew by too quickly. I didn't want to leave because I was happy there. There were always lots of people around and I loved to 'smooch' with my niece and nephews. After I got home, I let Jodie drift back into my life as easily as the wind blows the sand in a desert. I just didn't want to be alone and afraid anymore. I phoned her and asked her to sleep at my house. I didn't ask Mom because she wasn't home, and she'd probably say no anyway.

She came, and after supper we sat outside on the lawn. She asked me if I wanted a cigarette. Without hesitating I said, "Sure." I puffed it, inhaled it, and never felt a bit of guilt. It didn't taste very good but I didn't care. At least I wasn't alone. Then she told me she had a surprise for me and went into the house. When she came out she had a half-full bottle of something in her hand. She told me it was Lemon Gin. She said she stole it from home.

We got some glasses, poured the Lemon Gin in, mixed it with water and tasted it. It tasted awful and it was so strong it took my breath away. We added some more water and drank the rest of the bottle. It didn't take long before my head started spinning. We laughed at each other because we couldn't say our words right. They sounded all mixed up.

In the morning I had a real bad headache, and Jodie told me I had a hangover. She said, "You always get a hangover when you drink too much." I didn't like the headache, but I liked the fun we had last night. I knew I had crossed the line to the other side, but I didn't care anymore. I just wanted to be happy, have fun, and forget my past.

I still had to go to church every Sunday. When Mom and Dad weren't home, Norm came and picked me up. Church was okay. I still loved the music, but most of the time my heart was hard against God. He was somewhere way up there, and I was down here all alone. I could play church when I had to.

For the rest of the summer whenever Mom wasn't home, Jodie and I and another friend, Mary Ann, went uptown to the New Moon Cafe and drank Coke and smoked. Lots of times we ended up at a party somewhere. There was always lots of booze and guys, of course. There would always be good music, turned up loud, and I would dance and try to forget my crummy life.

It was late August and Norm's wedding day. Alice and Shirl were in the wedding, so they were home. It felt so good to be with them again. I missed them both so very much. They were so far away, and I was so lonely. It was a wonderful wedding and Sharon was a beautiful bride. Norm looked so handsome and he looked very happy.

After harvest, Harry's parents came to visit my mom and dad for a weekend. Harry's sister, Donna, who is a few years older than I , came along. We both loved Elvis, so when we saw that an Elvis movie was playing at the theatre, we decided to go. We weren't allowed to go to the movies, so we cooked up a story about going for a long walk. We headed straight to the theatre to watch 'Jailhouse Rock.' It was wonderful! The next night we told another "fib" and went again. Just for a second, I thought about "Love Me Tender." I shuddered, and put it out of my mind.

They went back to Saskatchewan and my life went back to the way it always was. My two friends and I found every party we could. We danced all we could and we drank all we could. One night the party ended up at my house. We asked a few kids to come over, but kids came from everywhere, until the house was full, standing room only. There was a blue fog in the house from the cigarette smoke and there was booze everywhere. We had loud "rock and roll" music playing but there was no room to dance. I knew I was in trouble when I saw my brother walk in the door. He was very upset. He told me I had ten minutes to get everybody out or he would call the police. He told me he wasn't going to tell Dad, but Mom would sure hear about it.

Mom never said a word to me, but whenever she was home she was much quieter than usual. I knew what was bothering her, but I wasn't going to talk about it if I didn't have to. She knew how wild I was but she never scolded me. I noticed that she was praying a lot more and sometimes I heard her mention my name in her prayers. She asked her Lord to watch over
me and protect me. It made me feel bad, but I couldn't let it bother me too long. After all, where was God when I needed Him?

Later that year Alice got married. She never told the family or invited them to the wedding. She called Mom one day and told her she was married. His name was Ron and he was a World War II veteran. He had been injured in the war, sohe frequently made trips to the hospital for a rest. She told Mom she felt sorry for him at first, but she ended up falling in love with him. There was only one problem - he was an alcoholic. Mom cried and Dad was furious.

Ever since I was a little girl, I was frequently sick with tonsillitis, but over the past few years I was getting worse. The doctor said that they had to come out. The day before the operation the nurse gave me some pamphlets to read about the surgery. It said that the chloroform they used to put you to sleep was safe, but there had been rare cases of people dying from it.

I got scared. I didn't want to die. I knew if I died I would go to hell, so I asked Mom to tell Norm to please come and see me before the operation. I needed him desperately. When he came into my room I started to cry, and I begged him to pray for me. I told him I didn't want to die and go to hell. He sat on my bed and hugged me real tight. He told me I wouldn't go to hell; all I had to do was ask the Lord to forgive my sins and everything would be fine. He prayed with me and I asked God to forgive me. I felt happy after that and I was ready to go to the operating room ... I guess by now you know, I lived!

School was out again and I made my usual summer visit to Saskatchewan. I did love it there. Everybody was always happy and laughed lots, they made me feel like I was special. I really loved Harry and I tagged along with him whenever I could. Church was good, youth group was good, and then there was Douglas. I had a crush on him and I think he liked me too, because whenever I looked at him in church I could see he was sneaking a peek at me. He had beautiful blue eyes, dark wavy hair - very good looking, but shy.

Very soon after returning to Medicine Hat I let the pull of the world draw me in again. I was wilder than ever. Jodie and I had our routine. New Moon Cafe, cigarettes, parties, booze: finally I hit rock bottom, not resisting any guy who said he loved me.

On one of the days I was forced to go to Redcliff, I needed some money. I knew Dad hid his coins in a jar in his closet. I had taken money from there before when I needed to buy cigarettes. This time I wasn't so lucky and Dad caught me with my fingers in the "cookie jar." He started yelling at me and I knew I was going to get a beating. Mom came running into the house, stood in front of me, and told Dad to beat her and leave me alone. I was so scared! It looked like he was going to hit her, but he backed away instead. He was mumbling to himself all the way out the door. Mom said, "Susie, Susie, what's the matter with you? Don't you care about anything?" I didn't answer her, but I thought, "No, I don't care about anything."

It wasn't long after that day that the chicken ranch sold. Dad didn't move to Medicine Hat, though; instead he bought a small irrigation farm at Seven Persons. There was no house out there so Dad built a small one. He never finished the inside of it, and there was no running water. He wanted me to come and live there with Mom and him. I said, "I'd rather die!" So of course I didn't have to go.

This was going to be my best summer ever because dad was going to teach me how to drive. I was really excited, but I was also afraid. I wondered how many 'lickens' I'd get until I learned. I decided I could take it. I had to - I wanted to be able to drive.

It sounded simple. Put your foot on the clutch. Turn on the key. Shift it into first gear. Step on the gas, let the clutch out real slow and drive. I did okay until I got to the step on the gas and let the clutch out real slow part. I stepped on the gas so hard it roared. Dad yelled, "Not so hard." I let up a little. He kept on, "Now slowly let the clutch out." I let it out. Jerk - Jerk - Jerk. Dad yelled, "Put the clutch back in." I did and it quit jerking. He said, "Give it a little gas and try it again." Jerk - Jerk - Jerk. I figured he was going to reach across the car and

77

crack me on the side of the head. He laughed. I couldn't believe it; he was actually laughing. After he quit laughing, he said, "Okay, let's try it again." This time I got it going without any jerks. We kept at it, and by the time we got back home I was doing pretty well. After that, whenever Dad came home I pestered him to take me driving.

I phoned Anne and asked her if I could bring a friend with me to their house this summer. She said I could. Jodie and I caught the bus to Swift Current and they picked us up. They liked Jodie because she was very friendly.

We went out with the youth group the first Friday night we were there. We decided we liked Pete and Douglas. We hoped we could see them again. After church on Sunday, Pete and Douglas came to Harry and Anne's for dinner, and then we took Harry's car and went berry picking in the hills behind the farm.

Douglas picked me up and carried me down the hill to the car. We sat in the back seat and I sat real close to him. I wanted him to put his arm around me, and kiss me. I don't know if I was too bold, or he was too shy, but he didn't do anything. When we got back to Medicine Hat I decided farm boys were too shy for me.

One night after Dad came home from the farm, Jodie, two other friends and I decided to take Dad's car for a spin. We carefully planned how we could get it out of the garage and down the back alley without Mom and Dad hearing it.

The plan was made. All four of us helped open the garage door because it was heavy, and it had to be lifted very slowly because it squeaked. After we got the door up, I would put the car in neutral and they would push until it was out of the garage. We had to slowly close the
door again so that nobody would see that the car was gone. I would get back in and steer it until they pushed it all the way to the end of the alley.

The plan worked. I started it and away we went! We drove up and down the main strip in front of the New Moon Cafe, and then we drove up to the ice cream parlour where the high school kids hung out.

We were on our way back home when I heard a police siren. My heart sank! I told the girls I was just going to keep driving because they weren't looking for us, anyway. The flashing lights came up behind me and I knew they were after me. The policemen motioned for me to pull over. I did. My knees were shaking so hard that I was sure he could see them. I knew I was in big trouble!

There were two policemen in the police car. One came to my door and the other one went to Jodie's door. The policeman beside me asked if I knew I went through a stop sign. I said, "No, Sir." He said, "How old are you?" I didn't answer him. "Can I see your driver's license, please?" He asked me again, "How old are you?" I knew I had to answer him this time or I'd be in real trouble. "Fourteen." He said, "Well, then, you don't have a driver's license."

One policeman took dad's car and the other one took all four of us to the police station. Luckily, Al Matson, the policeman who went to our church, was working. He was surprised to see me there. He must have felt sorry for me because he took me in a different room than the other girls. I waited for what seemed like a hundred years and finally he came in. He said he had called Norm and my mom. He said he didn't want to get me in trouble with my dad, so Norm was going to take care of everything. He told me I was one lucky little girl and that I should be very thankful. I was very thankful, but I wouldn't let him know that.

Mom wouldn't let me go out for quite a while, for stealing the car. But one day I had to run an errand for her. She needed some sugar to bake a cake. I walked real slow so that I could enjoy every minute of freedom. I stopped to look at some roses in a yard. I stopped at the street light when it was green. After it changed color a few more times, I finally moved.

When I got back, there was nobody there. All the stuff was still on the cupboard, ready to bake a cake. There was dish water in the sink with soap in it. I called, "Mom, where are you?" No answer. I went into the bedroom to look for her - she wasn't there. She wasn't in the bathroom or her bedroom. I noticed one of the soft chairs in the front room was out of place, but nobody was home. I got scared. Where did she go?

When the phone rang it startled me. It was Mom. She was at the hospital. Dad had had a heart attack and was in critical condition, but the doctor said he would live. Mom said that he drove himself the twelve miles from the farm to the house, while he was having his heart attack. It took him two hours, but he got home. Norm had to take him to the hospital.

When Dad got out of the hospital he was told by the doctor to rest. He didn't listen, of course, and went right back to the farm and went to work. I thought, "Good, go ahead and kill
yourself. We'll all be a lot happier." He slowly got better and by the time I went back to school he was back to normal.

I made it to high school - grade ten. I don't know how I got that far, because studying was not one of my favorite pastimes. I only did the bare minimum of homework, just enough to squeak through. This year I thought I might try a little harder to get good marks.

I liked math, partly because I was pretty good at it and partly because my teacher, Mr. Head, was a nerd. He was always doing something stupid that made us laugh. Very soon, though, school got to be a drag, and I started skipping classes again. I stayed home from school as often as I could. Same song; school called, I said I was sick.

One Friday night, the Harlem Globe Trotters were coming to our high school to play basketball. I had skipped school that day but I wanted to see them. I decided I'd take a chance and go to the game. I waited until the game had started, then I slipped in and sat on the bleachers near the door. I was going to leave early. I didn't want any of my teachers to see me there.

During the intermission, the Globe Trotters were doing some entertaining with the audience. One of them came over to where I was sitting, grabbed my purse and took a letter out of it. The letter was from Alice but he pretended it was from my boyfriend. He made up a bunch of stuff about love and kisses, and I knew as soon as everybody started looking at me that I'd be in trouble with the principal.

Next morning I got called into the Principal's office. He wondered what sickness I had that could let me feel good enough to go out by the evening. I told him that I couldn't help it if I felt better by evening. He didn't like my attitude very much because he told me if I skipped class one more time, I was out. I laughed to myself and thought, "As if I care."

Tragedy struck our family twice over the next few months. Alice was the first to feel the blows of heartache.

Her husband Ron had been in a lounge one night and as he was walking across the street to get to his car, a speeding driver hit him with his car. He died. She was alone with two small boys. Financially she would be all right, but emotionally she didn't know how she was going to raise her two small boys as a single parent.

Dan, a close friend of Ron's who was in the war with him, assured Alice that he would help in any way he could. He said he would help with the boys and help tie up the loose ends concerning the lawyers and the Veterans office.

The second tragedy hit Norm and Sharon. They had moved in with us for a few months while their new house was being built. I liked not being alone, but I didn't like having to stay home at night.

One day when I got home from school Norm was lying on the couch, moaning in pain. He rolled from side to side in agony. I asked Sharon what was wrong with him. Why was he so sick? She said that they weren't sure yet but they thought it was polio. It was polio, and he suffered for a long time.

Finally their new house was finished and Norm was well enough to move. I felt a little sad to see them leave. I had grown to love them both while they lived with us. There was a softness and gentleness in Norm's spirit that I didn't understand. I wondered how he could still love the Lord so much, and thank Him for everything in his life, even after his Lord dealt him such a low blow. It seemed to me that Norm loved his Lord even more.

Winter settled into the same old routine. Parties, booze and whatever I could think of to try to make myself happy. My marks were slipping at school again, but I really didn't care. I stopped going to church. I was too bad to try to pretend I was still good. When I left my church for the last time, I said good-bye to God. I told Him I didn't want Him in my life anymore and that I didn't need Him. That part of my life was over.

In the spring our boys' high school basketball team was going to Swift Current to play in a weekend tournament. One of my girlfriends, Sandy, was dating a player on the team. She wanted to go to Swift Current and she wanted us girls to go with her. We were going to take the bus and we could stay with a friend of hers there.

None of us could get any money, so we decided to hitchhike. The tournament started Friday night so we would have to skip school Friday. It took a while for us to get there because nobody wanted to pick up four girls. Finally we got smart: two girls with their thumbs up, two girls hiding in the ditch. If someone stopped, the two would ask if two more could come along. Some said yes, some took off. It took all day but we finally got there in time for the first game.

The weekend was fun. We partied and met some new guys. Two of them were in a 'rock and roll' band - right up my alley! They were playing at a local bar, so after the game on Saturday night, we went there. I guess we looked old enough to be in there because they didn't ask us for any identification. We partied hard, then the weekend was over. We managed to get a ride back with a guy who had brought his car. We told him we would give him some money for gas when we got home. We lied: we didn't have any money, but he fell for it.

Monday morning we all got called into the Principal's office. The other girls got a lecture; I got the book thrown at me. I was permanently expelled, finished, kicked out. They had called mom and told her I was on my way home. When I left his office I turned around and said, "Have a nice life!"

I knew dad was going to kill me when he found out, so I figured I better get my Will prepared. I didn't have much to leave anybody, but what I did have was Jodie's. When I got home Mom said she would figure something out, because under no circumstances could Dad find out.

Dad never paid much attention to his kids, except to beat on them, so it was easy to fool him. Whenever he came home I grabbed a few books that were lying around the house, and my loose-leaf binder with lots of paper in it, I pretended to be doing my homework. I copied a paragraph or two out of each book. After about an hour I quit. No problem! Homework done! That went on until school was over. Mom would have all summer to figure out what to do with me.

That was the first summer I didn't go to Harry and Anne's. My life was too messed up to live with anybody. They knew they couldn't handle me anymore, and my brothers couldn't handle me either.

The only person who wanted to take a chance on me was Alice. She came up with a plan. All she had to do was convince Dad. She told him that there was a beauty school in Lethbridge that I could attend. It was a ten month course. She would pay for it and when I graduated I would have a profession. I would be a hairdresser.

She had built a new house in Lethbridge, so she explained to Dad that I could help her with the housework, the yard work, and help her look after the boys. After much discussion, Dad agreed to let me go and Mom was relieved because now she wouldn't have to tell Dad that I had been kicked out of school.

I was happy to be getting out of Medicine Hat. I knew I would never have to stay alone again. Besides, Medicine Hat was beginning to be a real drag. The only hard part was leaving Jodie. How was I going to live without her? Alice told me that Jodie could come and visit, but I knew in my heart that I would never see her again.

I was almost sixteen years old. How did my life get so out of control?

CHAPTER THREE

Wasted Years:

Rebellion and anger

I liked Lethbridge immediately. It was big and had clean, wide streets. I felt clean. Maybe I could have a new start here? Maybe I could clean up my life?

I quickly settled into my new surroundings. Alice had a beautiful new home and two wonderful little boys who loved me. I could pretty much do what I wanted, but Alice did have a few house rules. I had to keep my room clean, help around the house and baby-sit the boys when she needed me. If I went out, I had to be in by 11:00 p.m. on weeknights and 1:00 a.m. on weekends. That seemed fair. I didn't go out, anyway, because I hadn't made any friends yet. We didn't go to church either, so my whole life was there in that house. That was all right, though, because for the first time in a very long time I felt safe and happy. I didn't even mind cleaning her hardwood floors.

When Ron died, his best friend, Dan, was a real help to Alice. He was a good friend and she leaned on him heavily. He spent a lot of time with Alice and slowly and unexpectedly their friendship turned into love, but Dan was married. He asked his wife for a divorce. She said "No." He moved out of his house into ours.

I thought that would be all right. He made Alice happy and he was good to the boys and he was nice to me too. He wasn't afraid of work. He looked after the vehicles and helped around the house and yard. He was easy to get along with and gave lots of compliments. "A real charmer," I thought.

The enrollment age at beauty school was sixteen. They let me start even though my sixteenth birthday was over a month away. I was glad because I was starting to feel a little lonely. I missed mom and Jodie. I knew I needed to get out and make some new friends.

The beauty school was upstairs in a building in downtown Lethbridge. The salon area had twenty-five styling tables and chairs. The sinks were along one wall and another wall had a whole row of windows. There was a separate room for our theory classes that had lots of tables. Some had mannequins on them and the rest were for taking notes. There was a big lunch room with lockers, and a long white table and white chairs. I decided that I liked it there and that I'd work hard at becoming a hairdresser. This was one school I didn't want to get kicked out of.

New students were allowed to start classes at the beginning of every month. I started with nine other girls and two guys. Making friends was not easy for me. I appeared to be strong and aggressive, but inside I was an insecure little girl who didn't think much of herself. By the end of the first week I had made one friend: Shannon. We found we had lots in common, including having a good time. Shannon and I made two more friends: Mavis and Deanna. That was our foursome.

After the friendships were made, the next step was a complete make-over. My long, brown hair was cut short and dyed jet black. It made me look older. I liked that because I always felt older than I really was. School was interesting. I liked the instructors, and practicing on the mannequins was fun.

Deanna and Mavis were from Lethbridge, so Shannon and I went out with them to a few parties; but they were tame compared to the parties I had gone to in Medicine Hat. I went out with a few guys but nothing interesting came of them. I was determined to get good marks at beauty school, and besides, I didn't need to party every night, anyway.

The minute I turned sixteen I tried for my driver's license. After the second try I made it. I was on top of the world when Alice said I could take her car to the drive-in movie. Life was good! It seemed like my life had just opened up, almost like a tightly closed rosebud that springs open to show all of its beauty. I wanted to try everything the world had to offer. Shannon felt the same way. We weren't bad, we were just in love with life.

I pierced Shannon's ears; she pierced mine. We had our palms read, our tea leaves read, and our fortune told with tarot cards. Deanna brought an Ouija board to school and we spent all our lunch breaks asking it questions. We couldn't believe how it always gave us the right answers. We went on double dates and supper dates, and we loved every minute of it!

We were so busy with life that I hadn't really noticed the two guys in our class. One guy was married and the other guy was a few years older than I . He was almost a head taller, about 5'9". He had nice brown hair, he was quiet and not too hard to look at. His name was Charles.

By this time, I was getting tired of black hair and wanted to try a different color. I wanted to be platinum blonde. I let Shannon practice on me. She bleached it and it turned bright orange, pumpkin color. I was not pleased!

The next day we put the peroxide mixture on again. Suddenly, my head got real hot, so I did a smart thing; I stuck my head out the open window. My head was steaming like it was on fire. The class thought it was hilarious! By the time we washed the peroxide off and applied a tint, I ended up a light ash blonde with hair that felt like the long green hairs on a cob of corn. What an experience!

I had been keeping my eye on Charles from a distance, so when he asked me out on a date I said, "Yes." He picked me up in his car, took me out to supper, to a movie, and home. He was fun, polite and didn't try to put any moves on me. I liked him. He treated me like a lady.

The ten months passed quickly. I wrote my theory examination and had to do a shampoo, haircut, perm and a set on a live model. Two provincial instructors came from Edmonton. The twelve of us who started together were tested together. I passed both tests and graduated. I was actually a hairdresser. I was pretty proud of myself. I had stayed out of trouble long enough to do something right.

Shortly after graduation, Alice gave me some news that shook up my security again. Alice worked in a Catholic hospital that was run by Nuns. She was living with a married man who was Catholic. Dan's wife had gone to the Mother Superior and insisted that Dan go back to her. If Dan persisted in his ungodly life style, Alice would have to resign her nursing position. The decision was made. They were moving to Edmonton. Alice would have a nursing position on Paediatrics at Holy Cross Hospital. Alice told me I was welcome to move with them. The choice was mine.

I had been dating Charles quite regularly and I didn't really want to leave him. I liked him. His family was fun and I got along really well with his sister, Shelly. I especially didn't want to leave my friends. If I stayed, I would have to find a job right away. I felt I was old enough to be on my own, so Shelly and I got a two bedroom apartment. It would be cheaper to share expenses.

Later, Charles found a job in Lethbridge and moved in with us. Shelly gave up her room and she and I bunked together. Having Charles live with us was awkward at first. I had a fairly healthy dislike for men, and living with one was uncomfortable. The difference with Charles, though, was that he just wanted to be with me. He wasn't out to get what he could from me.

After Charles moved in I saw very little of my girlfriends. Charles and I were inseparable. We went everywhere together and did everything together, but we didn't sleep together. He treated me like a princess and made me feel like a queen. He was kind, gentle, and soft-spoken, and his feelings were easily hurt. He was totally opposite to my dad. I liked that. After all, I did vow that I would never let a man walk all over me, like Dad did to Mom. I was sure Charles didn't have a mean bone in his body.

I was sixteen, infatuated with romance and I had a fairy tale view of what love was. It's called "puppy love," you know - the romance novel kind of love. I was in love with love. I was sure Charles was the man of my dreams; we would get married and live happily ever after. So the night he told me he loved me I thought I had died and gone to Heaven. I thought, "I'm so Lucky! Somebody really loves me!" I gave myself to him willingly. I thought love would make it right.

I couldn't have been more wrong, because after that everything changed. We were playing house. We dated less and stayed home more. The romance bubble was broken. I wanted an engagement ring. Two of my friends were engaged and planning weddings and that was what I wanted - marriage. Charles said he wasn't ready for marriage and we were too young, but I put the pressure on. I nagged until finally he gave in and we bought my rings. I had no idea of what a real love marriage involved. I just wanted to be married.

We went to Medicine Hat to talk to Mom and Dad about a wedding. We picked a date and Dad left all the arrangements to me. He gave me one hundred and fifty dollars to buy a wedding dress and we would get together later to discuss the plans. It was happening. I was going to be a bride just like I dreamed I'd be.

I looked at a few wedding dresses, but the idea of marriage was not as exciting as it was before. I started to drag my feet and finally, by mutual consent, we decided to postpone the wedding. The one hundred and fifty dollars? I spent it!

One Sunday afternoon I got a phone call from Mom. She told me that Dad had cheated on her again with a lady from Seven Persons. Her husband ran Dad off the farm and threatened his life. The farm was sold, the house was sold, and they were moving to Kelowna, British Columbia. They would buy an apartment building there and retire.

I managed to find a fresh amount of hatred for Dad, and a little less respect for Mom. How could she let him do that to her again and still stay with him? Did she like being cheated on? Did she have a hidden desire to be hurt? After I calmed down, I did tell her I was happy that at least now she wouldn't have to work so hard. Taking care of apartments was easy compared to all the work she did before.

Mom told me she sold the piano. My heart broke. That piano was a part of my childhood, a part of my innocence. But that was gone centuries ago, and the sale of the piano closed that part of my life forever. Medicine Hat was finally over.

Marriage started to look appealing again, after my friend Shannon's wedding. The wedding was so romantic and she looked so beautiful. I knew I couldn't ask Dad for money for a dress again. I was lucky to get money the first time. We decided we would go to Coeur d' Alene, Idaho, and elope.

Charles thought I was seventeen. I knew I wasn't old enough to get married without my parents' consent. I was arrogant enough to think that I could get away with being sixteen. The Justice of the Peace would just glance at my birth certificate, overlook my age, and we'd be married.

My heart was pounding so hard I was sure Charles could hear it. The Justice of the Peace looked our papers over and said, "Sorry, I can't marry you; you're under age." Charles looked puzzled. "What do you mean, under age?" The Justice of the Peace replied, "She's only sixteen; she needs consent." Charles never said another word. He turned around and walked out. I quickly gathered up the papers and ran after him. He was very upset!

We got in the car and started back home. He kept saying over and over, "Why didn't you tell me? Why did you let me go all the way to Idaho knowing you were lying about your age?" I was crying so hard I was almost out of control. I told him I was so sorry and I promised him that I would never lie to him again. I pleaded with him not to break up with me. He just said, "Leave me alone; I have to think!" It was a nightmare. I thought for sure he would ask for his ring back.

The next few days were very cool at the apartment. Charles kept his distance and never spoke to me. I knew I deserved it. I wished I could blink and it would go away, like it never happened. Finally, after about a week, he told me we needed to have a talk. I prepared myself for the worst. To my surprise he told me he loved me, and even though he couldn't understand why I wasn't truthful with him, he forgave me and still wanted to marry me. I couldn't believe what I was hearing! He forgave me. I promised again to always be truthful with him.

We gave notice on our apartment and moved in with Alice and Dan at Edmonton. We got written consent from Mom and Dad, and Alice and Dan were our witnesses; the Justice of the Peace pronounced us man and wife, and we were married. Seventeen, and all my dreams of being a beautiful bride were shattered forever!

It was December, a busy month in a beauty salon; so it wasn't hard for Charles to find a job. We rented a cute little furnished apartment and set up house. That lasted over the winter. By spring Charles was homesick, so we moved back to Lethbridge and in with his parents.

There were absolutely no jobs available, so we started looking for work in the smaller towns near Lethbridge. Pincher Creek is a beautiful little town that is nestled in the foothills of the Canadian Rockies. We fell in love with it at first sight. The town was booming and there was only one beauty salon there. They were crying for hairdressers. Charles' dad suggested we set up our own beauty salon. He would help finance it and we would pay it back with monthly payments.

We found the perfect spot downtown and rented it. We ordered the equipment, renovated, and set up shop. We had our own business. The Leading Lady Beauty Lounge. We rented a little old house a few blocks away, borrowed some furniture from Charles' parents and settled in to our new life.

Life became very routine. Get up, go to work, clean the shop after work, go home, make supper, do the dishes, clean the house and go to bed. Everything had to be clean; I was obsessed with cleanliness. Over tired, but clean.

The business wasn't growing as quickly as we expected. The big boom was unfortunately on its way out, but we made enough after expenses to have a decent income. The unexpected! I got pregnant. Pregnancy didn't fit into the plans of a growing business.

I was sick a lot and had dizzy spells, so I frequently stayed home. I finally had to quit altogether. I hardly ever went out after that because, truthfully, I was embarrassed to be pregnant. I felt like everybody was staring at me and I hated it.

Charles ran the shop by himself for a while but it was too much for one person. His dad suggested we hire someone, so we did. The extra expense was a hardship on our already close budget. Money was becoming a problem for us.

We all know females like to talk about their deliveries. I am a female. Eighteen years old; first baby. My pains started about 10:00 p.m. I went to the Pincher Creek Hospital at midnight. There was only one nurse on in maternity so she called my doctor. He said to keep him posted and he'd be in later. The pains were very close together and I was fully dilated. I had to walk from my bed to the delivery room. I walked with my legs real close together. I was sure if I didn't, the baby would drop out on to the floor. By 3:00 a.m. my doctor still wasn't there and I was ready to deliver. He did arrive in time and at 3:15 a.m. Monday, December 2, 1963, a son; Charles Matthew.

By spring we were almost broke. We tried to sell the beauty salon, but the boom was over and there were no buyers. We decided to sell the equipment separately, pay Charles' dad back and look for work.

Meanwhile in Kelowna, Dad decided he was bored with life in their apartment, so he sold it. He bought a twenty-three acre orchard in Rutland, a suburb of Kelowna. They were going
back to hard labor. Dad told us that if we wanted to move to Kelowna, we could help out on the orchard until we could find work. We didn't have any money to move, so Charles' dad paid for it.

We set up house upstairs at mom and dad's. Charles managed to find work right away in a beauty salon close to the orchard. I didn't look for work because Matthew was a real handful. He was colicky for nine months straight. Sometimes he cried so hard I thought he was going to pass out. Mom and I took turns walking the floor with him.

Helping me with Matthew was physically hard on Mom. She worked hard in the orchard all day, then insisted on helping me with the baby. She lovingly walked the floor with him at night. She prayed over him, cried over him, and sang hymns to him. She told him that she loved him and that Jesus loved him too. Mom helped me keep my sanity.

One day while I was walking the floor with Matthew, I realized that I hadn't heard from Alice in a long while. I asked Mom to fill me in on everything I had missed. She whispered, "Don't mention Alice's name in front of your dad, he'll get mad." I said, "Why, what happened?" She told me that Dan wasn't divorced yet and Alice was pregnant. Dad was furious at her and told her he disowned her and she was never to come home again. Nobody knew where she was. I was really upset! I hadn't disowned her. She could keep in touch with me. I wouldn't condemn her, but I knew in my heart that she wouldn't contact any of her family. She disliked Dad enough to just stay gone. I felt sorry for Mom, though, because I could see how hurt she was. She thought she would never see her precious child again. Her heart was broken. She cried and prayed lots and I knew Alice was heavy on her heart.

Bill was a pastor at a small Church of God in Kelowna. He tried very hard to get Charles and me to go to church. He hounded me to quit smoking and go back to the Lord. I hadn't forgotten that God wasn't there for me when I needed Him, and how unfair He was, but Bill was stubborn and kept persisting. Finally, we gave in and went. I could play church when I had to and it would get him off my back.

Our marriage was slowly going on a downhill slide. We really didn't fight; there was just no magic left. Charles was homesick and unhappy. I was beginning to realize how much he needed his dad for support. I wasn't much better. I was unhappy and bored with marriage. We never went anywhere or did anything. We didn't have fun anymore. We talked about it and decided to give it one more try and, if it didn't work, we would separate.

The marriage got better for a while; then it continued on its downhill slide. By that time, though, I suspected that I was pregnant again. That added to our problems. We decided we needed to work at our marriage for the sake of Matthew and the baby on the way.

Mom loved cattle, so it was inevitable that she would have a few milking cows at the orchard. She did the milking and separating. She made cottage cheese and sold it. She sold the milk and cream, and she sold eggs that her chickens laid.

To everyone's surprise, including Mom's, Dad let her keep that money for herself.

One morning during milking, a cow was going to kick Mom so she tried to get out of the way. She fell and shattered the wrist on her left hand. I wanted to rush her to the hospital for x-rays and whatever else she needed, but Dad wouldn't hear of it. He said, "I can fix it just as good as a doctor can. She'll be better off if I do it." I couldn't believe what I was hearing and I boiled with anger. I yelled at him, "What's the matter with you. Are you crazy?" She needs a doctor!" He yelled back, "No doctor!" I walked over to mom and said, "Let's go." Dad came towards me with his hand raised, ready to hit me. I threatened, "You lay a hand on me and I'll have the cops here so fast you won't know what hit you!"

He walked over to Mom and started twisting and turning on her wrist. She was in such agony, I thought she was going to pass out. The tears were streaming down her face and she was sobbing like her children did after they took a beating. She suffered unbearably, with only aspirin to relieve the pain. I was seething with anger so I was happy when Dad wouldn't speak to me anymore.

After that incident Charles said, "We need to get out of here." We packed our belongings and within a week we were ready to go. Before we left, Mom told me to go in the garage and take some apples with us. Dad followed me in and told me not to touch them. There was no fruit for me. I told him he was a real prize, got in the truck, and we were on our way back to Lethbridge. I cried for Mom. I would miss her. I wondered what she was made of that she could live with that man and not kill him.

We rented a large, one bedroom basement suite and Charles got a job at a men's wear store. His salary was low, but we managed with a strict budget. No extras for any fun things. Our only entertainment was going to his parents' house on the weekends to play cards. I looked forward to going there. We had a routine. His mom would make a delicious supper, the men would go in the front room and talk while we did the dishes. We played cards until the wee hours of the morning. We always stayed overnight, so whoever was up first in the morning would look after Matthew. Somehow it always seemed to be Grandpa.

Sunday morning, April 25, 1965, I woke up from a sound sleep at 8:00 a.m., had a labor pain, then another very soon after. I called the doctor, went to the hospital, and by 9:20 a.m., I had delivered a beautiful baby girl, Stephanie Dawn.

I was nineteen years old, had an unhappy marriage, and two babies. Fortunately my life was too busy to worry about it. Matthew and Stephanie were only sixteen months apart. They were both in cloth diapers and both needed to be fed. I made it harder on myself, though, because I never let Matthew feed himself. I couldn't stand a food mess on the floor.

They were both beautiful little babies and I had so much love to give them. Stephanie wasn't colicky at all and I was very thankful for that. It was almost like having two dolls to play with: two Snuggles.

That year I spent almost all my time with the kids. There was always something to teach them, and of course they were constantly teaching me: mostly patience! I was trying to grow up too. I loved to give them "butterfly kisses." In case you don't know, a "butterfly kiss" is when you blink your eyelashes very quickly on their cheek or eyelids. It tickled and they laughed. Or I gave them an "Eskimo kiss," which is rubbing noses together. I loved to smooch with them. For Matthew there was potty training, and learning to drink from a cup. For Stephanie there was learning to crawl, and later to walk. In between I was trying to keep Matthew from walking on Stephanie's fingers when she was crawling on the floor. I was referee when they had their little fights, and doctor when

I had to "kiss it better." Matthew loved to play in the sandbox in the back yard and splash around in his little swimming pool. Stephanie just loved to be held and cuddled. My kids were my life.

One day Charles came home from work and asked me if I wanted to go to Saskatchewan to see Harry and Anne. I called her to see if they would be home. The arrangements were made and the next weekend we were on our way. I was so excited! I hadn't been there since I was fourteen. It would be like going home.

Saturday night while we were doing dishes there was a knock on the door. To my surprise, there stood Douglas. I had forgotten how handsome he was. My heart actually did a flip! He was muscular, over six feet tall, had beautiful dark wavy hair and blue eyes that pierced my heart. He was married, so I wondered why he was by himself. I didn't go into the front room but I could see out of the corner of my eye that he was watching my every move. I knew that the excitement I was feeling could go nowhere. I was not going to be like my dad and be unfaithful.

After our trip to Saskatchewan I was even more discontent with my marriage. One problem was interference by his parents, and the second problem was still finances. It seemed we needed more money and had less of it. I decided I needed to find a job. There were no hairdressing jobs available, so I looked elsewhere. There was a full-time position for a carhop available at the A&W. I applied and got the job. The next problem to overcome was finding a good baby-sitter on such short notice. My friend, Shannon, told me about a lady named Vi Parsons who might be interested. She had three children of her own. Her youngest was Matthew's age. She was a jolly, middle-aged Ukrainian lady who loved kids. I liked her immediately, and the kids liked her too.

The extra money helped a lot and by spring we could afford to rent a two bedroom house. The kids had to share a bedroom, but they were too young to care. It was nice and bright because it had lots of windows. It had a small kitchen, but it had a huge living room, lots of room for the kids to play in.

Charles applied for a position as a fireman and had to go through some intensive training and testing to see if he was firefighter material. He was accepted and our lives changed drastically. He had to do shift work and I had to be alone some nights. I felt a little safer with the kids there but I still had that childhood fear of being alone.

The following summer we took another weekend trip to Swift Current to see Harry and Anne. I was secretly hoping that Douglas would visit again, and yet I hoped he wouldn't. He didn't come on Saturday night so I assumed he didn't want to, because he knew we were coming to visit. Sunday after church and dinner, he drove into the yard. Handsome man! He didn't come in this time. We all just visited in the yard and then he was gone. "Oh well," I thought, "it's better this way, anyway."

In the late summer of 1967, Dad had another heart attack and was hospitalized. Mom and Auntie Hilda were alone in the orchard and neither one could drive. It was almost plum-picking time and Mom needed help. I wasn't working anymore because Charles was making pretty good money and he wanted me to stay home with the kids. He said they needed their mom.

Our second vehicle was a little blue Volkswagen "Beetle." I packed it up, and the kids and I took off for Kelowna. Driving in the mountains with a Volkswagen and two small children is quite an experience. I had to floor the gas pedal on the way down the mountain so that I could get up the other side. I think that a few times a person who was just walking could have passed us. At least I had time to look at the beautiful scenery. Of course, the kids were very unhappy with each other that day, and most of the time it was World War III in the back seat. Finally, after twelve hours of driving, we arrived safely.

This was the first time I had ever been anywhere alone. I liked it! Neither Charles nor I were very happy these days. Living together was more of a partnership than a marriage: very little affection and a lot of duties. I decided I was going to enjoy every minute of my freedom.

Picking plums was harder than I expected it to be. The ladders were big and heavy and the boxes were very heavy when they were full of fruit. I had to learn how to drive Dad's old tractor so that I could pull the wagon that had all the boxes of picked fruit on it. Learning how to drive that tractor reminded me of the first time Dad tried to teach me how to drive the car. You remember, Jerk, Jerk, Jerk.

Mom gave each of the kids an ice cream pail and they picked the plums that they could reach from the ground. They felt very important, especially when Grandma praised them for doing such a good job. When the wagon was full of boxes of plums, I loaded them onto Dad's pickup truck and Mom and I headed for the packing house. Everything was going fine until I turned the first corner. Suddenly there were some loud bangs and I stopped short. To my horror, there in the middle of the intersection lay the plums. The top boxes were smashed and the plums were mush! I was so upset I started to laugh. Mom cried. We cleaned up the mess as best we could and continued on our trip to the packing house. The man there told me that I had piled the boxes too high and stacked them the wrong way; that's why they slid off. We packed the next load the right way and there were no more problems.

All too soon it was time to go home. I really dreaded going back there; life was such a drag. I didn't care what

Charles said, I needed to get out of the house or go crazy. I applied for a job in a department store and got it. Vi was willing to baby-sit again and I felt like I was let out of prison.

I looked forward to going to work. I made a couple of new girlfriends who liked to party. They kept asking me to go with them, but I always went home. They kept nagging me and finally I consented to go with them, "just this one time." It was fun. I had forgotten what it was like to laugh. It felt good.

Partying became a habit. I only went out when Charles was on the afternoon shift; 4:00 p.m. to midnight. It was like sneaking out to the show when I was young. The fear of getting caught made it all the more exciting. I didn't have to worry about the kids because Vi was looking after them and she was very good to them.

All I wanted to do was have a good time and forget my unhappy life. Subconsciously I wanted to get caught; that would be an easy way to get out of my marriage. The booze flowed like water, the music was romantic and easy to dance to and the guys were on the make, and so was I. They knew all the right words to say to a love-starved loser like me. I was just like my dad and I didn't care.

When Dad got out of the hospital his doctor had told him that he couldn't do any more hard work, so instead of selling the orchard outright, he decided to sub-divide it. The Real Estate Agency told him he could make more money that way. For a percentage of the profit the Agency would do the actual sub-division. Dad agreed, and after the contract was signed the procedure began. I was happy to hear the orchard would be gone, because I knew the work was too hard for Mom and Dad. They weren't getting any younger.

I had been having a lot of pain in the mid-section of my body. I went to the doctor thinking I had an ulcer. After some tests he told me it was my gall bladder. With a proper diet and no alcohol I should be all right. I didn't listen, of course, and after a party one night I had a gall bladder attack. The pain was excruciating. My doctor told me it had to come out.

The gall bladder surgery went well, but the day before I was to go home I got real sick, and had a lot of cramping in the abdomen area. Examination found an abscess on my uterus. I needed another surgery to drain it. A short time later I had to have a complete hysterectomy.

Charles became very compassionate and caring during all the surgeries. He even sent me a bouquet of flowers. When I got home from the hospital he took control and looked after me, the kids, and the house. This was the kind and thoughtful man I married. I wondered if there was hope for our marriage after all. I promised myself that if he stayed this way my partying would end.

News arrived that Dad was in the hospital again. The doctors said it was terminal. Most of our family went to see him, and to their surprise, Dad asked for forgiveness. He said he wasn't a good father and said he was sorry for everything he had done. Some of us forgave him and some of us didn't. After that Dad seemed to rally a bit so the doctor sent him home, but he was to stay in bed. He didn't listen, of course. The day after Father's Day 1968, Dad collapsed and died on the basement floor. Bill was there and he helped Mom make all the necessary arrangements.

I had a storehouse of mixed emotions. I felt guilty because secretly I had wished him dead, and now he was. I felt guilty because I hadn't taken time to call him on Father's Day. I felt sad because no matter what, he was still my dad, and I would miss him. I felt glad for Mom that she could finally be released from her unhappy marriage. I felt angry that Dad never had to pay for any of the evil things he had done in his lifetime. I wondered if by some slim chance, he might have made peace with God and gone to Heaven.

Mom was really wishing she knew where Alice was. She missed her so very much. She felt that Alice needed to know her dad was dead, and that she would be welcomed home with open arms. It seemed like an impossibility. How could we find somebody who didn't want to be found? Somebody in the family came up with the idea that the Veteran's Board would know where she was as she received a monthly widow's pension, because her late husband had been a war veteran. We contacted them and they told us they weren't allowed to reveal her whereabouts, but they would forward the message to her. It only took a few days and Mom received a phone call from Alice.

She was in San Diego, California. She was married to Dan and they had a child, a girl, Sheila. She was working as a nurse for three doctors who were ear, eye, nose, and throat specialists. She felt bad that she hadn't kept in touch with Mom. She loved her and missed her very much, but she would not come home for the funeral. Dad was a non-issue.

Norm and Sharon were expecting their third child. Two days after Dad died their baby boy, Daryn, was born. They had a hard decision to make. After almost eight years they were blessed with the little boy Norm had longed for. Should he stay home with his wife who needed
him, and his little boy that he had prayed for for so many years, or should he go to be with his mom and family who also needed him: Sharon was very gracious and agreed that he attend the funeral.

All the family was at the funeral except Alice. The pastor talked about a loving God who would forgive our sins if we asked Him. I listened very closely. It had been many years since I thought about Heaven and hell. I was sure there was a God up there somewhere, but He wasn't here, anywhere close. The pastor's voice faded into the background as my mind traveled back to that Christmas Eve when I received my first

Bible. I still had the Bible but I never opened it. I wondered what my life would have been like if that awful day at Jodie's hadn't happened. Would I love the Lord like mom did? Who would I be married to? The singing brought me back to reality. What a dreamer I was to think that God even cared about me.

The subdivision of the orchard continued after Dad died, except now Bill was helping Mom with the details. Mom received money from the Real Estate Agency every time a lot sold, and there was some life insurance money. Dad's will stated that Mom would receive half of everything and the other half was to be divided up between the kids.

With the money I received, Charles, the kids, and I, flew to California to see Alice. Everything was so beautiful; the palm trees, the flowers, the ocean. We were like kids in a candy shop. We went to Disneyland and took the kids on all the rides. We went to SeaWorld and saw Shamu, the killer whale. We saw everything we possibly could. Mom flew down with us but she was content to just visit with Alice. They had so much catching up to do. Next, I bought a 1968, V-8 automatic, two door hardtop; maroon and white Beaumont car. My very own car and she was beautiful!

It wasn't long until I became very restless. It was like something was chasing me, and if I didn't run as fast as I could it would catch and devour me. I couldn't sit still. I had to be on the move. Nothing satisfied me, especially my marriage. It was so routine and it was boring. I needed to have a good time and I needed to be with my friends. They knew how to have a good time. Who needed God anyway? I did exactly as I pleased and never thought twice about my marriage.

I asked Charles for a divorce. He said, "No." I told him the only thing we had left in common was the kids and they would be just fine without him. He could see the kids whenever he wanted, but as far as the marriage, it was over.

We lived in the same house, but we were as divided as the North and South Poles. We were at a stalemate.

Finally one night he said, "Let's talk." I asked him what it would take for him to give me a divorce. By his answer I knew he had been getting advice from someone; probably his best friend, his dad. He told me that if I wanted to run around and act single, I'd have to pay. I said, "What do you mean, pay?" He told me that he would give me a divorce if I gave him the Beaumont and signed a paper saying that he didn't have to pay me any alimony or child support. I could keep the Volkswagen and the furniture.

When I agreed, I could see by the look on his face that he didn't expect his little scheme to backfire on him like it did. He was so sure I wouldn't give up my car or financial support. He looked like I had slapped him in the face. I felt like doing just that because I had absolutely no respect for a man who would use his kids as bait for a settlement. He moved out and the kids and I were alone.

Now what? I had no job and only a little money left in the bank. I needed something that paid more than minimum wage. I had the full responsibility of supporting myself and my kids. My friend, Vi, told me I should try to get a job at a service station. I did find a job close to home, pumping gas. Strange as it seems, I liked my job. Vi, the wonderful friend she was, wouldn't take any money from me, at first, for baby-sitting. She said that as soon as I got back on my feet, we'd renegotiate.

I hardly ever went out at night. I couldn't afford to and I wanted to spend more time with the kids. I was usually pretty tired by evening, but I was happy. I know the kids missed their dad, though, and they were happy when he came to get them for a visit.

That summer Mom came to visit us. She brought a little cheque from the sale of another lot in the orchard. She filled my fridge and cupboards with groceries and bought each of my kids a new outfit. Matthew would be starting grade one very soon and Stephanie would be going to kindergarten. I was sure mom was an angel in disguise. I knew her Lord would truly bless her for the wonderful woman she was. I was actually glad when I heard Mom tell Matthew and Stephanie some Bible stories. She said bedtime prayers with them and told them that she loved them, and so did Jesus. God was okay for my kids, but I didn't need Him. After we put Mom on the bus, I went home and cried like a little girl. I loved that woman very much.

Over the winter I developed a friendship with a couple who always got gas at my service station. Their names were Lamar and Denise. The kids and I went to their house for supper one night and when we walked in, I almost turned around and walked out. Her house was a disaster! It looked like a war zone! There were kids and cats everywhere and it smelled like the garbage hadn't been taken out in quite awhile. I was a fanatic about a clean house and I could hardly stand it. I knew I would just have to close my eyes to everything, or I'd never make it through supper, let alone the whole evening. They were a wonderful couple and I would have to just accept them as they were.

After dishes were done, Lamar told me he wanted to show me what he did for a hobby. We all went into the garage and there it was, a beautiful white stock car with the number 22 painted on it in black. I could hardly believe that he was a stock car driver. I didn't actually know what a race car driver looked like, but I was sure he wasn't one. He was too tall and skinny. He started the car and revved the engine a few times. I was hooked. He invited me to come to the races with them when they started up in the spring. I told him I could hardly wait.

The first stock car race of the season, the kids and I went with Denise and her kids. I had never been to a race before so I was curious about everything. The track was a paved, one-quarter mile oval. There were two classes of stock cars. Lamar's was a street car that was stripped; and a racing engine and roll bars were installed. The "B" modifieds looked more like the race cars at the Indianapolis 500. After the time trials they lined up in twos, ten deep, fastest at the front, slowest at the back.

The grandstand was full and buzzing with excitement. The cars lined up at the starting line! All eyes were on the flagman! He waved the green flag! The race was on! The roar of the engines was almost deafening, but it was the biggest thrill of my life, next to Disneyland! The fans were cheering wildly for their favorite drivers. Many laps later, the white flag came up. One lap left. The checkered flag came up and the flagman waved it like a conductor directing a symphony orchestra. Lamar came in second.

After the races were over we went down into the pit area to see Lamar. I walked around and looked at all the cars. It was exciting! Lamar introduced me to some of the drivers. I guess I expected race car drivers to look like movie stars, but most of them were ordinary people with families. However, Lamar did introduce me to some eligible drivers. I was hooked on stock car racing!

I was shocked when one of the drivers called and asked me out on a date. His name was Mack and he was one of the drivers Lamar had introduced me to. I remembered him as being older. He had salt and pepper colored hair and hazel colored eyes. He wasn't really hard to look at, but what I remembered most was his politeness. He called me "Ma'am." I hesitated to give him an answer, then decided that I had nothing to lose. I'd go out with him. Besides, if Lamar introduced us, he was probably a good guy.

We went to a supper club and he was a perfect gentleman. We spent the evening "wining and dining." He loved to dance and was very good at it. When the evening was over, he walked me to my front door, then he was gone. I figured I hadn't made a very good impression on him because he didn't even offer a good night kiss.

After every race we went to the pit area, so it was easy for me to slip over to Mack's car and see if he even remembered me. When he saw me, he gave me a big smile and called me over. He was sorry he hadn't called, but they were having some problems with his car and it took all of his time to fix it. He asked if he could call me again. I said, "Sure."

All our dates were fun. We went to a supper club, ate, drank and danced the night away, or we went to the bar, listened to the music until closing, then went for Chinese food. We drank beer and worked on the stock car, and of course we raced! We played bridge with his sister and brother-in-law, or his mom and dad, or golfed.

Mack was a total opposite to Charles. He liked to talk and we discussed everything from his tour of duty in Korea to how to finesse in the game of bridge. He was very independent and didn't have to talk everything over with Dad before he did it.

He had gone through a bitter divorce. When it was all over, his ex-wife moved his five-year old son and infant daughter as far east as she could. He hadn't spoken to them or seen them since.

He told me he had never met anybody until me who he was willing to take another chance on. He said that he was falling in love with me. I was not prepared for that statement at all! I just wanted to have a good time, no strings. I wasn't even divorced.

He kept insisting that he loved me and wanted to be with me. I liked him a lot but it wasn't love. His maturity made me feel secure and protected. We had a lot in common, but I wasn't ready for any kind of commitment.

When he asked me if he could move in with us I said, "No." He made himself scarce after that. He missed several races and, when I called him, he didn't answer his phone. I thought it was over. I was a lot unhappier than I should have been and I missed him. Finally he called me. By that time I thought I probably did love him, and I gave in. I didn't even think about asking my kids what they wanted. I only thought of myself.

Mack and Stephanie hit if off right away. She was the little daughter he never got to know. Matthew, on the other hand, was not Mack's son. He resented Matthew because of it.

In the past, when the kids had their regular visits with their dad and grandparents, the visits went well. The kids came home happy. They enjoyed their visits and looked forward to them. After the last few visits, though, I noticed the kids were upset and seemed to be fighting more.

I asked them what was wrong. They said, "Nothing." I knew there was a problem, though, and I pestered them until finally Stephanie blurted it all out. Grandpa always tells us that our mommy is bad. He says you are a bad girl for having a man stay at our house. Stephanie said, "Daddy always asks questions about you and when we don't know the answer he gets mad at us." Then they told both kids not to tell me what they said.

I was outraged! I called Charles and told him that if that happened again, all their visiting privileges would be denied. We didn't owe them a thing. Charles didn't care enough about his kids to even pay child support, so as far as I was concerned he had no say in the kids' lives, or mine.

A few weeks later I was served with my preliminary divorce papers. The grounds, adultery. That was an ugly word to me. It was a word that made me think of my dad. I had vowed I would never be like him. Here I was, just like him.

We had a church wedding, something I had dreamed about all my life. I couldn't wear a long, elegant white gown of pearls and lace, but I did wear a pale pink lace dress that made me feel and look beautiful. My headpiece was pink and white with a short white veil. My flowers: pink roses.

Matthew was ring bearer. He looked so handsome in his little black suit. Stephanie was my beautiful little flower girl. She wore a cute little turquoise and white dress and carried a basket of white daisies. Matthew wore a white carnation boutonniere; Stephanie, a pink Sweetheart Rose corsage.

We invited immediate family from both sides and a few close friends to the wedding. It was a special blessing to have mom there. She stood by me all the years I gave her heartache and she never stopped praying for me. Harry and Anne came too. They never condemned me for my lifestyle, either. Al and his wife Fran were there. Fran so willingly and beautifully played the piano. Norm and Sharon ... Norm honored me by walking me down the aisle.

All the way down the aisle I was wondering if I was doing the right thing. But when Mack smiled at me all the butterflies in my stomach took flight and left. Tears filled his eyes when he said his vows to me. I thought, "He really does love me. I AM going to make this work!"

CHAPTER FOUR

A Glimpse of the Road Back:

Are you there Jesus?

The first four months of marriage were high energy: work all day, drink and dance at night, race on the weekends. My kids were at Vi's place most of the time. Lots of times we were so late getting home from the bar that she had put them to bed. Sometimes they stayed overnight: sometimes we took them home, asleep.

I was in love with racing. The speed and the roar of the engines gave me an adrenaline rush. So naturally when I was asked if I wanted to drive in a powder puff (ladies) race, "Yes," came out of my mouth before I even had a chance to think about it. Out loud, I said "THANK YOU, DAD, for teaching me how to drive!"

Race Day! I was driving Lamar's car, number 22. It was easier to drive than Mack's; something to do with the steering. I didn't care whose car I drove, I just wanted to drive. I sat in a stock car many times, but this would be the first time I actually drove. Lamar said I needed some practice laps to get used to the car and the track. "Just take it easy and build up your speed each lap." I had watched enough races to know what to do, but actually doing it was very different. I had no fear, so I pushed it as hard as I could. When I got back into the pit area Mack told me that if I drove like that in the race, I'd be a winner.

Next were the time trials. I had to drive two laps. On the second lap they clocked my speed. I came in the third fastest of ten women. That put me inside, second from the front. Lamar said that was a good position. He said, "Stay inside, watch close, and if anybody makes a mistake, make your move." Simple!

The night seemed to drag on forever. Finally it was the ladies' turn. I was so excited my body was shaking from the inside out. I slipped into a pair of white racing coveralls, put Lamar's racing helmet on, snapped it tight under my chin, climbed through the window, sat in the seat, strapped the seat belt on tight, and started the engine. The flagmen lined us up and we were off. We slowly circled the track trying to get close enough together to start the race. Fourth time around we got the green flag.

The roar of the engines was much louder in the car than it was in the grandstand. It was electrifying! But above the roar I could hear my thoughts. They were so loud in my head that I was sure there was a microphone under my helmet. "The straight-away, step on it; okay, the corner; foot off the gas a little; tromp on it; tromp on it; okay, straight away; faster, go faster, Susan; good, good, the car in front of me is losing control; oh no, she hung on; okay, okay, keep watching, maybe she'll spin out; the white flag; one lap left; I need to make a move if I want to win; Push, Push; last corner; straight away; checkered flag. Third; I got third!" I was disappointed but Mack and Lamar told me not to feel bad, I drove a good race. What a night! I absolutely loved it!

Saturday was my time with the kids. We had a ritual. We went to the mall. We laughed and talked. We ate hamburgers, fries and gravy, and drank Coke. Matthew especially enjoyed Saturdays because he didn't have to be near Mack. There was an underlying feeling of dislike developing between them, but I didn't think there was any real problem. It would be all right.

One night a phone call came for Mack. It was a man's voice that I didn't recognize. After Mack said hello there was a long silence. I wondered why he wasn't talking so I looked

112

over at him. Tears were streaming down his face. I panicked. I thought maybe one of his parents had died. Then I heard him say, "Bobby, my precious son."

When he got off the phone, he said Bobby had turned eighteen and was old enough to leave home. He was coming out west and was going to live with us. I said, "Don't you think we should have talked about it first?" I knew there would be trouble because I knew how he treated Matthew. If Bobby got all the love, Matthew was really going to get hurt.

May 28, 1971. Mack and I went to the bar, went for Chinese food, picked up the kids from Vi's, and went home. I drank too much and everything was spinning. I went straight to bed. When the phone rang, Mack answered it. It was for me. It was Al. He said, "I have some terrible news. Norm was in an accident with his semi. He is dead." I sobered up immediately. I told him I didn't believe him, he was playing some sort of horrible trick on me. He said, "No tricks." I started to cry, "Oh no, not Norm, please not Norm." I went numb. I knew Al was
still talking, but I couldn't hear him anymore. I held the phone in my hand and wept. "Susan, Susan," Al was calling me, but I couldn't answer. Mack took the phone from me and Al told him the whole gruesome story.

Norm was taking a semi-load of cattle carcasses north, from Medicine Hat to Calgary. It wasn't his run but because the regular driver hadn't had enough rest, Norm agreed to take it for him. About four miles east of Calgary on the Trans-Canada Highway, a car heading south stopped to let Norm go by so that he could turn left on to Conrich Road. A three-ton, gasoline operated, delivery truck was following the car. When the car stopped to let Norm go by, the truck behind was following too close to stop. Instead of turning toward the ditch to miss the car, he turned into the oncoming traffic lane, hitting Norm, head on. There was an explosion and tremendous fire. Three people dead. Norm, 37 years old, - Dead!

The clean up was horrendous. Charred bodies and body parts were found many feet away, mixed in with the carcasses. After Mack told me the whole story I went into the bathroom and vomited. I couldn't believe that anything that horrible could happen to Norm. He was such a good person and this was so horrific.

After a few hours I was finally composed enough to have a few clear thoughts. Mom would know by now too. She was all alone; I needed to call her and see if she was okay. Bill lived in Kelowna; maybe he was there with her. It took a long time for her to answer. I asked her how she was. She said, "It's Norm isn't it? I had a nightmare about him.
He died in it." She wept. I felt sick. Why did I call her? Over and over I said, "Oh Mom, I'm so sorry. I'm so sorry." She said, "It's all right, Susie, I'm okay. I'm okay."

Late the next morning Bill called me. He was at Mom's. She had settled down and was resting. The reason he hadn't told Mom that night was that he didn't want to disturb her rest. He knew she wouldn't be able to sleep for the rest of the night and he thought she would be needing her rest to cope with everything. He said he could have told her, though, because she was awake from that nightmare, and had been crying and praying most of the night.

I shut down. Mack tried to get me to talk about it. There were so many thoughts going through my mind. It was like trying to put the pieces of a puzzle together, but nothing fit. Everything was scrambled and out of place. He told me that if I couldn't talk about it, I should try to write down how I was feeling, on paper. If I didn't let it out it would destroy me. I wasn't a writer, but the words flowed quickly, from somewhere deep within.

The life of a brother has been taken away.

*The pain and emptiness I feel today, is unbearable to
the point of mental fatigue.*

*If there is a God? Tell me why, why do good people
have to die?*

*The horror of his violent death, leaves a rotten taste in
my mouth and an ache in my heart.*

I think back to the hardships of his short life ...
How could this tragedy happen?
He's leaving behind a wife with no husband -
Three children with no father -
A mother with no son -
A family with no brother -
I don't understand it, explain it to me, somebody!
I am so angry,
There is a gnawing in the pit of my stomach,
*The tears are always just below the surface, ready to
flow.*

*I don't want to see his charred body, and yet, I feel an
uncontainable drive to see him -*
just one more time,
to say good-bye,
to say I'm sorry if I hurt you,
to tell him I should have done more for him.
*I know he's in Heaven; his soul isn't in the torture of
hell.*

*I hope Dad is with him - so he won't be lonely, while he
waits for the rest of us to join*
him, on that important day in everyone's life.
Death!

I was afraid to go to sleep at night. If I died in my sleep
I'd go to hell. I should have been the one who died. Norm was
the good guy. Why did God take him? Why didn't He take
me? I deserved it! I had wished bad things on Norm when I
was young. It must be my fault! There was a slight chance that

I could accept a simple death, but mangled, charred bodies - that was too much. I just couldn't comprehend it! How could such a wonderful loving God allow such a horrible, ugly accident?

The funeral was like a church service. When the congregation sang they looked happy, but I could see tears. Something very strange was going on. I had "goose-bumps" all over my head and down the back of my neck. The policeman, Al Matson, sang a solo. He sang about how much Jesus loves us. I knew Norm loved Jesus with his whole heart. I almost fell apart when the pastor spoke these words:

"No man can live as great a life as Norm lived, without faith. His faith in God bore up under various strains and never wavered. He had unshaking faith in the Bible: not once did he question it. He had faith in his fellow man, both in and outside of the church.

"Norm was a man of deep feeling. He felt deeply about anything that had the slightest tendency to harm the church he loved and served so devotedly. He was deeply moved by gratitude and helped to strengthen many aspects of church life. He never hurried away following a service, but was "always in the midst," giving hand clasp, offering praise, expressing appreciation and giving encouragement and kindly comments.

"No one questioned that he displayed New Testament love for his wife Sharon, loving her as we read, 'Husbands, love your wives, even as Christ loved the church.' He was a fine father, possessing excellencies greatly to be valued. Two lovely daughters, Kim and Shawn, and a son Daryn, which he especially felt was God-given, blessed their union ...

"It is hard for us to accept that he is gone, but there is joy in knowing that he is forever at God's right hand.

"So, until the day dawns and the shadows flee away - we will remember him."

Due to the state of Norm's body, no one, including Sharon, was allowed to see him. It was a closed casket, so as the pall bearers carried Norm's body past me, on the way out of the church, I had to say good-bye. I reached out and touched his casket. The moment I touched it I felt a tingling go from my fingertips, up my arm, to the side of my face. It was as if his soul was touching mine. I took my hand off as quickly as I had put it on. Then I wept.

The trees and grass seemed unusually green at the graveside. There was not a breath of wind. It was as calm and peaceful as a sleeping child. This was it! This was where it ended! At the very second the pastor said, "Ashes to ashes," a gale force gust of wind blew across the coffin, across us, then it was gone. As quiet as a moment before.

I didn't want to admit it, but I knew without a doubt that God's presence was there. His presence blew across Norm and took him home to Heaven. If I had doubted that there was a God, after that funeral I knew in my heart that God was real. That day, I had my first glimpse of the long road back to Jesus!

Lack of sleep became commonplace with me. I was afraid to drive too fast, afraid to go to sleep, afraid of being alone: all my old fears, plus some new ones. I did remember about Heaven and hell. I watched television until the early morning hours. One night while I was paging through the channels, I tuned in to Jimmy Swaggart. He was preaching hell-fire and brimstone. He pointed his finger right at me and said, "If you don't repent right now, hell awaits you." My heart started pounding so fast I couldn't change the channel fast enough. I was really under conviction! Maybe I should give my heart back to Jesus? I don't want to go to hell. Night after night the same routine. I argued. "If I get saved, look at all I have to give up; dancing, smoking, drinking. On and on the list went. I thought I was going insane.

I received word that instead of buying flowers for Norm's funeral, people donated money, on behalf of him, to the World Mission Living Memorial fund. Enough money had been sent to Brazil to build a church in his honor. A plaque was placed on the church that read, *"In Living Memory of Norman Mueller: December 13th, 1933 to May 28th, 1971."*

In one sense that news made me happy; in another it hardened my heart. I thought, "Surely, God could have found another way to build that church in Brazil?" It was too much for my emotions to handle. I had to shut it off. Once again I said good-bye to God. I was sure it was forever.

Slowly but surely Charles stopped picking the kids up for their visits. It was so gradual that I hadn't even noticed it, until Matthew asked me when he could see his dad again. I told him I'd find out.

Charles said he wouldn't be picking them up anymore, for two reasons. One: He found himself asking the kids too many questions about what I was doing. It was an obsession with him. Second: It hurt too much to have to leave them every time. It was easier not to see them than to say good-bye. I couldn't understand his logic, but that was the way it was going to be. I told the kids their dad wasn't going to be picking them up anymore and I never gave them a reason. They were being rejected by their dad and it hurt them. No more was said about it.

Bobby arrived at our house with all his belongings, ready for a long stay. Our family life changed from that day forward. Things were exactly as I expected them to be. Bobby was perfect and could do no wrong; the apple of his dad's eye. Mack spent practically all his spare time with Bobby. Bobby looked like his dad, acted like his dad and thought like his dad. Mack's rejection of Matthew became more evident with every day. Finally he just quit talking to him. It was like Matthew didn't exist. I got angry.

I told Mack that if his attitude didn't change toward Matthew, our marriage would be over. He said, "Just how do you expect me to act? I haven't seen Bobby for ten years." I understood that, but I asked him how he thought Matthew felt being rejected by his dad and by his step-dad. All Matthew wanted was a father. I told him if he wanted our marriage to work, he would have to make an effort to include Matthew in his life. Things got worse and Matthew's hurt turned into anger.

Bill was building a new house for Mom with her money from the sub-division of the orchard. She called to tell me it was complete and she was living in it. She was finding it hard to cope with Norm's death, but she was happy with her new house. I shared my concerns with her regarding Matthew. She said, "Why don't you let Matthew and Stephanie come out for the summer and stay with me? Maybe by fall things will be better." I asked the kids if they wanted to go stay at Grandma Mueller's. They agreed it would be fun.

While the kids were at Mom's that summer I got another inheritance cheque. Mack wanted to up the class of his race car to a "B" modified. He asked if we could use this cheque to buy one. I said, "Sure." After all, I loved racing too. He found one in Calgary and bought it. What a car! It did look like a baby sister to the "Indy" cars.

In a few weeks the Stock Car Club was going to host an international "B" modified race meet. There would be cars from all over Western Canada and some from Montana. Mack was
excited about racing his new car. Unfortunately his pit crew was having all kinds of tire problems. He spun out on his time trials so he had to watch the races the first night. He was not happy.

The last race of the night a driver from Montana lost control of his car. It rolled over on its roof and caught fire.

These cars burned high octane fuel, so the fire was extremely hot. The driver's seat belt wouldn't release so he was hanging upside down, on fire. A couple of other drivers burned their hands trying to get him out. It seemed like a hundred years went by until they came with fire extinguishers and put it out. By that time, the driver's racing coveralls had melted onto his body. The grandstand was silent. We heard him screaming in agony, then he was quiet. I immediately thought about Norm and I went to the washroom and vomited. The driver died three days later.

A powder puff race was scheduled for the next weekend. After watching that driver burn the week before, and thinking about Norm lots again, I didn't want to enter. I told Mack I was afraid I would crash and burn. He said that would never happen in the kind of car I was driving, so I agreed to race.

I had another adrenaline rush, but this time it was fear. I did my time trial; came in ninth, of ten cars. I was so afraid. My foot was shaking so hard I thought it would jump right off the gas pedal. In the race I did everything wrong and spun out. Race over! I was scared to death. I vowed I would never race again.

Things were changing in our marriage. Mack was becoming too possessive. I was very independent and needed breathing space. He wanted to cling. When we went dancing he didn't want to dance, but if I danced with someone else he got jealous. He didn't like me working at the service station anymore because I was too friendly with the men.

I, unfortunately, had a terrible temper. Just like my dad. So we had some really big fights. I "saw red," as the saying goes. I wanted Mack to back off and give me my space. He finally did and he started going to the bar after work, and usually stayed until closing. I didn't care because he was becoming a real "So and So" and I was liking him less and less.

I started going to the lounge with my girlfriends. The pasture looked greener on the other side. When I went out alone it made Mack a little crazy. He would accuse me of cheating on him, then he would say he was sorry and tell me he didn't want to lose me.

When the kids came home I knew it wouldn't be any better for them. In fact, I imagined it would be worse because Mack was so wrapped up in Bobby. Sometimes the tension was so thick in the house that I could have cut it with a knife. Everybody was upset and nobody was happy. To Mack, Matthew didn't exist. Matthew dealt with his rejection by staying in his room or watching television. Both were a way for him to escape from reality.

Finally I said, "This is enough," and made Mack tell me what was going on. Why was he being such an idiot? I said, "What's wrong?" He said, "Nothing, nothing." I said, "You're lying. Give me an answer." He broke down and cried. Bobby was leaving in the spring to join the army. I was livid! "You mean you put us all through hell just because your precious "so and so" son is leaving?" I thought, "You "So and So." You're going to pay for this!"

I did quit my job at the service station, but certainly not because Mack wanted me to. It was a drag working there and I needed a change. I found a job at a factory, making dishes. It was hard work and boring, but it was something different.

Home life was getting more and more difficult. The kids seemed to be fighting all the time. Most of the fights ended up physical, with Stephanie getting the worst of it. I knew Matthew was hurting and angry, but he kept it all inside, except one night. Mack came home from the bar and wanted me to make him some supper. I told him supper was at 5:30 p.m. and he had missed it. If he wanted to eat, he had to make it himself. He went into a rage, yelling and swearing at me. He knocked things off the shelves in the front room, pushed over some easy chairs, yanked a big picture off the wall and broke it over my head. Then he left, slamming the door behind him.

The pain exploded at the top of my skull and ran down the rest of my head. My head was throbbing. I was so angry, I was shaking and crying at the same time. I told myself to stop acting like a baby, to be strong like Mom was when she was beaten. I hardened by heart towards Mack; I vowed he would never touch me again.

After Mack left, the kids came downstairs. Matthew was so angry he said, "If I had a gun, I'd kill him!" Matthew's anger had turned to rage. He went to his room and punched his pillow so hard and so many times, that his arms tired out and he couldn't punch any more.

Help came in the form of a television commercial. The Lethbridge Community College was advertising an upgrading program for high school drop-outs. All that was required was that a test be taken to establish the grade level where each individual was. I filled out an application, was accepted, tested, and told I had the equivalent of a grade eleven education. I was surprised, because I had only completed grade nine and part of grade ten. I would start in January and graduate with a grade twelve education at the end of June. That meant there would be a lot of homework. I was prepared to do that.

I was hoping that after I graduated I could get a better job; one that wasn't so hard and tedious. I was a little concerned about remembering how to study, but I assumed it would come back to me in a big hurry. I made a promise to myself that I would give it all I had. Come hell or high water, I would do this.

School was very difficult at first. But the professors were very understanding and helpful. They were aware of the problems an adult student can have adjusting. Before long I was finding school very interesting. It seemed easier to learn now than when I was young. It seemed that I could understand

122

better. My brain was like a big sponge, absorbing everything it heard. Maybe the difference was that I wanted to be there.

Going back to school does change your home life. It was kind of fun to sit at the kitchen table with my kids, doing homework. I had a lot of homework and burned the midnight oil many times. I even pulled an all-nighter to finish a huge assignment for my English class. I wondered if I was cracking up, because I even liked Biology (my worst subject in high school.)

There was a down side to going back to school. That was Mack. He was not happy about me spending so much time "in the books." So when he got an opportunity to coach a womens' hockey team, he took it. He would be gone lots in the evenings for practices and they traveled to other cities for games on most weekends. That took the pressure off me, and the kids were a lot happier when he was gone.

I did go out with him some weekends, but I found my attitude had changed. I didn't want to drink very much because I needed to be in control of my mind. I needed all my brain cells intact for school. I drank less and danced more. Mack didn't like me dancing with other men, but I was caring less and less about what he liked and didn't like.

Many times at the bar, I found myself wondering if this was all there was to life. "There must be something more fulfilling than seeing how drunk I can get, or what person I can make a pass at on the dance floor. There has to be more, or there would be no reason to better myself, nothing better to hope for."

June came and finals would soon be here. I was doing very well to this point. I had worked hard and managed to keep an A+ average the whole term. One day one of my professors asked me, along with several others, to stay after class. I couldn't imagine why. I knew I hadn't done anything that I needed to be reprimanded for. He gave us good news. None of us had to write finals. We had done so well all year that they felt our marks were good enough for a pass mark without finals. We had proven ourselves all year. I was proud of myself. Twenty-nine years old, and finally a grade twelve graduate.

I knew that my luck was changing for the better when Vi told me about a bookkeeping job at the Lethbridge Flying Club. Her husband Roy was the chief flying instructor and he said I should apply. He said I probably would get the job. I filled out an application and was called immediately for an interview. According to my application they knew I had no formal training as a bookkeeper. I assured them that I was willing to learn and would take whatever courses I needed. They said I could take a class if I wanted, but it wasn't necessary as their accountant would be training me personally. Their bookkeeping system was very basic. All the involved areas would be taken care of by the accountant. I thanked Roy for helping me get the job. I wouldn't let him down.

The accountant was there for two weeks. I found bookkeeping to be very easy. I understood it quickly and enjoyed it as well. I settled into my new position with ease. I was accepted into the flying club fold by both the executive and the instructors. I loved my job! It was a dream come true.

I was eager to learn everything about flying. When I wasn't busy I would go to the mechanics' shop and watch them work on the planes. I listened when the instructors were teaching a class. I asked all kinds of questions. There was so much to learn, it was overwhelming at times.

One day when it was too windy to fly, all of the instructors and a few pilot regulars were sitting around having coffee. Colin, one of the instructors, said that after coffee they were going to clean the planes. He asked me to go to the mechanics' shop and get some "prop-wash." I assumed it was some kind of special fluid they used to clean the propellers.

When I asked the mechanic he burst out laughing and said there was no such thing: they were initiating me to be "one of the guys." When I went back in they were laughing like little boys who were up to no good. I said, "Very funny, boys. Don't die laughing." But inside I was pleased that they had accepted me.

A couple of the instructors continually pestered me to take flying lessons. Every time they saw me they would say, "Come on, let's go up." I told them I would rather crawl than fly with them and that Roy was the only good instructor there. I finally got tired of being pestered and asked Roy to take me up. He gave me a quick lesson on all the necessary instruments. He showed me how to keep her steady and how to bank left and right. He lifted his hands in the air and said, "She's all yours." The beautiful blue sky turned to black. I was terrified! I said, "Please Roy, I can't do this!" He reassured me that he wouldn't let anything happen. I started to shake. I pleaded with him to take me down. I didn't want to die; I didn't want to crash and burn. I know he thought I was being ridiculous, but he took me down right away. I told him I was sorry. He said that not everybody was cut out to be a pilot. He didn't know that I was afraid of dying because I didn't want to go to hell.

Summer, 1975. A wedding invitation arrived from Swift Current. Harry and Anne's oldest son, Lindsay, was getting married. I replied that three would be coming. I didn't ask Mack to go along. I told him it would be a "dry" wedding, so he wouldn't enjoy it anyway. I could hardly wait to see Harry and Anne again. I hadn't seen them since Norm's funeral, four years ago.

This was the first Christian wedding I had been to in many years. The ceremony was lovely. It was very evident that they not only loved each other, but they loved God, too. I wondered if it was possible to have the kind of love their pastor was talking about. I really doubted it.

After the ceremony, everybody was standing outside visiting. There was a tap on my shoulder. I turned to see who it was and before I could blink, Douglas grabbed me and gave me a wonderful long kiss on the mouth. I didn't resist. I thought, "WOW!"

When the kiss was over, he gently pushed me an arm's length away and said, "You look beautiful." I said, "Thanks!" He was so handsome my heart melted like ice cream on a hot day. I said, "Aren't you still married?" When he grinned, I knew he was. I said, "You're terrible!" but my mind was definitely still on that kiss.

At the reception, I could see that the people sitting near me were really disgusted when I pulled out my cigarettes and smoked one. I thought, "You hypocrites. How many of your kids smoke behind your back? This is the way I am: if you don't like it, too bad!" I could see that Mom was upset with me too, so for that reason alone, I put my cigarettes away.

The kids went back to Kelowna with Mom to spend the rest of the summer. They were happy to be with Grandma. She was very good to them. While they were with her, she took them to church, and told them that she loved them, and so did Jesus. I was planning to have a good time, so they were actually better off with her.

I was on the make. When my girlfriends and I weren't at one of the lounges listening to music and dancing, I was out with some of the pilots from the flying club. My marriage was pretty much over, so why not? Besides, it was kind of a thrill to see how much I could get away with.

That October, Harry and Anne were celebrating their 25th wedding anniversary. They were having a big celebration in their community hall at Hallonquist. Seeing them twice in one year would be great. The kids and I went alone again, so I was really hoping Douglas would be there. He was!

They had a program with lots of singing, poems, tributes, gift opening and lunch. Harry and Anne were still in love after all those years. They looked as happy as they did on their wedding day.

At lunch time all my old friends from the youth group (oh so long ago) were sitting in one area, visiting. I asked them if I could join them. Douglas was there too, so that made it even better. There weren't any empty chairs available, so Douglas told me to come and sit on his knee, which of course I did. It was so much fun talking about old times, it seemed as if I'd never been away. When Karen came over, I figured I had better get off her husband's knee. He told me to stay where I was: his marriage was pretty much over, anyway. I could see she was hurting, but I figured it wasn't my problem. All too soon the weekend was over. I didn't want to go home.

Mack and I did our own thing. However, periodically we did go somewhere together. One such occasion was the "Wings Parade." It was a banquet and dance put on by the flying club to honor their new graduates. They would receive their diplomas and pins, the pin being wings. The evening started out to be a lot of fun but slowly turned into a disaster. Mack got jealous when I danced with one particular pilot. He thought the guy had the hots for me so we ended up in a fight. He left. I started to drink heavily. Vodka - "Harvey Wallbangers."

By the time the dance was over I was almost in a stupor, so Vi and Roy took me home. I up-chucked so much that I had nothing left in my stomach. When I got the dry heaves, it felt like my stomach was trying to come out of my throat. Vi put me to bed in one of the kid's beds to sleep it off.

I had promised the kids I would take them to a movie on Sunday afternoon, but I couldn't get out of bed. My head had a siren going off inside of it and it felt like it was being squeezed by vise-grips. My ears were ringing like a telephone.

127

My mouth felt like it was full of cotton. My breath was like the dragon lady's, and my stomach was on fire. I couldn't see straight. Everything was blurry and out of focus. My body was shivering like I was freezing to death. All I could do was roll from side to side, moan and groan, and cry. My kids were really scared.

They tried to wake me up. They put cold face cloths on my forehead. They brought me water and Coke to drink. I said, "I think I'm going to die!" They started to cry. "Please don't die, Mom!" I passed out again. I was flat on my back the whole day. By bedtime Sunday I could finally lift my head off the pillow. The kids made me a slice of toast and brought it to my bed. I was able to keep it down, so I figured I would probably live. I promised myself and my kids that I would never do that again. I asked the kids where Mack was. They said he hadn't come home at all. I wasn't surprised, because I had been told he was seeing a woman from his hockey team.

I was true to my word. Whenever I went to the lounge I had a glass of "Baby Duck" wine or a glass of Coke. At times I couldn't stand the smell of liquor so it made me gag, or actually feel sick again. I settled down quite a bit, and spent more time at work. I enjoyed being with the pilots who hung around the club. Most of them were business men; many of them owned their own businesses and airplanes. They were nice guys. Some were even nice enough to go out with. I stayed away from home as long as possible. The kids were at Vi's a lot. I felt that right now they were better off with her. She could at least be there for them. I knew I had made another mistake. I was actually in a worse situation than before. I had to get out of the mess we were living in. I would start looking for a place to live that was affordable, but I needed to be careful how I handled it. Mack was very strong when he was angry, so I was afraid, yet excited, about being on my own again. The decision was made. The kids and I were going to go it alone, again.

July, 1976. Another wedding in Swift Current. This time it was Harry and Anne's second oldest son, Jeffrey. The reply was the same as last time. Three would be going. Stephanie was very excited about going to this wedding because she was asked to sit at the guest book table. She had never done anything like that before and she was looking forward to it. I bought her a new dress and she was anxious to wear it. Matthew was happy about going too, because he was good friends with Harry and Anne's youngest boy, Bert. They were almost the same age and they loved to play together.

Weddings are beautiful and this one was no exception. I was very distracted, though, because Douglas was in perfect view from where I was sitting. He was very easy to look at. I could see that he was checking me out too. He was alone, so I assumed that he and his wife had split up.

After the ceremony there was the usual visiting on the lawn. Douglas came over to me and asked me if I wanted to go have a few drinks before the reception. He said that I knew everybody who would be there, all the old gang. The kids were not happy with me for saying yes. They didn't want any more men in their lives. They didn't know who they belonged to any more, and didn't want any more men to reject them.

I was a little nervous when we got there but everybody was very friendly. They seemed genuinely happy to see me. I had one drink that I nursed the whole afternoon. Donna and I laughed lots as we reminisced about the time we told our parents we were going for a long walk and went to see the Elvis movie, "Jailhouse Rock." We talked lots, laughed lots; we had fun. The time slipped away and before long we realized we were all going to be late for the reception if we didn't get going. Donna told everybody to come back after the reception and we would finish the party.

When we got to the reception hall there were no parking spots anywhere near it, and I still had to get my gift out of my car. Needless to say, everybody was seated when the four of us walked in. It seemed as if a hush came over the room and everybody was staring at us. I imagined they were condemning me for being with Douglas. I didn't care because I thought most of them were probably hypocrites anyway. Besides, it was nobody's business what I did. I didn't have to answer to them.

Back at Donna's house, the party took a different tone. There was lots to drink and good music to dance to. When Douglas and I waltzed, he held me so close it must have looked like we were welded together. It felt like we had been together all our lives. He whispered in my ear, "Let's get out of here." I nodded, "Yes." He asked Donna to keep her eye on Matthew and Stephanie for a while; we were going for a drive.

The minute we got out the door, he kissed me. We were trembling; it felt so right. There were no other people in the whole world; there was just us. If only he had done this, oh, so many years ago when we were fourteen, our lives might have been very different.

In the car I snuggled up as close to him as I could get. I wasn't going to let him get away again. We drove around for a while. He showed me where his mom and dad lived and where the church was. When we got to the place where he worked, we parked and talked. He told me about his job and his farm. He told me some of the reasons his marriage was on the rocks. I explained that my marriage was over too, and I needed to do something about it. After a very long time he pulled me close again, and kissed me. This kiss was different than the first one. More loving, more gentle, more meaningful. We gave ourselves to each other without any reservations or shame.

It was late when we got back to Donna's and the kids and I still had to go to the farm. Douglas asked me for my phone number so that he could call me. He wanted to see me again. He gave me his work phone number and his mom and dad's phone number. He was staying in their basement.

I did a lot of thinking and planning while we were driving back to Lethbridge. By the time we got there I knew what I was going to do. I told Mack our marriage was over and I was getting out. Monday morning I called work and told them I would be in later. I went looking for a place to live and found a small house close to the airport. Immediate possession! I called the movers and two weeks later the kids and I were on our own. I took everything including our new car and car payments. He kept the race car. Now he was free to move in with his girlfriend.

When we got settled I called Douglas at work and gave him my new address and phone number. He called me that evening and we talked for over an hour. The next few months were like a honeymoon without the marriage. He came up almost every weekend and called me two or three times during the week. His phone bill was out of control. Some weekends I popped tons of popcorn and we took the kids to the drive-in movie. Sometimes just the two of us went out for a romantic supper, then back to the house to "be together."

I made a few trips to Swift Current too. One weeknight I rented a plane from work and had Colin, one of the instructors, fly me to Swift Current. Douglas wined and dined me with steak and lobster and wonderful dancing. His mom and dad were gone to Saskatoon so we slept in the basement. It felt like I was part of the family anyway, because I had known his parents for so many years.

We made plans to be together the long weekend in September. I would leave the kids with Vi and drive to Swift

Current. We would stay in a motel, and I would meet his friends and he would show me his farm.

It was the best weekend of my life. Douglas shared his dreams and plans with me. He wanted to buy more land and get better machinery. I encouraged him to follow his dreams.

I knew I was falling in love with him. In fact, I could honestly say I had never felt this way about anybody, ever, in my whole life. I was the luckiest girl alive, and the happiest. I could hardly contain myself when he told me he loved me. This was it! The man of my dreams! Finally, after all those years, the two of us could be together.

Just before noon on Sunday we went for a drive. He drove to the parking lot at the Church of God and parked. Church was still in. He pointed to Harry and Anne's truck and asked me if I wanted to wait and say "Hi" to them. I declined. While we were having lunch he told me he had to ask me a question. I wondered why he just didn't ask it. Why did he need my permission? He said, "Will you and the kids move down to Swift Current and live with me?" I absolutely was not expecting a question like that. But I absolutely would not refuse.

Later in the afternoon we went for a drive in the country. After he showed me where his land was, I assumed we would go back to Swift Current. He started driving in the opposite direction of Swift Current. My heartbeat quickened as we neared Harry and Anne's farm. I asked him what we were doing here. He said he thought I might want to talk to them about something. When I realized what he meant, fear gripped my heart. Would they understand?

They were so happy to see us it was like a family reunion. I told them Douglas had asked me to move in with him and I wanted to know what they thought about it. To my surprise there was no judgment at all. Anne said we were adults and could make our own decisions. Then she said the nicest thing, "It will be so good to have some of my family here."

By the time I got back to Lethbridge that weekend I was totally swept off my feet: head over heels in love. A few days later a letter came from Douglas. He told me he loved me and sent a dollar bill to prove it. On one side of the dollar he signed his name in black felt pen and on the other side, also in black felt pen, he wrote "I love you," three times.

As moving day approached I did have some reservations. Not about loving him or living with him, but about living together in a small town where everybody knew each other. People would undoubtedly talk. I reassured myself that it was none of their business. If they were talking about me they would be giving somebody else a rest.

Saturday, October 1st, 1976. The movers packed us up and we were on our way to Swift Current, Saskatchewan. Hopefully, leaving Alberta would give us a happier life. After all, I would be with the first real love of my life.

I don't know what made me say it, but before we left Lethbridge I asked Douglas if we could go to church in Swift Current. He said, "I don't see why not!"

CHAPTER FIVE

I Hear You Lord:

Decisions, Decisions

I realize that every story can be seen differently by each person involved in that story: Douglas and I agree that our marriage has been like a roller coaster ride; some very highs and some very lows. However, this is how I, Susan Arlene, perceive my life in Saskatchewan.

Douglas' mom offered to let the kids and me stay at their house, but Douglas and I couldn't sleep together. She is a wonderful Christian lady, and although she didn't agree with what Douglas and I were doing, she never said a word about it. Her offer was gratefully declined. We rented a motel suite with a kitchenette and stored my furniture in his parents' garage until we could find a suitable apartment.

The first Sunday morning we were in Swift Current, as Douglas promised, we were going to church. It had been previously arranged that Harry and Anne would go with us for moral support. We were late getting there so we had to sit near the front. It seemed like the whole service stopped short while everybody watched us walk in. That didn't happen, of course, but I was feeling very uncomfortable, like a fish in a fish bowl.

The music was very good. I even remembered some of the hymns they sang. I didn't sing out loud, but I sang them in my mind. A guy about the same age as us gave his testimony. He told us how the Lord had convicted his heart about his sins, and how with his wife's help, he gave his heart to Jesus. He was very soft-spoken, and cried as he talked. Anne whispered to me that he was a friend of Douglas'. It was hard for me not to cry too. He closed his testimony by saying that giving his heart to Jesus was the smartest thing he ever did, next to marrying his wife.

The congregation had just hired a young pastor and his wife from the United States, Pastor Ed and Janette Hyatt. He was only twenty-four years old, but he said the right words to convict my heart. I was sure I was the only person in the whole church, and that he was speaking directly to me. This was not my living room; I couldn't turn the television off and make him go away. I had wanted to go to church; now I had to sit through it. I don't know why, but we decided we would go to church again.

Thanksgiving Sunday we were invited to Harry and Anne's farm for a turkey supper. They said to come in the afternoon so the men could shoot some skeet. To my surprise the pastor was there, shooting skeet with the men. Didn't he know it was Sunday? Didn't Men of God keep the Sabbath? How holy could it be to shoot skeet on Sunday? He definitely was a pastor like I had never seen before.

Moving to a small town from a big city was quite an adjustment for the kids and me. Everybody in Swift Current seemed to know Douglas, and I knew that people were talking about us. I could tell by the way they glanced at me that they were wondering if I was the reason Douglas and his wife broke up.

We didn't do a lot for entertainment. We went to one or the other of the two clubs in town, and did some wining and dining, or we went visiting (mostly relatives). We spent many hours at Harry and Anne's, which was wonderful for me. It gave me a real opportunity to get to know my sister. We felt comfortable with them, and they didn't judge us. Our friends all seemed to be from his married past, so I always felt uncomfortable. I couldn't help but wonder if they were comparing. I hoped we would make some of "our own" friends.

Everything happened at once: We found a three bedroom duplex and moved in on December 1st. A few days after we got settled in, I got a bookkeeping job at the John Deere Farm Implement Dealership. Douglas and I suspected that there would be some friendly competition between us, because he was a salesman for the Case Farm Equiment Dealership in town.

The month of December is filled with celebrating. There are lots of house parties and staff parties; Swift Current is no exception. We were both looking foreward to Douglas' Christmas party. There would be a turkey supper with all the trimmings, followed by a dance. We went with the intention of having a good time, and we did. The liquor flowed like water. The band was excellent and we danced the night away. When we were waltzing he held me so close, it felt like we were sharing the same bodies. When he whispered in my ear, "You're my kind of woman," my heart melted. I thought, "How lucky I am to have this handsome, loving man in my life." I could honestly say that for the very first time in my life, I was really in love.

December is also a month of gift giving. Douglas showered me with expensive gifts. He bought me an expensive watch. He bought me a beautiful mink coat, and he paid off my car. He asked me to marry him, and on Christmas Eve he gave me an engagement ring. When the light caught it, the diamonds sparkled with every color of the rainbow. It was beautiful and I cried. I couldn't believe how good my life had turned out. This wonderful man who I was with really loved me. He gave me all the affection I so desperately needed, and he made me feel like I was the most important person in his life.

A brand new year. 1977. I expected it to be the most wonderful year of my life. As soon as our divorces came through, we were going to get married. I had waited all my life for the happiness I was feeling. I was convinced that because we both came from Christian backgrounds, we would both come back to the Lord, and that would complete our wonderful, perfect lives. Unfortunately, bubbles burst.

Douglas talked to his kids on the phone, but they had never been to our house. This was going to be the weekend. Everybody was a little nervous because we didn't know what to expect. Would his kids like us? Would my kids like his? It went badly! It was exactly the same as when Bobby came to live with Mack and me, except this time the rejection involved all three of us. I'm sure his kids felt uncomfortable around us, and because they hadn't seen their dad in quite a while, they basically stayed by his side. Consequently there was no discipline at all and very definite favoritism, complete with a personal catering service. It seemed like my kids and I weren't there. We were invisible and I didn't like it. I was hurt and angry.

When he got back from taking his kids home, he broke down and cried. That upset me more, so I confronted him. I asked him why he had ignored us. He denied that he had. I asked him why he couldn't treat all the kids equally. He said that he did. I wasn't getting through to him so I kept questioning him about each of his unfair actions. Finally, he blew up. He told me how bad he felt about leaving his kids without a dad: how he was to blame for the whole mess, and now his kids had to suffer because of it. I told him it wasn't my fault he left his kids. I said, 'And what about us? We're suffering too. You moved us all the way down here because you wanted us in your life, and now you ignore us like we don't exist." He said that if I moved down here to see what I could get out of him, I could go scratch myself. I wasn't going to get "one red cent" of his. Everything he owned was going to his kids. I told him I didn't remember asking him for "one red cent," only for his love. Here I was again, facing the cold stark realities of love. Only this time I was living in the middle of nowhere, with nowhere to go and no one to turn to. After a couple of days Douglas was over his guilt feelings and things were fairly normal again. There was no apology, but he was back to his loving and considerate ways.

Also in January, Douglas had a chance to purchase two quarters of farm land that were close to his other land. One quarter had a house on it that the owners had been living in. It would be a good chance to enlarge his land base. Previously, he had opportunities to purchase more land and move to the farm, but Karen didn't want to live on a farm. Now he had another opportunity, and he took it. This, in fact, was one of the dreams he had shared with me the previous summer. I was willing to live on a farm. I never backed away from a challenge.

It turned out to be quite an adjustment for the kids and me. A large city - to a small city - to a farm that had only one other living creature on it, a grey cat. The house was very old, but it had all the modern conveniences except one, a flush toilet. All it had was a carry out pail (port-a-potty). Douglas said we would have to make it do until he could get a chance to put a toilet in.

Everything in our personal lives changed when we moved to the farm. We rarely went to the clubs in town because we started to run around with a few couples from the area. We all liked to party, and for a while we made our rounds to all of the couples' houses. It didn't take very long until I was staying home, and Douglas was going out with "the boys" somewhere. He was always prepared for a party and had two or three different bottles of liquor in his truck at all times. Many times when I got home from work Douglas wasn't there. It wasn't uncommon for him to stay out all night drinking, or for him to drive as far as our yard and either pass out or fall asleep. I had never been in a situation like that before and I didn't like it. I didn't like being excluded, and I didn't like wondering if he'd be home when I got there. He never called to tell me where he was. He could have fallen off the face of the earth, and I wouldn't know it until the next day.

Just when it was time to start seeding in May, it started to rain. Rain, of course, was a good reason for the boys to go out and drink their heads off. One Thursday night when I got home from work, Douglas wasn't home. He didn't come home all night. The next morning Stephanie was sick, so she stayed home from school. Matthew had already gone on the school bus, and I was getting ready to go to work. Douglas finally got home and quietly came in the house. I was angry at him, as I usually was when he had been drinking all night. After we said a few unkind words to each other, I thought it was all over. He left the room and I continued to put my make-up on. A few minutes later he came back in the bathroom and told me he had to talk to me. He told me he was sorry, but he thought he still loved Karen, and he was going to see if she would take him back. He turned around, walked out the door, got in his truck, and left the yard. He never looked back; he was gone.

I lost it! I cried so hard that Stephanie came running to see if I was wounded. There are no words that can adequately express how I felt. I was completely devastated. I had given up my home, my life, and my friends in Alberta, to live with the one true love of my life. Now he was discarding me like a piece of used furniture. My heart was broken! My mind was numb! My soul died inside of me! I couldn't think clearly! I knew I couldn't go to work! I didn't know what to do, or where to go! Then as if an answer to an unspoken prayer, I remembered Anne. She could help me. She would know what to do. I had to get over there. I told Stephanie to get in the car and we headed for help. Somehow Anne would get me through this, because I couldn't bear it alone.

I was hysterical by the time I finished telling Harry and Anne the story. They couldn't believe it. They felt bad for me, but they didn't know what to do, either. Anne asked me if she could pray for me. I didn't really listen to all the words as she prayed, but I heard enough that I could feel my spirit start to settle down. When she was finished, she asked me if I would mind if she called Pastor Ed and asked him to come out and talk to me. I wasn't really sure that I wanted to bear my soul to a preacher, but maybe he could help me.

It seemed like an eternity until he got there. As soon as he came into the house, he came over to where I was sitting. He didn't say a word; he just put his arm around me. I sobbed like a child that had been beaten. Finally, he spoke. He told me that Jesus loved me so much that He died for me. If I wanted Him to come into my heart, all I had to do was ask Him. He would forgive my sins, cleanse my soul, and give me strength to endure the heartache I was feeling. He would give me a brand new life and a new start. He asked me if I wanted him to pray with me. I hesitated for a long while, then with Pastor Ed's help, I asked God to forgive my sins and come into my heart.

I didn't feel the earth shake, and I didn't see beautiful fireworks go off in the air before my eyes: I just felt an incredible peace in my soul. Tears were still just below the surface, and my heart still ached, but I felt different inside. It felt like an evil, black-hearted twin inside of me left and took the weight of all the years of sin right along with her. I felt very light, like a free spirit.

Stephanie was hurting too. She had been crying and was visibly upset. I asked her if she wanted to ask Jesus into her heart too. She said she did, and Pastor Ed prayed with her too. I was happy for her because I knew that if she felt like I did inside, with Jesus in her heart she could cope with what was going on.

I called the school bus driver and told him to drop Matthew off at Harry and Anne's. He had to bring their youngest son Bert home, anyway, so I knew it would work out all right. We stayed until quite late into the evening. I avoided going home as long as I could. I didn't know if I could handle being there. I wasn't sure what would be waiting for me. Fortunately, Douglas wasn't home.

The reality of what I did never sank in until much later. I went to bed as soon as we got home, but my eyes were wide open most of the night. Sleep was the last thing on my mind. Douglas didn't come home all night so I assumed that everything had gone the way he wanted, and that he and his family were back together. I didn't know how I was going to handle it, but I felt more at peace about it. I knew I wouldn't fall apart again. I hadn't had Jesus in my heart since I was a little girl and I had to get used to it again. I knew He was right there: all I had to do was talk to Him and He would hear me. It was all so overwhelming.

The last time I glanced at the clock, before I fell asleep, was 5:00 a.m. Around 8:00 a.m., I woke up when I heard the front door open. Douglas was home. I didn't know what to do. Should I lay as quiet as a mouse and pretend to be asleep, or should I get up and face the bad news, head on? It was Saturday. I didn't have to go to work, so I chose to stay in bed. He came in the bedroom and sat down beside me on the bed. He looked very sad. My heart was beating very fast. He told me that Karen wouldn't take him back. She didn't trust him and wouldn't take a chance on him. He spent the evening playing with his kids and slept on the couch. Then he asked me if I would take him back.

My first thought was that God had answered my prayer in a hurry! My second thought was one of disbelief. I couldn't believe that he had enough nerve to think I'd take him back, knowing that I was his second choice.

He continued. "There is something else I should probably tell you before you decide what you're going to do. After my marriage broke up, I was dating someone. We were still dating while I was going to Lethbridge to see you. The night before I went to Lethbridge to move you here, I went to her place to say good-bye to her. I told her that I loved you, that you were moving down here, and that we would be getting married - I slept with her." I rolled over, buried my face in my pillow, and wept. He left the room.

I cried until I had no tears left, then I got up and went into the living room where he was lying on the couch. I told him that I had something to tell him too. I said that while he was gone I had become a Christian. He would have to decide if he could handle that. He looked like I'd slapped him, but didn't say a word. I told him that we both needed time to think about what had happened. We'd talk tomorrow, after the kids and I got home from church. The rest of the day and evening was cool and quiet. The kids stayed in their rooms most of the time, and I did laundry and cleaned the house until it sparkled. Douglas divided his time between working outside and sleeping on the couch.

Sunday. It seemed like a thousand years since I gave my heart to Jesus. I really needed to be in a place where people would actually love me. I could hardly wait to get to church. When I reached into my purse to get my car keys, I saw my cigarettes. At that moment I realized that I hadn't had a cigarette since Friday. I had smoked for twenty-one years, and just like that, the craving was gone. I threw the cigarettes and the lighter in the garbage and went to town.

Church was different today. I couldn't quit smiling. I sang all the words to the hymns and I meant them. I didn't squirm in my seat, and I didn't have to daydream to keep from listening to the sermon. I heard every word. When Pastor Ed prayed, I prayed. I felt so full - so full of Jesus - I could hardly contain myself. I took it all in, like a sponge filling up with water. After church Anne told me that my face looked like it was glowing. I told her it was!

I put off thinking about Douglas until our drive home. A million thoughts were attacking my mind. Should I throw in the towel, pack up and run for my life? Do I have the strength to try and make it work? Can I ever trust him again? Do I love him enough to forgive and forget? Will he be able to accept me as a Christian? Will he even be home when I get there?

Douglas was home, and he looked a little happier than he had earlier that morning. The kids quickly went to their rooms. They didn't know what to expect, and neither did I. We made some small talk and then got right into it. I asked him how he felt about my becoming a Christian. He said he wasn't happy about it. He wondered how we could go out together and still have fun, now that I "couldn't do anything" anymore. Silence! Finally he said, "I guess I'll have to learn to live with it."

I still didn't know exactly what I was going to say, so I started by telling him that he had hurt me more than he could ever imagine, because he was the first man that I ever really loved. My love for him was like a school girl's, because I never doubted him. When he told me he loved me, I believed him. I trusted him with my heart and he broke it. He sat very quietly, so I continued. I told him that I didn't want to lose him, and I would try to forget the whole thing. At that point neither one of us had anything else to say. There were no tender moments of wonderful love and affection. There was just an unspoken agreement to stay together.

Pastor Ed gave me a new Bible from the church. It was a more modern version than the Bible I had gotten for Christmas so many years ago. I knew I would need it, because I was an infant Christian who would be wearing spiritual diapers for a long while. I had so much to learn.

I started to read my Bible right away. My mind was opening up to the spiritual things I read. I wept when I read about Jesus and the Cross. How He suffered! I read for hours at a time and I underlined everything that I thought was important for me to know. I could finally understand that ,even though I rejected God and told Him I didn't want or need Him anymore, He had never left me.

I even attempted praying. I had no great or wonderful formula for prayer. It was very basic. I thanked God for dying for me and I pleaded with Him to save Douglas and Matthew.

Matthew and Stephanie joined the youth group at the church. The youth leaders were a couple that let the kids have fun, but also had certain rules that had to be followed. They led the Bible studies as well as the activities. My kids loved it.

The Lord answered half of my prayer one Sunday morning at church when Matthew gave his heart to Jesus. He was very happy. I couldn't remember seeing him that happy in a very long time. He told me that when he asked Jesus to forgive him, all the rage and bitterness he had inside left. He still felt the rejection in his life but he didn't feel like killing anybody anymore.

One night the kids came home from youth group, very upset. They told me that some people in the church were saying that I wasn't a Christian because I was still living in sin. Until that very moment, I had not thought about the fact that I was still living with Douglas and professing Christianity. It bothered me. I didn't want to choose between Douglas and Christianity. I didn't want to move out because I was sure that if I did, Douglas would find somebody else. I wanted to be a Christian, but I sure didn't want to lose Douglas. When I told him what people were saying, he said that if I felt I should move out, I could. It was up to me. I decided to let people talk.

Douglas thought that we should probably get married sooner, rather than later, to "silence the gossipers." We decided that it would be as soon as harvest was over. When we went to see Pastor Ed to ask him to marry us, he said he couldn't. Some people on the board were against it because I was still living with Douglas and calling myself a Christian. But Pastor Ed's greatest concern was that Douglas and I were serving two different masters. He said there was some very definite scripture in the Bible about being "unevenly yoked." I was very upset.

Later, when we were alone, I was very verbal to Douglas about how I felt about judgmental Christians. I just couldn't believe that Pastor Ed couldn't marry us. Douglas said that the preacher had to do what he thought was right, and that I should settle down. We would just have to find somebody else to marry us. He was actually more understanding than I was. I was resentful. I felt like saying that if this is Christianity, I don't want it. In my heart I knew I didn't mean it, but I sure wanted to be married by my pastor.

November 10, 1977 was a wonderfully warm Autumn day. The trees had given up their leaves, dropping them to the ground. The leaves were a brilliant gold and yellow, and they spread themselves over the grass like a beautiful carpet. This was the day I had waited for all my life. The marriage wasn't going to be as picture perfect as I dreamed it would be, but we were fairly happy.

Our "church wedding" took place in the judge's chambers in the Court House. Harry and Anne had given us their unwavering support from the very beginning. Our way of thanking them was to ask them to be our witnesses on this very special day.

As we were waiting for the Justice of the Peace to arrive, I let my mind drift back to the very first wedding I ever attended - my sister Sophia's. I remembered how I looked in the mirror and saw myself as a beautiful bride, and imagined that my groom was tall, dark, and handsome. Now a lifetime later, my childhood dream was coming true. Douglas was definitely tall, dark, and handsome.

We didn't have a church elegantly decorated with flowers and candles. A piano and organ weren't playing beautiful wedding music. But surrounding us were some very important people that truly loved us. Douglas' mom and dad, along with my mom, whole-heartedly gave us their blessing. Matthew and Stephanie ... I hoped that all the hurt they had already gone through in their young lives would end today.

The ceremony was brief, but the Justice of the Peace had some very good advice for us. He told us that we should build each other up with kind words. We should submit to each other. We should treat each other with respect and be faithful to each other. He almost sounded like a preacher. We said our vows, exchanged rings, kissed, signed the register and we were married.

It may sound like our wedding wasn't meaningful. Of course, that is false. I believe with all my heart that Douglas was God-given to me. I also believe that if I hadn't been so wild when I was young, and/or Douglas hadn't been so shy, our wedding could have been the first and only one for both of us.

After the ceremony, the rest of our families joined us at a Chinese restaurant. After supper everybody was invited to Douglas' mom and dad's place for a very informal reception. We visited and opened gifts. As soon as the coffee was made, it was time to cut the wedding cake. The cake was in the shape of an open book. The icing was snowy white, and there were six pink roses arranged around the writing. On one side of the cake was written "With all my love." On the other side, "Today and always." After we posed for pictures, Douglas kissed me the same way he had kissed me on Donna's front steps over a year ago. The day ended perfectly when he told me he loved me.

We had decided earlier that we wouldn't go on a honeymoon until winter. My wedding gift to Douglas was a two week honeymoon trip to Hawaii. I booked it for the last week of January and the first week of February. Sandy beaches and palm trees would be the perfect setting for a honeymoon. The hardest part was the waiting.

Shortly after we got married, winter settled in and covered the countryside with a beautiful blanket of white snow. One Saturday morning I woke up early and couldn't get back to sleep. Instead of rolling around until I woke Douglas up, I decided to make myself a cup of fresh coffee, sit on my favorite chair in the front room, read my Bible and pray. I turned the lamp on because it wasn't quite daylight. I inhaled the wonderful aroma of freshly brewed coffee, and nestled into my chair.

While I was praying a picture came into my mind. It was an aqua colored, eversharp pencil with a silver ring aroung it. It had a silver clip on it that allowed it to be clipped on to the inside of a pocket. The eraser was white. I didn't know why that picture came into my mind, so I opened my eyes. The pencil was still there but it was almost life size, right there in my living room. I was frightened, so I quickly closed my eyes again and asked the Lord what was happening to me. A voice in my head said, "I want you to write a book." I opened my eyes immediately. The pencil was gone. I shook my head in disbelief and chuckled to myself, "Me write a book? What a dreamer!"

I read until the sun came up. There had been a heavy fog during the night and all the trees in the yard were covered with a thick covering of frost. The sky was very blue and the trees glistened and sparkled as the sun's rays spread across them. I felt such peace in my soul: I was sure the Lord was right there in the room with me.

I glanced at the tree directly in front of the house and saw two chubby little birds sitting on a bare, frost covered branch. They sat about six inches apart and were facing in opposite directions. The voice came back into my head and told me that what I was looking at would be the cover of the book I was going to write. The title was TWO: ALONE. Just as quickly as the voice entered my mind, it was gone. I was a little bewildered, yet I felt an incredible peace. I felt like I was stationary and everything around me was floating.

After my spirit settled down, I tried to analyze what had happened. There must be some kind of meaning to what I saw. I asked the Lord to please show me what it meant. There was no voice in my head this time, I just knew what it meant. The two birds were not love birds. They were just two plain old chubby birds. They were together, yet far apart. They shared the same branch, yet they were alone. Thus, Two - Alone.

After I became a Christian I bought a beautiful large picture of Jesus. I hung it on the living room wall so that when I really needed His presence in my soul, I could look at Him and talk to Him. He was right there in front of me. I looked at Jesus and told Him I couldn't write a book. I didn't have anything to say. I took another glance at the tree, but the birds were gone.

I had some very definite misconceptions about living the Christian life. I assumed that things would automatically change for the better and I assumed that Douglas would become a Christian right away. The Bible said that if I prayed and asked for something, and believed it, my prayers would be answered. I assumed that all our problems concerning the two sets of kids would vanish like a puff of smoke. I assumed that Douglas would quit drinking with the boys, and I assumed that I could forget how much Douglas had hurt me. When things didn't happen as I assumed they would, I started to question if Christianity was what I really wanted, or had I been too wicked in the past, and God couldn't forgive me? I packed a bag for all my mixed-up emotions and invited them to come on our honeymoon.

The aroma of the beautiful orchids and tropical flowers greeted us as soon as we left the plane. Beautiful Hawaiian girls placed a lei of real orchids around every man's neck. Handsome
Hawaiian men placed a lei of real orchids around each lady's neck. They took our pictures and we were on our way to Honolulu.

Our motel room was on the fourteenth floor, facing the ocean. The view was breath-taking. The smell of the ocean was heavenly and it displayed shades of blue and green that I'm sure are unnamed. Beauty beyond description!

The next morning at a buffet breakfast sponsored by the airline, we were encouraged to sign up for sightseeing tours. The pineapple was as sweet as honey, and the Hawaiian music made me feel like I was swaying in the soft Pacific breezes. I wanted to sign up for everything, Douglas didn't. I argued that we probably would never get to Hawaii again so we should see everything. He didn't want to stand in long lines, waiting for a bus. We were both stubborn and wanted our own way. Somebody had to give in. Douglas wasn't happy, but he gave in.

We met a couple from Swift Current that were on our plane. We spent a lot of time with them and enjoyed their company. One night the guys wanted to go to a "strip" club. We girls objected, but were overruled. I decided I might as well get with it, and ordered an exotic Hawaiian drink made with vodka. The room was dimly lit until the flood lights came on, exposing two homely, vulgar women. I hated it there and asked Douglas if we could leave. He said, "In a while." I told him I needed to go right away. We left, but on the way out he said my Christianity was a pain in the ass!

The second week, we flew to the island of Maui. There was very little to do there and Douglas was bored. Fortunately for me, the couple from Swift Current was there too. We rented a car and the four of us toured the island from one end to the other. The week crawled by and finally we were on our way home.

The cold, stark realities of marrying an unsaved person are painful. Douglas didn't want me to be a Christian, but he didn't want me to "not" be a Christian. I tried to stay strong in my faith, but I failed. I wanted to live for the Lord, but I wanted to please my husband. I felt like Paul. "I don't understand myself at all, for I really want to do what is right, but I can't. I do what I don't want to do - what I hate. I know perfectly well that what I am doing is wrong, and my bad conscience proves that I agree with these laws I am breaking. But I can't help myself, because I'm no longer doing it. It is sin inside me that is stronger than I am that makes me do these evil things. *Romans 7:15-17 (TLB)*

The next few months were like a roller coaster ride. There was spiritual warfare going on for my soul, and my marriage. The forces of evil really wanted me back, and my marriage to break up. Jesus wanted me to stay with Him and have a happy, healthy marriage. The devil brought out the heavy artillery. I had the "Armour of God," but I didn't know how to use it.

The war touched every area of my life. My marriage was attacked first. It started small, like a single cancer cell. I noticed that Douglas stopped telling me he loved me. He stopped calling me "Hon." He pulled away when I tried to touch him. He moved away when I sat beside him on the couch. Douglas was withholding from me the very thing I so desperately needed, my overwhelming need to be loved. When he pushed me away, I felt hurt and betrayed. My emotions were like an open wound. I was super-sensitive. Everything hurt me. The more I pressed him for love, the more he pulled away. I was like a bear with a thorn in its paw.

A group of our friends decided to go to a farming show in Regina and asked Douglas and me to go along. There were too many people for one vehicle, so we took two. Douglas wouldn't ride in the same truck as me. He wouldn't walk with me when we viewed the exhibits. He wouldn't sit beside me at supper, and he wouldn't drive home with me. To him, I wasn't there. I was devastated. I was really feeling sorry for myself, so when they passed the bottle of whiskey around, I drank lots, and I drank it straight. I hated whiskey, but I didn't care. I didn't want to be able to feel anything. I wanted to be numb and I knew the whiskey would do that to me. My head was spinning wildly, but I managed to get home before I got sick. After I had up-chucked my entire day's intake, Douglas ended my awful day by telling me that I disgusted him.

When he said that, all of the past came back to me. I remembered that he was going to leave me for someone else. I couldn't get past it. It was always on my mind. "He doesn't love me. I'm his second choice. I don't deserve to be happy. I AM no good." My self-worth was nonexistent and my self-esteem was on par with a worm. I asked Douglas things about his marriage; when he told me, I got jealous. I always compared myself to "her" and always came up short. We were very unhappy.

Douglas and I were both spoiled and we wanted everything our way. Immediately wasn't soon enough. We never listened to each other and we only worried about "how I feel." During a fight, we picked up on one issue, or one sentence, and got stuck on it. Neither of us heard another word. He told me I was the problem. I told him he was the problem. We both lost.

Then there were the kids. My two are the oldest. Matthew, then Stephanie. Mitch is the oldest of Douglas' two.

Vanessa the youngest. There are seven years between Matthew and Vanessa. Matthew and Mitch got along pretty well, most of the time. However, one day after they had gotten on each others nerves, they had a falling out. Mitch pulled rank and told Matthew that just because he was living with his dad, that didn't make Matthew his son. He finished by saying that blood is thicker than water. From that day forward, there was an invisible wedge between them. A cautious friendship. Stephanie and Vanessa never really got along, and as time passed, their resentment for each other deepened. Eventually, Vanessa quit coming to the farm.

There was still favoritism shown between the two sets of kids. My kids lived with Douglas every day, but his kids received more attention in one weekend than mine did all year, especially Matthew. It caused a lot of grief. My kids resented him and his kids. His kids resented me and my kids. There was always a very uncomfortable undercurrent of hurt and distrust.

Douglas also played favorites with my kids. Matthew was quiet and tried to stay out of Douglas' way. Matthew was always ignored. Douglas hardly ever spoke to him. Douglas did show some affection toward Stephanie, but that made her feel bad because she knew that hurt Matthew and me. Whenever his kids' visits were over, we always had a fight. He got angry, went out drinking and I cried. It was a family tradition.

I set myself and my kids up for the ultimate rejection when I asked Douglas if he would adopt my kids. His reply was, "Why should I adopt your kids, when I can't even have my own kids?" He continued, "And don't ask me for any money for them; they are your responsibility. Their dad doesn't support them. Why should I?" I felt sick. I was too hurt to cry.

Karen would call Douglas and add insult to injury. She knew exactly what buttons to push to start the guilt factory producing. The kids needed straightening out, he wasn't there for them so he needed to call them and settle whatever the problem was. They needed some extra money for this project or that activity. She even scolded Douglas for not spending enough quality time with Mitch when he was at the farm. Whenever he got off the phone, he was one, "hurtin' puppy." Of course, it was all my fault. Then came the fight, his exit, the family tradition continued. We said things to each other during our fights that will probably never be totally forgotten.

Next, the forces of evil attacked my Christianity. It didn't seem like God was going to help me out. After all the praying I had done, after I claimed the promise in the Bible that, "All things are possible," our marriage wasn't getting any better. The Bible said that all I had to do was, "pray and ask and believe." I did that too, and things got worse. Finally, I did what every baby Christian does; I tried to fix our marriage all by myself.

I tried to buy Douglas' love and affection. I paid him a hundred dollars a month to help with utilities. I gave him all of the money back that he had spent to pay off my car. I bought all the groceries and I bought all the clothes. I paid for the dentist, the optometrist and the pharmacist. None of that helped my marriage.

I decided maybe going to church more regularly would help. Maybe God would finally help me. To my surprise, Douglas started going to church with me. Things started to improve. We actually did some fun things together. It felt like God had given him back to me. We started curling earlier in the winter, so when we were asked by Douglas' boss and wife to curl in a bonspiel in Lethbridge, we accepted. We started visiting Harry and Anne quite regularly again. I had almost forgotten how much we laughed at their house. We took a trip to Iowa and Illinois. We didn't have one fight while we were gone and it seemed like our marriage was on the mend. Hope

154

reigned supreme when Douglas actually took the time to teach Matthew how to drive the old Massey 44 tractor. I was afraid to blink. I thought that if I did, "all good things" would vanish into thin air.

I must have blinked, because the next time Mitch came to visit, the cycle was in effect again. Again, I spent less time at church and more time trying to find ways to get my husband back. I started to smoke again, but I hid that from Douglas and I would have a drink when we were with our friends. I tried to keep reading my Bible, and one day I read something about being a "wine bibber." Guilt overwhelmed me and I was on my knees asking forgiveness, and promising not to ever have another drink! My peace of mind was just out of reach, and I was miserable. "During this period I exercised what is called 'bellhop religion.' We ask God to come into our lives to carry our bags of problems, our many parcels of pain; then when the problems are resolved, we say, Thank you very much. We'll call you again some day when we have more luggage too heavy for us to manage alone. Without even a tip or a courteous nod in His direction, I dismissed God when I'd finished with His services." *(1)*

From the time God gave me the vision of the book I was supposed to write, I wrote everything down in a journal. I decided that I would never be the person God wanted me to be, and I wrote my final entry. "Dear Lord, I can't do this. I am tired. I am drained. It hurts too much to live for you. It hurts too much to live without you. There is no hope. I have to turn You off so that I can disappear from your view. I know You will always be there, just a breath away, but I'm tired of hurting, tired of being afraid. Maybe some day, I'll find you again." With that entry, I closed the book and the war was over. The forces of evil won.

A few weeks later the kids came home from youth group and told me that there were a couple of people from the church who were saying that I wasn't really a Christian. They said that when I asked for forgiveness, I didn't really mean it. If I had meant it, I wouldn't be having such a struggle to live right. That was the final straw. I decided that the church was full of judgmental hypocrites. I said, "Who needs it?" and once again turned my back to God. He, however, did not turn His back to me.

One cold night in February, Douglas went drinking with the boys. When he got home, I was sitting on the couch watching television and having a cigarette. When he saw me, he hit the roof. He told me I couldn't do anything right, not even be a Christian. I mouthed off to him and stood up to leave the room. He slapped me real hard on the side of the head. I got a sharp pain in my ear and there was a loud ringing in it. It felt like my eardrum was broken. I started to cry. Douglas was so angry his whole body was shaking. He yelled, "I want you to pack your "so and so" bags, and get out of my house. I don't care where you go, or what you do, just get out. I'm going out and when I get back, I want you gone." He got in his truck and spun the wheels so hard the gravel flew; then he was gone.

After he left, the kids came out of their rooms. They were upset and angry. I told them to pack a few things in a suitcase because we had to leave. We would stay in a motel for a few days until I could decide what to do next. On the way to town Matthew said something I will never forget. He said, "If I wasn't a Christian, I would kill him!"

It was almost midnight and I was tired and emotionally drained. We stopped at the first motel we saw. It was expensive, but I took it for two nights. Two days later we moved into a cheaper motel. We needed to find an apartment as soon as possible, but it was the middle of the month and nothing was available. We would have to wait. Life, if you can call it that, continued. The kids went to school; I went to work.

Smoking was a very hard habit for me to break. It was one of the better tools the devil had to use against me. Smoking is addictive and gives a false sense of security. I needed to smoke to cope. This time, however, the Lord wasn't going to let me go. He convicted my soul to the point of tears. He hounded my soul. I was in such despair and anguish, I thought about killing myself, but I was a gutless wonder and knew I couldn't do it. Next to the rape, this was the lowest point in my life. I had reached bottom.

The kids were worried about me. One night while I was lying on the bed, Matthew came and sat beside me. He put his arm around me, and with wisdom far beyond his fifteen years, he told me that I should call Pastor Ed. He told me it hurt him to see me this way and that he was sure the pastor could help me. After wrestling with Matthew's idea for a few hours, I called Pastor Ed. He came over immediately.

When he came in , I broke down and wept. I told him what had happened at home. I told him I was smoking again and I wasn't a Christian anymore. Instead of agreeing with me, he asked me how I felt when I had a cigarette. I told him I felt guilty and ashamed. Then he said something I will never forget. "Well, then, you haven't lost it." He continued by telling me that every time I had a craving for a cigarette, I should tell myself to wait until the next craving. I should try to talk myself out of it: one cigarette at a time. He said, "Don't give up, just keep trying. You'll win." (The battle would take two years, but I did win!)

Then he told me that I had to make a choice and stick to it. I couldn't sit on the fence anymore. I had to choose one master. I knew I didn't want to serve the devil anymore, all he ever did for me was try to destroy me. When I was down he kicked me, and he enjoyed it. He didn't want me to serve the Lord, and he didn't want me to be happy.

I decided I might as well take a chance with God. I had done absolutely lousy on my own. Maybe with Jesus beside me to help me, I could become the person He wanted me to be. I knew I needed to love Him more than I loved myself. I needed to rely onHim instead of trying to fix things myself. Only He could put my broken life back together.

After Pastor Ed prayed with the kids and me, he shared a few things that I could cling to. He told me to forget my past sins, because God had. Then he said, "If you can't see Jesus because of your pain and tears, don't look at the pain. Jesus is outside the pain. Look at Him there." After he left, I knew that this time I would make it!

I found an apartment that would be available March 1st. Harry and Anne, my faithful, faithful friends, helped us pack and move. I took all my furniture except the fridge and stove, and I kept my car. Leaving the farm that day was the hardest thing that I had had to do in a very long time. I didn't want to move out and I told myself that living with Douglas, even though he didn't want me, was better than living without him. I should have stuck with God in the first place. I had tried to serve two masters, and I ended up not even serving one right.

I could only afford a two bedroom apartment, so Stephanie and I shared a room. She was almost fourteen and wasn't real happy about that. In fact, she wasn't happy about a lot of things. She was disillusioned with Christianity and hurt about getting kicked out of our home. I added to the problem by sharing "all" my problems with her. It was too much for her to deal with. She had her own feelings of hurt and rejection to deal with. She felt that God had let us down and she was struggling with living for Him. Finally she couldn't cope anymore and gave God up.

Matthew also felt hurt and rejection, but never let his love for Jesus waiver. He was still very quiet, but it seemed like he was able to cope better than Stephanie and I. In actuality, he was burying everything deep in his heart. He appeared strong, but he was crying inside.

If I was going to make this living for Jesus work, I knew I would have to get involved. I joined a Bible study group where I learned so many wonderful things about life with Jesus that I never knew before. Every problem of today has an answer from yesterday in the Bible. I learned how to pray, and I realized that I had friends who really cared about me. They hurt with me, and they cried with me. I learned about tithing. There was no financial support from Douglas, but I gave ten per cent of my income and the Lord blessed me for it. I gave freely and willingly, and I can honestly say I was never broke. I attended Stonecroft Ministries Banquets and was elected to the position of Special Feature Chairman.

When Baptism Sunday was announced in church, I knew I had to be baptised. It would be the first baby step of obedience. I invited Douglas to come to church that Sunday. I was sure he wouldn't come, but I had to show him that I was committed to living for Jesus.

As I walked down the steps into the baptismal tank, my whole body tingled. It felt like the Lord was right there beside me. I gave a short testimony; then Pastor Ed immersed me in the water. I closed my eyes and I could feel the water covering my body. I imagined that the water was sin in my life. I was covered by sin for so many years. When Pastor Ed lifted me back up and the water dripped off of me, I finally felt clean. My sins were washed away. They would go down the drain, along with the water. Douglas wasn't there.

I must confess, however, that when I was all alone, day or night, my heart still ached. Love doesn't just die when it gets stabbed in the heart. It can have enough cosmetic surgery to carry it through to the next heartache, but it takes a long time to die. I regularly pleaded with God to give Douglas back to me. My prayers seemed to go only as high as the ceiling.

One day at work the hurt I was feeling was particularly unbearable. I wasn't able to concentrate on my job. My office was upstairs beside the staff lunch room. I went into the lunch room to cry and pray. I didn't turn the light on, so it was dark. Out loud I pleaded with God to give Douglas back to me. I begged, "Please give him back to me Lord, please!" A soft audible voice answered me. He said, "Yes, my child." I was puzzled. I thought my mind was playing tricks on me, so I said it again. "Please give Douglas back to me!" Again the voice said, "Yes, my child." I knew it wasn't the devil talking to me because I wasn't his child anymore. At that moment, my soul knew that the Lord was there, speaking to me. I pleaded, "When, when?" He answered, "Soon." As quickly as He came, He was gone. The room felt like it was full of electricity. I almost expected the lights to come on by themselves. The hairs stood up on the back of my neck, and I was covered with an undescribable peace.

I went back into my office and reflected on what had just happened. I started to doubt. Why would God talk to me? It had to be a voice in my head telling me what I wanted to hear. I was confused. I called Pastor Ed and asked him how I would know if it was God who spoke to me. He told me that I would have peace in my soul. I had that. He told me that if it came true, it definitely was God. I would have to wait for that answer. I assumed that it hadn't been God who spoke to me in the lunch room when I heard that Douglas had, yet again, asked Karen to take him back. Her answer was the same.

Next I was told that Douglas had a girlfriend. What made it hurt more was who she was. If you guessed that it was the one he slept with the night before he moved me to Saskatchewan, you are right! I was told she was staying with him at the farm. She was living in my house, and sleeping with my husband. She considered herself to be a sex symbol,

160

because she was telling all our friends that her name was "Marilyn Monroe."

Our friends told me where she worked, lived, and the make and color of her car. They told Douglas that he had better smarten up and get his wife back where she belonged. My soul was tortured. I was driven by something that was stronger than I was, and I watched her. I drove past her work place, and her house. I watched for her car, and I watched for Douglas' truck. When her car was home I was happy. I knew she wasn't with Douglas. I dreamed of letting the air out of her tires or putting nails under them. I wouldn't actually do it, but I enjoyed thinking about it. I watched their every move. I was overwrought with grief.

I developed pains in my chest and down my right arm. I was sure it was my heart, and I was going to die. I was frightened enough to see my doctor. After an ECG and a long discussion, he advised me to go to Al-Anon. They would teach me how to cope. I was desperate enough to try it.

To my surprise, Al-Anon was based on some of the same principals as Christianity. They said I needed to rely on a higher power. That would be Jesus. They said to let go, and let God. That would be complete faith and dependence on God. They said, "If you pray, why worry? and if you worry, why pray?" That would be to "... understand how incredibly great His power is to help those who believe in Him." *Ephesians 1:19 (TLB)*. I felt that what I was learning at Al-Anon would definitely help me when Douglas and I got back together.

On my way home for lunch one day I saw Douglas and his girlfriend in his truck. She was practically sitting on his knee, and they were laughing. By the time I got home I was ready to fall apart. I took my Bible, knelt beside Matthew's bed and prayed. I asked God to show me what I should do - show me some verse in the Bible that would give me some assurance

161

that I could survive. I opened the Bible to Colossians. It said, "to set my mind on the things above, not on the things here on earth. For you have died and your life is hidden with Christ in God, I have put on a new self, ... Christ is all, and in all, Let the peace of Christ rule in your hearts..., Let the word of Christ richly dwell within you ..., It is the Lord Christ whom you serve, For he who does wrong will receive the consequences of the wrong which he has done, and that without partiality." *Colossians 3:1-25 (TLB)* I knew without a doubt that God was in control.

From that day on, I also knew my calling was to grow strong in the Lord. I only had to answer for myself. I wanted Douglas back, but if the Lord didn't give him to me, He would give me the strength and power to overcome the pain. I had come to terms with my heartache and I felt I could be happy again.

The early part of May I got a phone call from our lawyer. He asked me to take my name off the title for the home quarter of land. The home quarter goes to the wife in case of death or divorce. The lawyer was told by Douglas that I would sign off, that I didn't receive anything from any of my other husbands, so I shouldn't expect anything from him. I laughed. I told the lawyer that Douglas was dreaming: he was always so afraid that I would get some of his money. Our lawyer apologized for calling. He hadn't wanted to call, but Douglas insisted. He said, "He is being a bit of a stinker."

In the middle of May I got a phone call from Douglas. He wanted to see me. He asked me to come to the farm so we could talk in privacy. When I walked in the door, he grabbed me and gave me one of those wonderful kisses that he had given me when we were dating. He took my hand and led me to the living room, where he sat beside me on the couch. He said he wanted a fun-loving woman, one who could do all the things he enjoyed. I had hoped he was going to tell me that he loved me and wanted me back, but I could see that wasn't going to happen. I told him I couldn't be the kind of woman he wanted, that I had made my choice, and I would be a Christian no matter what. He carried on for a while then told me he was going to look for a young, good-looking woman who could supply all his needs. On my way out I said, "Go ahead, do whatever your little old heart desires."

About two weeks later he was waiting for me at my car when I got off work. He wasn't as confident this time. He wanted me back and he was sorry he had cheated on me. I got angry. His little affair was over and I was supposed to jump right back into his arms and forget, yet again. This was the moment I had been waiting for, but when it happened, I felt uncomfortable. Reluctantly, I agreed to meet him for supper.

While we were eating, he told me again how sorry he was for what he had done. He wished it hadn't happened, and asked me to forgive him. He told me that if I did take him back, he never wanted to hear about his affair again. He didn't want a daily menu of "adultery." Finally, after all these many, many months, I had my chance to tell him what I felt. I told him I wasn't one of his women. I was Susan Arlene. I didn't want to be compared and I didn't want to hear about them, either. He had to stop trying to make me over. I was going to live the Christian life and I didn't want to hear about that every day.

By June 5th, the kids and I were back home on the farm. His old furniture was gone and mine was back in place. As I unpacked the last box, I asked God to help me forgive Douglas and forget how he had hurt me. I prayed for strength to move on. I knew it would be a struggle and I knew I had to keep my eyes on Jesus. I hoped that I had made the right decision.

Douglas did his best to show me that he cared. He took me out for a romantic supper on my birthday and our anniversary. He had flowers sent to the restaurant and signed the card, "Love Douglas," but the relationship was always strained. There was almost too much pain to overcome. The pureness of the first love was clouded with heartache. I felt love for him, but it was different. It was almost a guard-your-heart kind of love. We did have some fun times, some wonderful times, but I always wondered, "What if?" I didn't want to wear that sign on my forehead anymore that said, "Hurt me!" I prayed that Douglas would become a Christian. I knew that if he gave his heart to Jesus, he would be able to leave all his guilt behind and find his own peace.

On one of Mitch's weekend visits we took him to church with us. It was summer and childrens' camps were being promoted. Mitch wanted to go, so Douglas signed him up and paid his registration fees. A few weeks after Mitch got back from camp, Karen called Douglas and she was angry. She told him that the counselors had forced Mitch into giving his heart to Jesus, and now all he did was fight with Vanessa. The only thing Douglas heard was that Mitch had been forced into becoming a Christian. He got very angry at everybody, including the pastor. I took his verbal abuse and defended my Christianity again. I told him that if Mitch gave his heart to Jesus, it was because of the Holy spirit, not the counselors. Eventually he simmered down and treated me fairly decently for a while.

We had one more hurdle to jump that summer. It was mountainous. Karen called and said that she and the kids were moving to Northern Saskatchewan. There was no explanation, no discussion. She had made the decision and it was final. Douglas took it better than I thought he would. He was angry, riddled with guilt and unhappy, but he didn't blow a fuse. I was sure that "this" move was going to be hard on everybody.

CHAPTER SIX

I Taste the Wine; I Smell the Roses

The sting of the serpent

I was slowly regaining the "joy of my salvation." However, my soul was extremely burdened for Stephanie and Douglas, and I prayed for their salvation regularly. I was positive our home life would improve if Douglas gave his heart to the Lord.

The new 1979 Buick station wagon Douglas picked me up in was beautiful. After a test drive, and his famous sales pitch, I was sure we needed it. I could drive to work in a brand new car! We could buy it if I made the payments. My mind raced! How could I afford to buy all the food, clothing, etc., etc., for my family and make a car payment too? The 1974 Pontiac I drove now worked just fine. If I said no would I lose him again? I decided yes would make him happy and he would stay.

Bill had quit the ministry and moved to another city to find work, so Mom was alone in Kelowna, and lonesome for her children. Anne and I convinced her to sell her house and move to Swift Current. In late October, Mom's entire household was packed on our three-ton truck, headed for Saskatchewan. Having Mom close would be a real treat.

Our marriage had been running fairly smoothly, so I anticipated a happy Valentine's Day. Douglas gave me a card, but instead of it being romantic, it was humorous. I wasn't impressed! He signed it, "Guess Who?" I couldn't hold back the tears. He chuckled, "What's the matter, don't you like my card?" I whispered, "You could have at least signed it "Love." He got angry, ripped it up, and threw it in the garbage can. He retorted, "You're always talking about feelings and love. I have no love to give you right now." With that remark, he left. It was very late when he got home, and he reeked of alcohol. "He doesn't love me," I thought, " but he sure loves his booze." He was always remorseful the morning after, and today was no exception. He apologized for tearing up the card, but nothing else. I wondered why I had so desperately wanted him back in my life.

I could tell by the way Douglas was acting that he was either feeling bad that his kids were so far away, or he was feeling guilty that he had left them (probably both). A week before Mitch's birthday, Douglas announced that he had sent him a card. I asked if he had signed my name too. He snapped, "No! Can't I have anything to myself?" I cried, we fought, he went drinking. We were on a merry-go-round, heading back to where we started.

Anne and I were horrified when Mom told us she had cancer and had to have a hysterectomy. It was agreed that Harry and Anne would take her to Saskatoon for her radiation treatments after she recovered from her surgery. I was working and most of our spare time was taken up renovating a two-story house we had moved to the farm.

Renovating is a tedious and expensive undertaking. I helped with some of the smaller expenses by purchasing all the light fixtures, blinds and draperies. After year-end was complete at work, all employees received a "profit share" cheque from our employer. My cheque was large enough for me to purchase a bedroom suite, dining room suite and a complete set of furnishings for the living room. We moved in to our new, old house on the first Saturday in October. I thanked the Lord for allowing me to live in this beautiful home, and I dedicated it to Him.

On my birthday Douglas called me at work. He had made supper reservations at one of the fancier restaurants in town, and I should go there directly after work. The atmosphere was definitely romantic. The white linen, and elegant glass and dinnerware trapped the glimmer of the candle light. To say the least, I was impressed. After we ordered, our hostess brought me a beautiful bouquet of flowers. The card said, "Love, Douglas." My heart was full.

The already perfect evening ended with one more surprise. In a couple of weeks our church was holding a marriage retreat at a local motel. Douglas was taking me to it. I wondered why he as being so nice. I didn't care, though, because this was the Douglas that I fell in love with.

The marriage retreat was a nightmare. It was too intimate for Douglas because it involved sharing our feelings and renewing our marriage vows. When we were supposed to be in our rooms sharing our innermost thoughts and feelings, we were watching television, going for coffee, or swimming in the pool. When the speaker and his wife led us in marriage vows, he wouldn't look at me. We were the only two in the room who never spoke, and both of us wished we were somewhere else.

The retreat ended with prayer. The lady praying singled Douglas out by praying for him to give his heart to Jesus. He would be so much happier, and on and on. He said, "Let's get out of here." I was upset too, because I knew that embarrassing him would do more harm than good.

We drove home in silence. While we were parking the car, one of his drinking buddies pulled up and asked him if he wanted to go for a drink. He said, "You bet I do." I expected him to be gone all night, but he was home by 11:00 p.m. He was sorry for leaving, but he was upset about that lady's prayer and he couldn't handle any more talk about feelings.

The next few months was a mixture of wine and roses. I could smell the roses when the Lord gave me words to write poetry. I could smell the roses when I read, "The Lord is close to those whose hearts are breaking." *Psalm 34:18 (TLB)* I could smell the roses when I realized how very much God loved me. "For I am convinced that nothing can ever separate us from His love. Death can't, and life can't. The angels won't, and all the power of hell itself cannot keep God's love away..." *Romans 8:38 (TLB)* I could smell the roses when Douglas bought me an electric organ. I felt the bite of the wine when his words, "It's too bad you only know one song," mocked me.

I felt the bite of the wine when Douglas told me that he was fine, but I needed a counselor. I felt the bite of the wine when he went out night after night. Where was he? Who was he with? Was he too drunk to drive home, or would he even come home? I felt the bite of the wine when he came home drunk and verbally attacked me for being a Christian.

I forgot everything I learned at Al-Anon and I marked my kitchen calendar every time Douglas drank. There were many marks. When he realized what I was doing he was furious.

I was furious when he informed me that we wouldn't be going on a summer holiday. His kids had holiday plans with their mom! If they couldn't go, nobody would go.

Douglas invited his kids to his home town reunion. I went along, but he distanced himself from me. I couldn't handle the rejection and went home. When Douglas finally realized I was gone, he came home and verbally attacked me. As he was turning to leave, I grabbed his arm and pleaded with him not to go. I was hysterical! He slapped my face and pushed me to the floor. I crawled to the corner, curled up in a ball and wept.

Douglas continually lectured my kids about money. He never gave them any, but always had lots of advice. When Stephanie asked Douglas if she could go see her dad, he said, "No - do you think I want to get kicked in the head?" How could he continually hurt and reject us, and openly affirm his love and loyalty to his kids? Was there no justice in this world?

I was like the mother bear that protects her cubs. Douglas was the same. We divided camps! "My kids - Your kids" was the battle ground. The war was on, but the battle was already lost. Our marriage and family life were the hostages and the serpent was the victor.

It occurred to me that our only hope of staying together would be if Douglas gave his heart to the Lord. I started a campaign. It was up to me to single-handedly save him. I had read my Bible; it told me that if I claimed its promises, Douglas would be saved and our marriage healed. "Ask, and it shall be given to you..." *Matthew 7:7 (NAS)* "With men this is impossible, but with God all things are possible..." *Matthew 19:26 (NAS)* "And everything you ask in prayer, believing, you shall receive." *Matthew 21:22 (NAS)*

That didn't work, so I tried to talk him into the kingdom. It wasn't until I read, "Wives, in the same way be submissive to your husbands so that, if any of them do not believe the word, they may be won over without words by the behaviour of their wives," *1 Peter 3:1 (NIV)* that I realized I needed to take my hands off and let God do His job. My attempts to "save him" had pushed Douglas into reverse. God's plan for Douglas was far superior to mine. However, I found it to be almost impossible to submit to someone who didn't show love for me.

My thirty-sixth birthday started out like any other day. It would be my choice as to whether it would be a happy or unhappy day. When Douglas told me that he was taking me out for supper, I decided on a happy day. There were no flowers or fine china at this restaurant, but the food was delicious and the conversation was pleasant. Throughout the evening, Douglas fussed with one of his pant legs and his left foot and shoe. I was nervous that he had some kind of a hurtful bombshell to drop on me. I would have to wait and see!

169

Ah! The weekend! Douglas would shower while I enjoyed my morning ritual, a cup of Folgers coffee. Later we would go to Swift Current to buy groceries. Douglas was in the bathroom for such a long time that I was beginning to wonder if he drowned. I knocked on the door and asked him if he was okay. After a long pause he answered, "I'm not sure. The left side of my body is numb and so is my head, tongue, and teeth." I panicked! "You must be having a stroke or a heart attack, or something. We need to get you to the hospital right away. I'll call the doctor; he can meet us there." He told me to settle down, that we would see the doctor when we got there.

They did a battery of tests and determined that it was not his heart, and they would need more tests to pinpoint the problem. Days turned into weeks and all the tests came back negative. His condition worsened and his speech became slurred. His head was numb, his face swollen, and he was exhausted. More tests. Negative results. As a last resort, the doctor ordered a spinal tap. Douglas would need to go into the hospital, as he would be on twenty-four hour bed rest after the test.

We were not prepared for the results. Douglas had Multiple Sclerosis. The prognosis: paralysis. We were in a state of shock. He was sent to a neurologist who explained the disease to us. "There is no cure and no medication." Douglas needed plenty of rest. He should stay active and he should stay working, but he shouldn't tire his muscles, and no stress. Most importantly - he shouldn't give up hope! In other words, keep living until you can't walk anymore.

Our lives changed dramatically. Douglas had to go to bed early because he was extremely tired. I usually went to bed late, but now I had to go to bed when he did. If I went later and happened to wake him up, he tossed and turned, sleepless, for the rest of the night. The next day he felt like a train had run over him. Sharp or loud noises sounded like a gong in his head, and the noise from a room full of people almost drove him around the bend. The kids and I walked the floor like it was covered in eggshells. If we happened to break one, it was like a sonic boom to Douglas. Douglas developed double vision. He wouldn't let me drive him anywhere, so he had to close one eye while driving. If both eyes were open he saw two vehicles. He often wasn't sure which one was real and which one was duplicate. He had to quit drinking because the alcohol intensified his symptoms. He was easily aggravated and very restless.

But he took the advice of his doctor and didn't give up. I was amazed at his positive attitude. He was not going to let his problem defeat him. He dealt with it, and he was moving on. Slowly his vision returned to normal. The numbness wasn't as severe and he wasn't quite as tired. He could stay up a little later, and gradually could tolerate more noise. Oh, yes - he could start drinking again.

I was almost emotionally recuperated when I received another blow. Mom was dying. The cancer was galloping through her body. She was in the hospital and would soon be gone. I visited her on my lunch hours, but I wasn't there as much as I could have been. Douglas rarely came with me; hospitals were not his favorite place to be. My screwed-up thinking told me that if I was gone every evening until visiting hours were over, as well as Saturdays, Douglas would always be gone drinking. I convinced myself that I couldn't deal with that too.

Saturday, December 19, 1981, we were invited to the staff Christmas party in the small town where Douglas worked. Mom was very close to death, but I opted to go to the party. I left the phone number with Matthew; I'd see Mom after church tomorrow. The drive to Vanguard was quiet. The wind was very strong. When the headlights caught the blowing snow in their beam, it reminded me of the little domed Christmas ornament that displayed a multitude of white dots when it was shaken. Storm-tossed, yet peaceful. I shivered when a white bird flew up from the ditch beside me, across the highway in front of us, and out of sight. At that moment, I knew the Lord had taken mom home.

Just like at Norman's funeral, I could feel the presence of the Lord at Mom's. This time, however, I wasn't fighting with the Lord; I was worshipping Him. There were many tears, but I was happy for Mom; she was finally home with her precious Lord, and her precious son. My entire family was at the funeral. Sharon and her children came, and so did Shirl.

Losing Grandma Mueller was especially hard for Matthew and Stephanie. They had spent many days with her. She filled many roles for them: grandma, mother, father and spiritual leader. She loved them as much as it was humanly possible to love, and they reciprocated that love. Matthew was able to put his feelings into a reading that Pastor Ed read as her eulogy. He titled it *The Best Christmas Gift.*

"Her body lay on the hospital bed. Some spoke of her glassy eyes. Three score and seventeen years she prayed. She prayed me out of hell. That I will never forget! She said she had no pain, for some strange reason; only the Lord knows why. She fought her whole life for the Prince of Peace. She gave her all, her heart, her mind, her self will, and her life. She lay there in confusion, not knowing that she touches us as we see her. That Godly woman went through hell her whole life, as her children know. Just ask them. But though she went through this, the Lord did not forget her. He opened the door to Heaven and walked down the stairway to her side. He took her new, young, beautiful body. He said to her, "You gave your life to me; I want so badly for you to come to me. This is your reward: peace, happiness, and joy, for all eternity. This is My Christmas gift to you." Then He took her hand and they walked up the stairs to Heaven, where she was greeted by a multitude of people. She stood there before the Father, Creator of the universe. Oh, how I envy her. The Lord is going to do the same for me, as I gave my life to Him. Death - we can't escape it. No one can hide from it. Thank you, Jesus, for dying for me, as Grandma died. I understand a little more now what it means when someone says that Jesus died for us on the cross. Remember the true meaning of Christmas this year. The Cross! Look at your tree and the presents under it, and remember Jesus and the gift of life He wants to give you. This is my best Christmas ever. Thank you for making it that way, Jesus." So ends the legacy of a godly woman: "My Mom."

Douglas' doctor suggested we take a vacation. Douglas needed to rest. Coincidentally, my nephew was getting married in San Diego in late January. We would take our motor home. In early February we would meet a couple from our church who were venturing to Phoenix, Arizona, with their fifth-wheel travel trailer. Each day of the seven weeks we spent in Arizona, Douglas regained strength.

After he got M.S., Douglas assumed that his farming days were over. He acted quickly. He rented his land to his brother and booked an auction sale to sell his machinery, but by the time we got back from Arizona he knew he had made a mistake. He felt good enough to farm his own land, but it was too late - the contracts were signed. For Douglas, not being able to farm his land was like having a burr in his sock. Very irritating. He still sold farm equipment, because he was a born salesman, BUT - he missed farming.

Matthew graduated from high school in June and enrolled in Bible School at Camrose, Alberta, for the fall semester. I had quit my job to go to Arizona for the winter. Douglas informed us that he would pay for Matthew's first semester, but after that, either I went back to work and paid for any further tuition costs, or Matthew would have to get a student loan.

I hadn't dealt with my guilt feelings concerning Mom. I felt guilty that I had been more worried about Douglas' drinking if I didn't go home than I had been with her dying. I felt guilty that after church on Sundays, I went to Douglas' parents for dinner and the afternoon. If Harry and Anne didn't visit her, she sat alone. I hadn't taken time off to take Mom to any of her cancer treatments, except one. Guilt penetrated my soul like the sting of a wasp. I was super-sensitive and I took everything personally, so we fought most of the time. The issues were always the same. Your kids - my kids, lack of love and affection, alcohol, and his being gone all the time. We said many hurtful things to each other, mostly in retaliation. Emotionally I was a wreck.

One Sunday afternoon, there was a knock on the door at Douglas' mom and dad's. There was Karen, big as life. She had come to visit. They fussed over her like she was the Queen of Sheba. I didn't fit into their "Do you remember the time we...?" discussions. I had to get out of there. I felt so hurt that I couldn't breathe. They wouldn't even miss me if I left.

I held myself together until I got to Mom's grave. I felt so unloved, so unwanted. I pleaded with Mom to forgive me for not being a good daughter. I cried until I had no more tears: then I prayed. "Lord, please help me, I'm dying inside. I'm so lonely and unloved. Please give me strength to live at my house. I want to be happy again. I want to be like Mom, and love You as much as she did. I want to have a peaceful and gentle spirit, like she did." As I sat quietly and drank in the beauty of her soul I really missed her: I could sense that she had forgiven me.

I immersed myself in church work. I needed strength to get through each day. Teaching the older youth Sunday School class was a real challenge, and I had to be on "my spiritual toes." I directed a major youth play, produced and directed a musical pantomime for the girls in my youth class, plus I was

174

on the Board of Church Growth and Evangelism. I was too busy to think about my problems.

When 1983 ushered itself in, I wondered what the year would have in store for us. Maybe there would be happiness instead of heartache. I hadn't forgotten my graveside visit. I still wanted to be like Mom. Somehow I needed to find the inner strength that she possessed. Somehow I had to learn how to let go of the heartache my kids and I had endured and let God deal with Douglas. I quietly made a commitment to the Lord to try to put Him first in every area of my life. I wanted to learn how to find joy in serving Him, because I believed the scripture that said, "Delight yourself also in the Lord, and He will give you the desires and secret petitions of your heart." *Psalm 37:4 (TAB)*

Douglas was given an opportunity to rent a large amount of farm land from his cousin. There were many factors to take into account. He would have to reinvest in some machinery. Was he healthy enough to farm that much land? Would there be too much stress? The biggest hurdle was the contract itself. His cousin insisted on a cash rent agreement. That would be acceptable unless we had a crop failure. If that occurred, we would have to take money from our pockets to pay the land rent. Douglas informed me that I would have to help, and that meant I would have to learn how to summerfallow. After much number crunching and discussion, we decided to take a chance.

When Douglas realized that M.S. and alcohol don't mix, he reluctantly gave it up. He wasn't drinking, but he sure wanted to be. The "dry drunk" mentality can be brutal.

He was more critical of me than usual. Unfortunately for me, he seemed to get more enjoyment out of criticizing me in front of our friends and his kids. When I took the garbage out, I put it in the wrong place. When I offered to help him do things outside, he said he could do it himself. When I tried to

175

touch him, he pulled away. When I tried to question him as to why he was always angry with me, he wouldn't answer. When I asked for grocery money or spending money, I got a lecture on how good I had it, or how lucky I was. Hadn't he bought me diamonds, furs and trips? If I needed money, I should go back to work. I said, "Keep pushing, I'll never go back."

Hate hardened my heart, but it kept the hurt away. I prayed for Douglas to become a Christian, but my heart was full of unforgiveness. I felt unworthy to be in God's presence, because I didn't want to forgive Douglas, especially when he didn't think he ever did anything wrong. All our problems were my fault in his mind. I didn't want the Lord to take his hands off me, so I decided to get honest with him. I prayed, "Dear Lord, I need to tell you something that you already know. My heart is full of hate and unforgiveness. Forgive me, Lord. I know unforgiveness is wrong, but I can't let go of it. It's my protection. If I empty my heart of it, I'll drown in the blood of my broken heart. Please be patient with me! Please don't give up on me! Please love me!"

My kids were living in my nightmare too. I couldn't, and wouldn't, inflict any more pain on them by sharing my pain with them. So other than the Lord, Harry and Anne were the only people I had to talk to. They were my life support. Besides, nobody would believe me. I was the import into the community, and Douglas was liked by everybody.

Without my noticing it, the Lord was answering my prayer. Every once in a while I felt a little flicker of "like" for Douglas. If life was good at home, I would let the guard of my heart down, just to test the water. If there was the slightest bruise, the guard went up again. Eventually I lowered my guard to half mast and left if there. It could go either way at any time.

Karen was having trouble with their kids. In every problem, she would call Douglas and ask him to phone his kids and straighten them out. Every call to them was a lecture and a scolding. I actually felt sorry for them. I surprised myself when I told him to stop yelling at them all the time. He was starting to look like the bad guy. The next time she called, he told her that he had yelled at them enough, and if she couldn't handle them anymore, they could come and live with him.

When Stephanie announced that she would be joining Matthew at Bible School in the fall, I couldn't help but reflect on the events that led up to her decision. Mom was steadily growing weaker as the cancer galloped through her body. Anne and I didn't think she would be able to look after herself much longer. Stephanie volunteered to move in with Mom and look after her. They became very close. Grandma Mueller was one of a kind. She was a woman of God. She loved Him with all her heart and she shared that love with Stephanie many times. Mom displayed unselfish love for her, and anyone else that came in contact with her. She prayed daily for Stephanie and told her so. Mom's kindness and generosity softened Stephanie's heart. After mom died, the "Hound of Heaven" continued to pursue Stephanie until she couldn't live without Jesus anymore. Once again, she gave her heart and soul to Him.

Stephanie had been dating a young man for some time and they were in love. Not coming from an evangelical background, he absolutely couldn't understand why she had quit drinking and smoking. They had been thinking about marriage, so he certainly wasn't about to let her go off to Bible School. He was putting intense pressure on her to give up her "religious experience." He wanted things to be the way they were before. In essence, she had to choose between two people she loved.

The breakup was extremely hurtful for Stephanie. He was hurting too, but he was also angry, an explosive combination. He maligned her to his family and their friends.

177

He spread   lies about her and harassed her unmercifully. September couldn't come soon enough for Stephanie.

Douglas astounded me. He supported Stephanie's decision to go to Bible School. The same circumstances applied to her as they had for Matthew. He would pay for her first semester, but after that she was on her own. Even more astounding, he gave Matthew our old Pontiac to drive while they were in Camrose.

With both my kids gone, I started to relax a little. I wouldn't have to fight for their rights anymore. I wouldn't have to defend them or protect their feelings. When his kids came to visit, there wouldn't be any more competition for Douglas' love. Douglas relaxed too. When his kids came to our house, he didn't have to feel like he was betraying them by living with my kids.

Hope reigned supreme when Douglas started going to church with me. We always sat two rows from the back - left side, next to the window. When Pastor Ed's message spoke to Douglas' heart, he read the song book, or whatever else he could find. I was so happy that he was going to church, I didn't even utter a defense when we had "roast preacher" for dinner.

My kids' biological dad, Charles, had an unmarried uncle who died and left all his money to his family. Matthew and Stephanie's share would be about seventeen thousand dollars, over a three to four year period. They decided to use the inheritance to pay tuition for Bible School. They were both taking a four-year course that would give them Bachelor of Theology degrees. Douglas was angry. Waste all that money on Bible School! After they're done there won't be a job for them, and the money will be gone, like a puff of smoke!

My friend, Gail, and I started a catering company: Copper Kettle Catering. We were planning to take our two families to Disneyland on a vacation. Catering would help us pay for the trip. We had a blast! Douglas and Pete were our meat carvers, as well as our taste testers. The biggest drawback to catering, of course, is leftovers. How many things can you do with left over turkey and jello?

Douglas and his family were devastated when they were informed that their dad was terminally ill with bone cancer. Douglas' mom had prayed her entire married life for her husband to become a Christian. The Lord rewarded her when he asked God to forgive him of his sins and come into his heart.

The family participated in a hospital room vigil. Dad was never alone. Day and night, one of his children and their spouse were at his bedside. The trauma of watching his dad slowly die, and many weeks of sleepless nights, was taking its toll on Douglas. He was dreading his dad's impending death, as he and his dad were close. Dad's decision to become a Christian was really speaking to Douglas' heart, too. His soul was in turmoil.

Friday was our turn to sit with Dad. We drove to town in silence. Douglas seemed nervous. He squirmed in his seat a lot. He didn't seem to be comfortable. Instead of driving straight to the hospital, he went to church. I said, "What are we doing here?" He didn't answer. He went inside. I followed. He headed directly for Pastor Ed's office. I couldn't imagine what Douglas was going to say to him. I gasped when he said, "Let's go out to the altar. I want to get saved!" Pastor Ed was thrilled to oblige that request. We knelt at the altar and they prayed the sinner's prayer. We all shed tears of happiness. This, this very moment, was what I had prayed for. I whispered, "Thank you, Lord! You did hear my prayers!"

It was strange having a Christian husband. I felt a shyness in his presence; like a new bride on her wedding night. I wasn't sure how to act or what to say. Douglas even looked different. The tension and worry lines were gone from his face and he looked happy. I expected our marriage to be miraculously healed. Unfortunately, the symptoms that caused the disease were still there. This cure wasn't going to produce immediate healing; it would be an ongoing process.

Within a few days, Dad was gone. Early one morning, with Douglas' mom and me at his bedside, he gave up his spirit to Heaven. After the funeral, as Douglas was reflecting on his dad's life, he confided in me that this funeral had been much easier to endure because he was a Christian. Tears were still shed as he said his good-byes, but his sense of loss wasn't as severe. The Lord had carried Douglas through his first valley.

California, here we come! Four adults and six teenagers. What a test of fortitude! The airplane flights and motel rooms were booked and a fifteen-passenger van was rented. We were anticipating a wonderful holiday. There was only one rule - NO fights! We experienced every possible tourist attraction in Southern California, and we were awestruck with the magnificent lights of Las Vegas. Matthew and Mitch traveled together. Pete and Gail have two daughters, so their youngest paired with Stephanie. Vanessa and their oldest daughter were a team. I was apprehensive about how our four kids would get along, in such close quarters for two weeks. To my surprise, everybody had a terrific time.

All too soon it was over. But the trip had started to mend some broken fences. Was there a possibility that the fragrant scent of roses that occurred when Douglas became a Christian could be strong enough to take away the bitter taste of the wine?

CHAPTER SEVEN

Two: Alone

I speak but no one answers

The next ten years were seasoned with a mixture of emotions. We tasted happiness, sadness, and all flavors in between. However, the flavor of spiritual growth was the ingredient that enabled me to survive the heat of the oven.

The Flavor of Happiness - Seasoned with Laughter:

Because of Douglas' M.S., we decided to spend our winters in Arizona. Our first stop was generally a week in San Diego, California, at Alice's house. Then we went to Phoenix for three to four months.

The winters in Arizona were happy times for us. We traveled together with a couple from our church, Roland and Adalene. They became our constant companions and good friends, and they were excellent examples of people who lived their Christian life.

We were "snowbirds" that flew south to explore. We wanted to see it all and do it all. We met a couple from North Dakota and another couple from Minnesota. They became part of our "crew." At the age of thirty-seven, Douglas and I were the youngest couple in the group and were "adopted" by our new friends.

We had sold our motor home, so we bought a small travel trailer that we left there, on a lot in the resort. Eventually we traded up to a brand new, one-bedroom park model, fully furnished. I loved it!

For the first few years, site seeing was our top priority. We visited every tourist attraction in the Phoenix area, as well as the Tucson area and Mexico. Overwhelmingly, the beauty of the Grand Canyon made me aware again of just how majestic our Creator is.

We had a steady stream of visitors from Canada: family and friends who wanted to see how "snowbirds" lived. These were wonderful times filled with excitement and laughter. We spent hours combing the newspapers, looking for specials that would aid us in our new hobby, coupon shopping. We were adventurous, sampling many new foods native to the area. I guess you could say that we ate our way across the south!

On weekdays we participated in many of the activities that our park provided. We played pool and shuffleboard. We golfed and watched major league baseball training. After Douglas taught me how to swim, we were in the swimming pool every warm day. On Saturdays we went to the flea markets and on Sundays we went to church. Most evenings, we played games: men against women, of course. Some warm evenings we sat outside and visited, and some evenings we actually got the opportunity to watch television. Oh, yes, we girls were always ready to go shopping!

The desert in bloom is an awesome sight. The arms of the mighty Suguaro Cactus stretch toward the heavens as they hoard tons of water in their trunks. They adorn themselves with delicate white blossoms which they display with grandeur. There are numerous varieties of cactus, each producing magnificent flowers in every color of the rainbow. In March, the wondrous scent of the orange trees in blossom fills your nostrils with an indescribable aroma.

The highlight of our winters was the live drama, "The Celebration of Easter." It portrayed the last few weeks of Jesus' life, His crucifixion, resurrection and ascension. Real horses, camels and donkeys joined us in a seven-thousand-seat church auditorium. Each year, when I saw Him - Jesus - my eyes couldn't leave Him. My heartbeat quickened and I was filled with excitement and anticipation. I could hardly believe it. He was right there. I was seeing Jesus.

I watched in horror as the soldiers put a crown of long thorns on Jesus' head. They beat His head and body with a stick, and spit on Him. I could see the blood start to flow from His head. Jesus was in pain.

When Jesus passed by our seats, He was carrying His cross. I wept so hard that my body shook. I could see His anguish. He was battered and bruised. He moved very slowly, because He was weak from the pain and the heavy load He was carrying.

Jesus had to lay on the cross and stretch out His arms. Bang! Bang! Bang! The soldiers drove a nail through one of His hands. I couldn't look at the awful scene anymore, so I quickly closed my eyes. I heard that terrible sound again. Bang! Bang! Bang! They nailed His other hand to the cross. Jesus moaned in agony when they drove the nail through His feet. I opened my eyes just in time to see the soldiers pick up the cross and drop it into the hole they had made for it. He was suffering there for me!

The last time I saw Jesus, I watched in silence as he ascended up into the spire of the church, hundreds of feet above us. He really was the Son of God!

The Flavor of Unresolved Feelings:

The same old problems we left behind welcomed us at the door each time we returned from the south. Almost methodically, we reverted back to our old ways. Douglas reclaimed his old attitudes and habits, and I reclaimed my old feelings of being unloved and unwanted.

I was very insecure about our marriage, so I pressured Douglas about not loving me. I pressured him about constantly flirting with other women while withholding his affection from me. I pressured him for being gone all the time and I was especially unhappy when he went hunting for a week. I was alone in the house and afraid.

Food was my comfort. My weight was an ongoing problem. I'm sure I've lost, and gained, a thousand pounds in my lifetime. When I was slim I didn't crave compliments on my appearance, but when I was overweight I had absolutely no self-esteem. I wanted Douglas to build me up emotionally by giving me compliments. That never happened. Eventually, I started to look at myself in the mirror and say, "Susan, you look beautiful!" "Thank you," was my reply.

When Douglas was sarcastic or critical, I retorted with a smart remark of my own. When he insinuated that I was dumb or stupid, I told him that he was the only person in the room who didn't finish school. When we drove anywhere together, there was no conversation. My only company was the country music on the radio station.

On the rare occasions when we were home together in the evenings Douglas almost always went downstairs to the rumpus room, leaving me alone upstairs. He watched television, or talked on the phone for hours. Out of loneliness, I would go downstairs and try to start a conversation with him. It was always the same. He either didn't answer me, or he made another call, generally while I was in the middle of a sentence. I usually gave up and went back upstairs. Sometimes I just gave up emotionally, and said to myself, as Rhett Butler said to Scarlett O'Hara in *Gone With the Wind*, "Frankly, my dear, I don't give a damn!" But of course I did, and I always ended up being hurt or frustrated.

We were famous for nitpicking at each other. We seldom talked at home, so we saved our degrading remarks for when we were out. He always seemed to get more remarks in than I did, because I was already starting to get hurt feelings right after the first dig. We were both controllers. He wanted his way; I wanted mine. He told me I was spoiled, I told him to look in the mirror and meet my twin. If he wasn't on the defense, I was.

I am positive that the Lord was grieving because of our behaviour toward each other. We certainly weren't acting like children of the King. Fortunately for us, "His compassion never ends. It is only the Lord's mercies that have kept us from complete destruction." *Lamentations 3:22 (TLB)*
The Flavor of "Your Kids - My Kids":

A re-marriage with kids is not always an ideal situation. It is rare if the two sets of kids blend together as a family. It is not uncommon for parents to play favorites between families. Douglas felt that he had to care for and protect his kids. My responsibility was the same for mine. We both loved our kids and were proud of them, but unfortunately we were not able to handle most situations correctly, so we drove each other, and our kids, apart. We argued often, and we "fought dirty." We verbally attacked each other. We went for the jugular vein, and retreated only when one of us drew blood. It always ended the same: Douglas would get angry and tell me I didn't want him to love his kids. I would cry and tell him I never asked him to stop loving his kids - I just wanted him to love me and my kids too. He would retaliate by saying we didn't respect him, to which I would reply that respect isn't automatic - it has to be earned. Neither one of us would give up the reins of control.

Somehow, in the midst of all our strife, the Lord showed me that I had to relinquish my reins of control to Him. I had to be obedient and let go so that He could work things out His way. "For I know the plans I have for you," declares the Lord. "Plans to prosper you and not harm you, plans to give you hope and a future. *Jeremiah 29:11 (NIV)*
The Contrasting Flavors of Wholesome Pride and Unwholesome Sorrows:

Matthew is small in stature, and solidly built. He is five feet, seven inches tall, has light brown hair and green eyes.

Handsome! Even though he wears contact lenses, it is evident that he has those beautiful "Mueller" eyes. Matthew is a quiet person, but has a hearty laugh. He rarely shares his feelings and keeps everything inside. When he lived at home he needed a father figure to communicate with, but there was no possibility of that happening. Sometimes I tried to talk to him, but we usually ended up arguing, because I would point out something that he had not done or needed to do. He felt unloved by everybody, including his mom. So naturally, I was surprised to receive a beautiful letter from him the year he graduated from Bible School. "Mom, I love you! Love is a gift from God. God has given us both that gift. It hurts me when we argue, but I know you love me enough to tell me if I've done something wrong. I don't show it enough, but I love you with all my heart. Thank you for being patient with me. I hope I make you proud. Cards can't express how I really feel about you, so I hope my words will warm your heart. I pray that this Mother's Day will be a happy one for you."

Academically, things went well for Matthew, but he had to work hard for his passing marks. He did his internship at Fort Collins, Colorado. He was right at home there because he was in his favorite surroundings - trees and mountains. The congregation and staff fell in love with him, and vice-versa. His calling into the ministry was confirmed to him there. After harvest that fall, Douglas took me and Harry and Anne to Fort Collins for a surprise visit. It was a fun trip.

1987 was a happy year for Matthew. He graduated from Gardner Bible College with a Bachelor of Theology degree. He had earned a double major: Pastoral and Christian Education. I had no trouble convincing Douglas to take me and Harry and Anne to Camrose for the ceremony, but I couldn't convince him to stay the next day to visit. In the spring, Matthew gave an engagement ring to his girlfriend Janice. He was enrolled in Seminary in Edmonton, so after their wedding in October they took up residence there. Janice worked and Matthew went to school.

Janice was a likable, extroverted blonde. But problems surfaced almost immediately in their marriage. Janice wanted to be a nurse. Unfortunately, she wanted to take her training sooner rather than later. After much conflict, Matthew gave in to her demands. He put his plans of being a pastor on hold. He quit seminary after one year and found work in a hospital, in maintenance.

Later they moved to Janice's home town, which was both positive and negative for them. Janice's dad became the father figure that Matthew needed, and they got along exceptionally well. On the negative side, instead of working out their worsening marital problems together, Janice shared all of Matthew's faults with her mom and sisters. They didn't want their marriage to break apart, so they sought marriage counseling. They were advised to move elsewhere. They agreed, and moved back to Edmonton. Things started to improve and it looked like they might make it.

I was stunned when Matthew called and said that Janice had left and that they would divorce. He was devastated. There are no words to explain how crushed he was. This quiet, soft-spoken, gentle young man had to endure one more heartache. This was the ultimate rejection for him, especially after Janice told him that she knew the night before the wedding that she shouldn't be marrying him. She hadn't loved him then.

The devil started to work overtime on Matthew. He told him he was a real failure. He couldn't even keep his wife, let alone become a pastor. Who would hire a divorced pastor, anyway? Matthew battled the devil until he came to a place of deep depression. Finally, he gave up the battle and agreed with the devil. His life was indeed worthless, and he should end it.

187

Matthew had a 22-caliber rifle, but no bullets. He was working at a car wash cleaning vehicles. A co-worker found a bullet in a farm truck they were cleaning and gave the bullet to Matthew. It fit his rifle. He had the weapon and ammunition to leave this world.

The battle intensified, but took a different course. The devil was convincing and powerful, but through divine intervention, Matthew realized the devil was trying to destroy him. From somewhere deep inside his soul came a soft, gentle voice of comfort. Jesus was quietly telling Matthew how much He loved him. He wanted Matthew to live. Lovingly, and convincingly, the Lord defeated the devil and saved Matthew's life.

I wish I could say that, "poof," just like that, Matthew's emotions were healed, but that wasn't the case. Stephanie convinced him to move back to Swift Current where she felt he could start the healing process. He had family and friends there that loved him, and Pastor Ed would be able to counsel him back to emotional health. In August he moved back to Saskatchewan. Matthew was almost thirty and starting over.

I, too, felt Matthew's pain. I needed to express my grief to Douglas, but he just wasn't there for me. He told me he didn't want to talk about it. He couldn't handle it. He couldn't help me. I was on my own. Harry and Anne became my moral support, again.

McDonald's ended up being the location for some counseling sessions. Grandma Butler, Douglas' mom, gave many, many words of encouragement over coffee. Whenever I got to town I took my turn. Ultimately, Matthew had to find his own way in the healing process.

During Matthew's and Stephanie's years at Bible School, they developed a "college lingo" that Matthew frequently shared with us, along with his Biblical knowledge. Douglas was not impressed, however, and it caused their somewhat diminutive relationship to fade into obscurity. Douglas felt that money spent on Bible School was a complete waste. Matthew should have trained for a profession that would insure him a job when he graduated. Pastoral jobs were few and far between.

Moving back to the farm was not an option for Matthew, so he found an apartment in Swift Current, but was unable to find a job. His savings were almost gone and I had no way of helping him. As a last resort, he turned to welfare. His self-worth, self-esteem and every emotion in between hit rock bottom again. We added one more rock to his pile when I informed him that we wouldn't be home for Christmas: he was on his own.

Miraculously, a job fell into his lap. He would be the janitor for one of the local malls. It was evening work, but the pay was good. Slowly he started to feel like his life wasn't over; he would make it. He wasn't worthless.

Stephanie is a green-eyed brunette. She, too, follows the Mueller heritage of beautiful eyes. She is short, slim and beautiful. She has a magnetic one-note laugh that causes people to laugh along with her. Her uncle Harry tells her that when she laughs she sounds like a chicken that is laying an egg.

Stephanie and Matthew have totally different personalities. She needs to talk when something is bothering her, or she'll explode. She has followed me into every room in the house, talking until she could deal with whatever was hurting her. Sometimes I tried to get away, so I retreated to the bathroom. That was always my greatest mistake. She followed me right in, locked the door, and sat cross-legged on the bathroom counter. I was trapped. Nobody could come in and rescue me, and I couldn't leave. The bathroom was our 'special place'! I actually didn't mind, but I suspected that there was a more pleasant room in the house that would suffice.

After Stephanie completed her first year of Bible School, she wasn't sure that was where she wanted to be. At Bible School she was always compared to Matthew. That was not a bad thing because he was liked and accepted by the other students. However, she was wrestling to find her own indentity and worthiness.

She decided to move back home. She got a job at McDonald's and, within a short period of time, acquired a managerial position as breakfast coordinator. She rented a furnished basement suite in her Grandma Butler's basement. Douglas bought her an older car to drive to work, but she was unhappy. There were too many ghosts of the past in Swift Current, and the Lord was convicting her about going back to Bible School. She worked for a year, then gave in to the Lord's call to go back into training for the ministry.

Stephanie doesn't heal quickly or easily from hurt and rejection. She was struggling to find emotinal healing, while searching for a deeper walk with Jesus. She had effectively learned how to shut her emotions off. "If you don't feel, you don't hurt." So I was excited to see that now the closed rosebud of her soul was opening up to display a beautiful flower. Her letters to me indicated that she was starting to feel again. She was sorry for hurting me and she loved me. She was finding a closer walk with Jesus, and shared it in an article that she had written. It was printed in "Worth Reading," a pamphlet the Bible School published monthly. It touched my soul and made me especially thankful to the Lord for His faithfulnes and goodness:

"Good day. How is it in your part of the world? It's good today. No, actually it's terrific! Thanks for asking. Today, my world is beautiful. But that's just today. Sometimes my day is like a piece of paper that is scribbled thoroughly with black marks. Then other days, my world is very normal and routine. Oh...but today is beautiful. There is beauty in my soul...harmony...joy that flows like from a fountain. Yes, today is beautiful.

There are times when my world revolves around itself so much that I don't even notice when I bump into someone else's world. What a crime. To think that I could have taken a step into your world, but I didn't see it.

Sometimes I want to invite myself into your world, but I don't know how. I try to think of ways that I could do it, but they seem so purposeless. So, I don't bother. There are times, I admit, that I invite myself into your world in an abrupt way, but please be patient with me, for I am still learning.

When I feel down on myself, and my world looks grey, I pray to God to help me through the bleakness. He does that very thing! He says, 'Here Stephanie, touch this world, become a part of that person's world.'

When I've stepped out of my world, into someone else's, the world I return to doesn't look all that bad. As a matter of fact, I begin to see flowers that I've been stepping on, and I can see there are no clouds in front of the sun...it was just that my eyes were closed.

Don't let yourself be robbed by not looking at and touching someone else's world. Who knows, you might have trampled a rose garden!"

Stephanie felt the Lord was calling her into the ministry, so she was very excited about taking her internship. It was to be in Chicago, Illinois, with a pastor she was somewhat familiar with. Her excitement rapidly turned to horror as she realized this pastor was not in favor of female pastors. If a female is called to any kind of ministry, it would probably be in a Christian Education capacity - that was his mentality. He discouraged her at every turn. He severely criticized her speaking abilities and crushed her spirit. When she left Chicago she even doubted her Christianity. That pastor had effectively destroyed her calling and her dream. Somehow, the

Lord intervened in her life and restored her desire to finish Bible School. She changed her major from pastoral to Christian Education and enrolled in her fourth year.

As soon as winter reared its cold, white head, Douglas and I motored south to the land of palm trees and sunshine. Needless to say, we were absolutely speechless when we got a phone call from Stephanie, telling us she was engaged. She hadn't dated for many years, now "boom," she was in love. Len had enrolled in Bible School in January, and they would marry in the summer. We were in such shock that we didn't ask any pertinent questions. We didn't even know what he looked like. We asked her if she was sure this was the right guy for her. She said she was.

I was very unsettled about the whole thing and didn't sleep well. After about a week of restless nights, I had a nightmare. I saw Len. I couldn't see his face, but I saw his jet black hair. There was an aura of blackness around him. The presence of the devil was intense. I was terrified and had to fight my way out of the presence of evil. When I woke up, my body and sheets were wet with perspiration. I called Stephanie the next day and told her about my dream, and that I was very apprehensive about her relationship to Len. She informed me that Len's hair wasn't black, it was brown. I shouldn't worry, everything was fine.

Graduation was the end of April and her wedding was planned for early July. She was under tremendous pressure. There was the stress of changing her major, finishing her assignments, and finals. Not only was she adjusting to dating again, she was making wedding plans. They had plans to live in Edmonton, but would they be able to find an apartment and jobs, and on and on? She pushed herself to the brink of emotional exhaustion. I believe the reasons she didn't succumb to a complete breakdown were that I was on my face before the Lord and Mom's prayers for Matthew and Stephanie's protection were still before the throne. The Lord, in His tender mercy, saw fit to answer them. Stephanie graduated with her Bachelor of Theology degree in 1988.

We didn't see Douglas' kids a lot, but needless to say, he was very proud of them. Mitch graduated from high school and decided not to attend university. He stayed at home for a while as he was dealing with some fears in his life. Eventually he started to work for an electrical contractor as a shipper-receiver. He was proficient and worked his way up into a managerial position. As was the tradition, Douglas bought an older car for Mitch, which he drove for many years.

Mitch didn't stop growing until he was over six feet tall, a couple of inches taller than Douglas. He has fine features and is easy to look at. Very active, quick to make a decision, and eager to please best decribes Mitch. He developed a love for hunting and fishing, which are Douglas' two favorite hobbies. Douglas is always happy and eager to share his knowledge and time, to advise and participate in both activities.

Vanessa is the youngest. She went through a period of rebellion, a trait common to many teenagers. She didn't graduate from high school as her interests were leaning toward a modeling career. Douglas paid her tuition to a modeling school. She needed a vehicle, and was provided with an older car. She graduated and tried to work her way up in the world of professional modeling. Vanessa was asked to go to other parts of the globe to help further her career. She was unwilling to do that so her opportunites disappeared. She decided to change professions, so Douglas paid half her tuition to enroll in a beauty school. Upon graduating, she became a licensed beautician.

The Flavor of Health and Wealth:

From time to time I have pondered that if I found Aladdin's lamp, my three wishes would be for health, wealth and happiness. However, until such time as I find my very own genie, I will have to remain as average as most of society.

Thankfully, Douglas' M.S. is in remission. Of course there are still certain limitations he has to observe to maintain his strength. He needs to get his proper rest, and if he is overly strenuous and tires his muscles, he suffers the consequences by becoming weak and fatigued. Stress is still the worst, and can cause immediate problems for his body. God has kept Douglas out of a wheelchair, and for that we are continually thankful. God is faithful.

Douglas encountered one other health problem. His doctor removed a small, malignant growth from his shoulder. No radiation treatments were required and cancer has not returned to his body. And as for me, other than the normal problems that go along with being a middle-aged female, the Lord has blessed me with good health.

Discussing money has always been a priority of Douglas', so many times over the years I have had occasion to become angry and resentful toward him concerning his attitude about it. But, financially speaking, we have not done without anything. On a personal level, though, I have had to pry out every penny. On one occasion, I wasn't allowed to call Alice in San Diego, and phone calls to my kids were few and far between. When I did call, it was like a recurring nightmare. I would get nicely into the conversation and Douglas would start nagging in the background. "Hang up. You've talked long enough!" He doesn't do that anymore, but if he did I know I wouldn't be obeying him.

Farming is the type of profession in which you can be rich and poor in the same year. That causes a "love - hate" relationship with farming. We made some mistakes, one being cash-renting seventeen quarters of land. A drought forced us to sell wheat harvested on our land in order to pay the cash rent to our landlord. Other than that, we've had bumper crops, average crops, and below average crops. Farming hasn't made us rich, but it has provided us with a very good living. God is faithful.

The Flavor of Family and Friends:

Because of the age difference between me and the rest of my family, I didn't have the opportunity to have a close relationship with them. When my kids and I moved to Swift Current, I was thrilled to be able to develop a friendship with Anne. We spent a lot of time with her and Harry, and she became my best friend. There wasn't one thing that I couldn't share with her. She was my shoulder to cry on and my encourager. She and Harry were my emotional support system, and they were there when I needed them.

Because of our winter visits to San Diego, I was also able to become good friends with Alice. I could share my life with her in the winter, but the rest of the year she was too far away to hug - and long distance costs money.

Our family, "the Muellers," drifted apart after mom died, so when a family reunion was suggested, Anne and I took it upon ourselves to organize one in Swift Current. Harry and Douglas gave us very little help or support, but we planned it anyway. All of our family came, including Sharon, and Shirl. About three quarters of my nieces and nephews and their families attended. We laughed, cried, and we agreed to have a family reunion every three years. The next one was to be in San Diego, then Calgary, Alberta.

A couple of things became very evident at our reunions. Of the seven Mueller children, over half were divorced. Of the nieces and nephews, almost half were divorced. Very few of my brothers and sisters had forgiven Dad for the abuse they suffered, and very few had forgiven him for being unfaithful and abusive to Mom. Most agreed that our overpowering need to be loved and cared for had caused us to mistakenly choose the wrong mates.

Douglas was never comfortable around my family. He didn't like it that we always discussed our dad. He could never grasp the hurt and anger of physical and emotional abuse. I always felt that my family was being compared to his brothers and sisters, and coming up short.

Douglas is the youngest boy in a family of four - one brother and two sisters. His sister, Marlett, is a few years older than him. She has been very supportive of us over the years and I have a great love for her. I feel completely at ease with her, and trust her friendship. Marlett, as well as her husband Doney, are good friends to us. They spent a few winters with us in Arizona, and they accompanied us on many summer trips. Christmas season activities were not complete until one day was spent together with them, Harry and Anne and Mom Butler.

The breakup of a friendship is as painful as the breakup of a marriage. A mother bear is vicious toward anyone who endangers her cubs. I, like a majority of mothers, am the same. Friendships unravel in defense of children. However, as a Christian I don't have the luxury of unforgiveness. The Bible says, "...whenever you stand praying, forgive, if you have anything against anyone; so that your Father also who is in Heaven may forgive you your trespasses." *Mark 11:25 (NAS)* Friendships can be restored, albeit in a guarded capacity.

Gossip is friendship's enemy number two. "An evil man sows strife; gossip separates the best of friends." *Proverbs 16:28 (TLB)* Again, I don't have the luxury of unforgiveness. Compare a friendship lost through gossip to open heart surgery. The knife of gossip rips open the chest, and exposes the damaged, bleeding heart. It is far better to swallow a malicious story, and discard the odorous waste, than to feed it to another. Gossip is like poison. It kills friendships instantly.

As a precaution against any further heartache caused by broken friendships, I guard my heart. I choose who will be my friend with great care and, right or wrong, I keep them at arm's length until I am positive that they will not destroy me or my family.

The Flavor of Loneliness:

"Dear Lord - I Am So Lonely: Douglas is gone again, and my heart is heavy. I want to cry, I want to die - no one cares. Love is gone. His life is his own. He has nothing to share with me, his lonely wife. I am excluded. If I didn't have you, Lord, I couldn't make it. I, alone, wouldn't have the strength to live here. I am so sad, I could easily go mad, or pull my hair and yell and scream. Maybe I'll just go to sleep, and dream - of love."

I did just that - dream of love. Every dream had a different setting, but the story line was the same. In one dream, I was waiting tables in a diner when a trucker came in. He was tall, with dark hair, but I couldn't see his face. He came to my section. He was very nice to me. He told me he wanted to buy me a ring. When he saw my diamonds, he said he couldn't afford anything that expensive. He told me he loved me and held me real tight. Somebody called me, but I didn't want to go. Susan! Susan! I woke up. I looked forward to my dreams because in them I was really loved.

My being alone was usually a result of a fight caused by a total breakdown in communication, or by complete frustration. I needed to talk - he didn't hear me, or wouldn't listen. I wanted him to share his life with me - he was silent. I wanted him to be my best friend - he was the boss - I the servant. I wanted to be by his side - he kept me under his feet. I wanted his love - he had none to give. I wanted to go places with him - we took two vehicles. We were two chubby birds on the same branch, and we were alone.

One particular day I was very lonely and desperately needed to feel loved. I got on my face before God and wept. I knew that if something didn't change soon, the emptiness inside

197

me would explode and rip me in a million pieces. I prayed, "Please Jesus, hold me, please just hold me. I desperately need to be held. I am so lonely." He answered my prayer. I could literally feel His arms wrap around me. Jesus held me and rocked me as lovingly as a father rocks his child. Jesus loved me! Somebody really loved me!

The Flavor of a Growing Christian:

Parallel nature to the soul. Using the rosebush as nature's pattern, Douglas and I the souls. The seeds of Christianity were planted long ago when we were young. They lay dormant until the conditions were perfect for germination. Douglas and I sprouted under different conditions. We grew at different speeds and produced roses at different intervals. Some of our branches were pruned, and it hurt. We both felt thorns as life touched us. Finally we rooted in His word, reached for the Son, and grew in God's love.

As the first sign of growth, Douglas was baptised. Water produces growth in the rosebush and symbolizes obedience in the soul. Because my seeds germinated before Douglas', I attempted to help with his growth. I wanted him to feel the warmth of the "Son"-shine. In fact, forcing growth causes the soul to stagnate and become dormant. Only the Son was truly aware of all the thorns Douglas had to deal with. As soon as I let the Son do His job, the soul responded. Rosebuds appeared. The roses opened to display the beauty of the Son, in Douglas.

As I struggled to become the seasoned soul God wanted me to be, He gave me the words to compose the following poem:

Seasons of the Soul

The soul that is lost is like the Winters' night. Cold. Dark
and despairing. No hope of new creation, no faith for the
future, nothing to anticipate. Oh, what agony. Oh, what
heartache. What a barren land of wasted life. An eternity of
darkness.
But wait! What is this occurrence? "The Resurrection?"
What does this mean? Could there be hope? Is there a
chance? Ah! The darkness is lifting. The warmth is
replacing the cold. Glorious sunshine is flooding the soul.
First signs of Spring are appearing at last. The soul comes
alive like new buds on a tree. Seeds that were planted so
long ago are starting to sprout now - are starting to grow.
The soul is maturing. It's reaching for Heaven. Searching
for knowledge and finding - "The Son of God." It's starting
to root now - to grab hold and drink, quenching its thirst
from springs of the water of life. This peace and
contentment the soul is enjoying, will it last?
Blossoms appear and the soul is aroused. Oh, what beauty!
What a fragrance! The maturing soul is like a sweet-
smelling perfume that fills the air, that drifts up to Heaven
and enters the nostrils of God. Is growing a part of life? Oh,
yes! The reward for growth? The Father is pleased with the
soul.
Off in the distance the rumble grows loud. There's thunder
and lightning, hailstones and clouds. A storm is
approaching. The testing is here. The soul starts to shake
now. It wavers and falls. Why? Why? Why is this
happening at all? The anguish it feels as it stoops to its
knees is washed cleanly away, by tears of rain - and now the
promise - the rainbow at last. The testing is over. The soul
has survived. It conquered the testing, it conquered the tide.
Laughter and love o'erwhelms it again.

Radiant beams of the summer sunshine illuminate the soul.
Amazing! The soul is alive. The soul is like a garden. But
how can that be? Alas, I see! The Spirit of God has
produced in that soul the fruit of the spirit, the courage to toil
and the strength to grow - Rooted in the Word of God.
Why does the soul feel so heavy? So discouraged? Such
sorrow? Is it concern for the lost? Heartache for sinners?
The burden is heavy, but there's power in prayer. Prayer is
the answer. Prayer produces endurance - changes the soul.
The long summer is finally over.
It's on to the harvest. There's much rejoicing. The fields are
white for the harvest. The soul is willing to labor. Time is
drawing nigh. Others are looking for the light. Results of
the great commission? A bountiful crop. Bursting granaries
as the first fruit comes in. What comes after the harvest?
Thanksgiving! Of course! The soul lifts up its heart with
praise to the Father. The soul bows down and worships the
King. Gladness and joy overtake the soul.
The seasons have passed now. It's the Autumn of life.
Looking towards Heaven the soul longs for rest. It longs to
see Jesus. It longs to go home. Sleep comes at last and the
soul is transformed. The journey is over. The work is
complete.
'Way off in the distance - I hear a "Well Done."

If I left the impression that Douglas and I lived in hell
for ten years, I'd be lying to you. There were many storm
clouds that produced rain, but there was also lots of sunshine
that produced happiness.

I'll end this chapter with some sunshine. One morning
after Douglas had gone to work in the field, I found a note that
he left me. It was under my coffee cup and it read, "Susan -
Have a good day, and I do love you."

CHAPTER EIGHT

Sink or Swim?

Shall I drown or grow fins?

Swimming in a river can be dangerous because of its concealed obstacles. Swift moving under-currents can pull you under and drown you. Heavy rains cause murky waters that are filled with debris. If you let the debris hit you, you will sink to the bottom. Life is like that river.

For over a year, Matthew had been experiencing back pain. The janitorial work he was doing was becoming increasingly more difficult and the pain more severe. X-rays indicated that he had two perforated discs and would need surgery. Having surgery would cause a few problems. One, he would be unable to continue in his job and two, he would need someone to care for him when he got home.

Matthew and I were growing increasingly concerned about Stephanie. Unlike me, Matthew had been corresponding regularly with Stephanie and was aware of murky water and debris in her life. I became aware of her physical problems only because of a phone call we received while we were in Arizona for the winter. Stephanie had passed out in the bathroom and fallen onto the side of the bathtub. The side of her face, shoulder, and arm were black and blue and very painful. Tests revealed Wolfe Parkinson Whyte Syndrom. I am only able to give lay terminology for her medical condition. The heart has four main chambers: two on each side. Blood is pumped into the heart on one side, through the heart, and out the left side. Stephanie has an extra attachment on the lower left side of her heart. Factors such as extreme stress and/or overexertion can cause the blood to be pumped into the attachment before it is pumped out. When that occurs, the heart misfires, causing pain and an irregular heart beat. The longer it takes for the blood to go into the right place, the more beats the heart misses. If the disease progresses, heart medication is required and, eventually, surgery to insert a pacemaker.

Matthew and I conjured up a plan: ask Stephanie to stay with Matthew after his surgery. The two of them could convalesce together. Len agreed. I picked Stephanie up from the bus station early one April morning. As we were eating breakfast, just like the old days in the bathroom, she poured out her soul to me. Her story broke my heart.

Her marriage was ravaged by infidelity, and emotional and verbal abuse. All indications pointed to the death of a marriage. However, Stephanie was not going to join the Mueller family statistics by divorce. She would obey God's word and rely on Him to help her. She would stick it out. She would deal with it. The hurt and rejection, on top of her health problems, were too overwhelming for her. Every male in her life had failed her. She had retreated into deep depression. She was drowning. My nightmare had become her life.

As the days progressed and her depression lifted, Stephanie could see things more clearly. She understood that Len, not she, was the one who had destroyed their marriage, and that, against all she believed in, there could be no reconciliation. She confided in me that if she had stayed with Len, she would have died. She would have to grow fins and learn how to swim alone.

Stephanie had become a very private person, and asked me not to share her story with anyone. As was the case with Matthew, I assumed I wouldn't be able to talk to Douglas about it anyway, so I agreed. But I felt Stephanie's pain and I did need to talk about it, so I took it to the Lord. I prayed and I cried, but it felt like He wasn't listening to me. I couldn't find any peace for my soul, so in a moment of weakness, I did the unforgivable and confided in my sister. Anne was my best friend, so why couldn't I talk to her? Anne loved Stephanie like a daughter, and the two of them shared many secrets together in the past.

I got a phone call from one very upset young lady. She said, "Mom, you betrayed me. I asked you not to tell anybody about my marriage, and you didn't listen. I don't know if I can ever forgive you!" Her words cut deep into my heart, but I knew she was right. It would be a long time before Stephanie would fully trust and confide in me again. I would have to earn her trust.

I, too, felt betrayed. I developed a new-found desire to get on my face before the Lord and re-evaluate my walk with Him. I had to find out why my relationship with Him wasn't deep
enough to let Him carry my heartaches. Oh, I was involved in women's ministries in the church; I played the organ every Sunday; I went to Bible study and I prayed. Still, I felt more carnal than Christ-like. I was living in the "Valley of Dry Bones." *Ezekiel 37:1-10 (NIV)* I felt like God wasn't reigning in my heart.

I was unprepared for Douglas' sudden interest in Stephanie's situation. He asked me to tell him the whole story, including my deteriorating relationship with her. He cried with me when I told him about the hell Stephanie had been living in, and he got upset at my sister when he heard that, because of the two-part betrayal, Stephanie was now sharing her hurts with Anne. For the first time in our marriage, Douglas was there for me. He was very supportive of me and participated whenever I needed to talk.

I had been independent my whole life. I did whatever I had to do for the survival of my kids and me. Nobody ever walked on my kids or me and got away with it. Neither Douglas nor I had unpacked our bags from our previous marriages, so we brought our luggage right along into our marriage. The bags were heavy, but when Douglas finally gave me his emotional support, I reciprocated by emotionally allowing his kids in my life. I was certain that if this emotional partnership continued, our marriage could finally get out of the murky river.

Vanessa had been living with her boyfriend Rick for quite a while, so when they announced that they were engaged, Douglas was happy for them (and relieved). He hadn't approved of their living arrangements, but felt that he couldn't judge them because we had done the same thing.

The wedding would be in Saskatoon in late August. Douglas had told my kids many times that, if they ever got married in seeding or harvest time, he wouldn't be there. Late August on the farm is harvest time. Unfortunately, there were no facilities available in June or July and they didn't want to wait until fall. Douglas would have to find a way to do both.

That June I was asked to make a toast to the bride and groom at a friend's daughter's wedding. I felt honored, and accepted the challenge. It would be relatively easy to find good things to say about Chelsie, but we had only spoken with the groom a few times.

I decided that after I said all the nice things I could about them, I would give them some tips on how to have a happy marriage. My marriage was not overly successful, so I combed through numerous books and came up with some good suggestions. I didn't need a degree in counseling to see that Douglas and I had a passing mark in the "don't do" section. Grade your marriage as I graded ours.

Do you make selfish demands? Do you spew forth degrading remarks about each other in front of others? Are you sarcastic and critical? Do you need to control every situation, but you can't control your anger or your tongue? Is your marriage lacking companionship, affection, romance and communication? Can you admit when you're wrong - and can you forgive? After God, do you put each other first? Finally - do you use withholding sex or the silent treatment as a weapon to get your own way?

If you passed the test of doing things the wrong way, here are some solutions. Demands should be left to terrorists. Build each other up with compliments and encouraging words. Find a positive characteristic in your spouse and share it with your friends. When you point your finger at your spouse's faults, remember, three fingers are pointing back at you. Leave power struggles to the politicians. Don't yell or scream at your spouse, unless your house is on fire. Make your spouse your best friend, and vice-versa. Say, "I love you," once in a while. You won't choke on the words. Learn how to listen and talk when it hurts. Share a laugh. Share a tear. Does it really matter who is right? Only if you've never made a mistake can you not forgive your spouse's mistakes. Remember the destruction weapons cause. Finally, and probably the hardest for most couples to do, honor God by putting Him first. Pray together, and pray for each other. Read God's word together and worship together.

While I was researching marriage, I caught a glimpse of the fact that I had to change. I couldn't change Douglas and I didn't have to answer to God for Douglas' actions. I was only accountable for the things that I said and did. God is the judge.

With the help of Mitch and Rick, I planned a surprise bridal shower for Vanessa at our house. They would come down on the pretense of making plans to go hunting for deer with Douglas in the fall. I invited everybody in the country that knew Vanessa. My house was full. Douglas assisted in our scheme by taking the three of them on a tour to inspect the crops. When they returned and she saw all the vehicles in the yard, she was reluctant to come into the house. Under protest, she entered to a big "Surprise!" from all of the guests. She was surprised and pleased. The gifts were beautiful - the lunch delicious. I felt a genuine warmth in my heart when Vanessa gave me a big hug and a special thank you. She was happy that I cared enough to do this for her.

I made a promise to myself that, no matter what was said or done, I would not ruin the wedding for Douglas. I knew it would be very difficult because I wasn't the mom, but I made a vow to myself to keep my mouth shut, bite my tongue instead of saying something I shouldn't say, and smile. Karen had never remarried, so I would be the only "step" there. Stephanie would attend the wedding - Matthew declined.

After the rehearsal, Douglas and I were invited to Karen's house for lunch. It was an awkward situation and we felt uncomfortable being there. However, Rick's parents made an extra effort to make us feel at ease, as did the kids and Karen. We decided that things had gone fairly well, so we could relax and enjoy the rest of the wedding celebration.

Vanessa was a beautiful bride. Having the face and figure of a model was definitely an asset. Douglas looked superb in his black suit and white shirt. His salt and pepper colored hair made him look distinguished. He was still a very handsome man. Consequently, I felt a twinge of jealousy when Douglas and Karen were alone together in a room with Vanessa, and I was excluded. Twinges continued as they both walked her up the aisle, and Karen sat close beside Douglas during the ceremony. I was true to my word and hoped that I'd have some tongue left after I bit it so many times.

Pictures in the park - what a beautiful setting. I smiled when I was excluded from the pictures, and I smiled when the bridal party looked at me like I was from outer space. But when Karen put her hand through Douglas' arm, I could smile no longer. I burst into tears and headed for the truck. As luck would have it, when all the wedding pictures were taken, Vanessa wanted to have a picture taken with her dad, me, Rick and her. I wasn't there, so Douglas sent Mitch to the truck to get me. I knew I was in trouble when he saw that I had been crying. After pictures, the ride back to the reception was very cool, and I knew that, at some point in the weekend, I would have to experience his wrath. True to my word, however, I kept my mouth shut.

Douglas stood beside Karen in the receiving line. I stood alone in the lobby, as I was not asked to join them. Rick's mom finally felt compassion for me and led me straight to Douglas' side, where she informed Karen that I should be included. Douglas ignored me throughout the entire supper and reception. So, by the time we were on our way back to Swift Current the next day, the third world war was about to erupt. Neither Douglas nor I could keep our mouths shut any longer.

I'm sure passersby could see the tires and sides of the truck bulge as the words of hurt and anger exploded. The last words Douglas said to me for the rest of the entire trip were, "When I saw you walk to the truck, I felt like telling you to keep walking." The hurt was gone, the anger was gone, only the hate returned. My stomach muscles tightened and cramped and my throat closed up. I wondered if I could ever get over what he had said to me. It would be a long time before I realized that, "You don't ever get over it. You either 'die,' or you allow God to transform the suffering into creative work like the wings of the morning, after the darkness of the night." *(1)*

A wall of hurt feelings had developed in my heart and I couldn't see Jesus anymore. I had to get back on my face before God. I had to be totally honest with Him again, and tell Him how much I hated Douglas. I told Him that I knew it was wrong, but I couldn't (nor did I want to) forgive Douglas. God had to be told how angry and hurt I was. Still, I was afraid that if God took His hand off my life, I would perish. I knew that He wouldn't leave me or give up on me when I read, "There is nothing you can share out of the agonizing hurts and depths and hates and rages of your soul that God has not heard. There is nothing you take to Him that He will not understand. He will receive you with love and grace." *(2)*

There is a young man who comes to our church; his name is Anthony. He lost his wife to cancer and was left to raise his three-year-old son Adam. Some of our friends and family decided that it would be a wonderful idea for Stephanie and Anthony to meet. We agreed that the two of them would make a fine-looking couple. Stephanie is beautiful and Anthony is no slouch either. He is short like Stephanie. He has thick auburn colored hair, a moustache, and nice blue eyes. He is a teacher in a small town near Swift Current, and he has a beautiful red Stealth sports car.

People who we thought were our friends, for reasons unknown to us, took it upon themselves to keep Stephanie and Anthony from meeting. But, against all odds, they did meet and the attraction was immediate. At that point a campaign evolved that would hurt Stephanie emotionally. Stephanie had been hurt many times in her life but, had she known the hurt she was going to have to endure at the hands of those individuals, she would have run for her life. They would not take prisoners! When Stephanie and Anthony started dating, the smear campaign got under way. Family and friends were starting to take sides, and unfortunately Stephanie was the target. Stephanie was emotionally exhausted and visibly in pain, so when I asked her and Matthew to come home for Thanksgiving dinner, she was only too happy to "get out of town!"

Fall is hunting season. Mitch and Rick were coming from Saskatoon for Thanksgiving. It had been decided earlier that, after dinner, Douglas, Mitch, Rick and Matthew would go "spotting" deer. Mitch and Rick arrived early, so rather than

208

wait for Matthew to come from Swift Current, Douglas decided to go without him. As Douglas was leaving the yard, they passed Matthew in the driveway. Douglas waved at Matthew, but didn't stop. Matthew was, yet again, the unwanted son. Matthew was hurt - Stephanie was furious. As usual, I invited Harry, Anne, Marlett, Doney and Mom for dinner. With Harry and Anne's help, Matthew and Stephanie calmed down and were prepared to enjoy the rest of the day.

At dinner, there appeared to be only three people at the table: Mitch, Rick and Douglas. Douglas was very impressed with his new son-in-law. The rest of us didn't exist, and all my family noticed it. The atmosphere at the dinner table slid from cool to frigid. When the three hunters went outside to "line up" their rifles and Matthew wasn't included, Stephanie and Matthew left: one angry, one hurt. At the end of that very long day, after everybody left, Douglas scolded me because my kids left in a "huff." "How do you think that made Mitch and Rick feel?" he asked, to which I replied in anger, "I hope they felt worse than Matthew did!"

I often wondered why people didn't notice the way Douglas treated me and my kids. Or did they notice, but didn't care enough about us to defend us? I assumed that everybody must think that Douglas was the real cat's meow. Nobody would believe me anyway if I told them what went on in our house. Is it any wonder that Matthew has very little desire to participate in our family life.

How deep would I sink into despair before I cried out to God to keep me from drowning in my heartache? Could He hear me whisper His name when my lungs were full of water? Maybe I should just give up and let myself drown.

Everybody, unless otherwise programmed, has a built-in desire to survive. My survival would come through Jesus and His work. My desire to survive was not built around an escape from my home life, nor was it a chore. It came from a new-found love I had in my life. His name was Jesus. I became a "Martha." I was chairperson for the committee that planned a Christmas party for two hundred and fifty women. I directed a Christmas play, and I produced, and directed a women's pantomime. Both were to be presented to the congregation at our Christmas service. Twice a week I had practice with other musicians and a worship team, to prepare for Sunday morning worship. Needless to say, my church work was a real aggravation to Douglas.

But when I was home alone in my prayer closet, I was a "Mary." I sat at Jesus' feet and there I learned again that, apart from Him, I have nothing. And apart from Him, I am nothing. There at His feet, He taught me how to swim!

CHAPTER NINE

"Yet Shall I Trust In Him"

"Though He slay me..." Job 13:15, KJV

My couch sits in front of the French provincial windows in my living room. I kneel before God at the middle cushion - a box of Kleenex is on the right cushion and my portable phone on the left cushion. I bury my face in the cushion, or I lift my face to the heavens as I pray. This is my prayer closet.

In the quietness of my house I could sense the closeness of the Lord. At times He was so real I could hardly breathe. Other times my body tingled in His presence. There on my face, before my maker, the Lord gave me a word that would give sustenance to the lives of my kids and me for years to come. One particular morning, God's presence was especially real. I wasn't even sure if I was breathing, and I couldn't lift my face off the couch. He spoke to me and said, "Do you love me?" Because He had spoken to me before, I knew it wasn't just a voice in my head. In my mind I replied, "Yes Lord, I love you." He continued, "Then trust me." Out loud I answered, "I do, I do!" The quietness of the morning returned, and the peace in my soul overwhelmed me. I was left with a very strong urge to share what had happened, and also the word "trust" with Matthew and Stephanie - which I did.

Trust - all three of us would learn what it meant to depend heavily on the Lord: to have hope when there was none; to commit our lives to His care, regardless of the outcome; to believe that He was in control, even in the pain; and to have faith that He would do what was best for us.

Matthew was having a hard time dealing with the most recent act of rejection. The pain was very deep. He needed to talk to someone he trusted. He chose Pastor Ed. He shared his struggles, including the events of Thanksgiving dinner. Can you trust your Pastor as much as you trust the Lord? Would he give advice that just puts a band-aid on the problem, or would he tell you the truth? Cruel as it may seem, "...you shall know the truth, and the truth shall make you free." *John 8:32 (NAS)*

Pastor Ed sensed that Matthew was stuck in his heartache. Not only was he feeling the pain of rejection, he was strongly feeling the pull of the Holy Spirit to listen to God's "call" on his life. Pastor Ed advised that Matthew should grab hold of the Holy Spirit's nudging, and continue his training for ministry.

Concerning rejection, Pastor Ed gave some harsh-sounding advice. He said, "Matthew, Douglas is not going to be the one who changes. You have to accept the fact that he will never love you the way you want him to, and he will never be the dad you are looking for. Accept it! Deal with it, and move on with your life! If you don't, you will be forever frozen in your pain."

At first, Pastor Ed's words seemed uncaring to Matthew. He would have liked to hear the band-aid solution. But after much prayer and soul searching, he accepted Pastor Ed's advice as being in his best interest. He knew he had to deal before he could heal. Matthew enrolled in a class that was being offered at our church. The program was in the form of a support group, with a leader that taught twelve steps to emotional healing. Matthew had to acknowledge each of his hurts and insecurities and accept healing for them. He had to admit his faults and shortcomings and ask God to help him change his attitude. Lastly, he had to surrender to the Holy Spirit and recommit to his calling. At the end of the program, a new Matthew emerged. He had walked through the fire - and the old chunk of coal turned into a diamond.

After considering five different seminaries, Matthew narrowed the field down to two. If he attended the Church of

God Seminary at Anderson, Indianna, he would be thousands of miles from home. But, on the plus side, learning Greek wasn't a requirement. If he attended Trinity Western in Langley, British Columbia, it was only hundreds of miles from home. But Greek was required for the degree he wanted. Matthew was fearful, as Ancient Greek is difficult and he has to work very hard for passing grades. He prayed repeatedly for help to make the correct choice. He wanted to go where the Lord directed him. Somehow, he needed a clear confirmation.

One afternoon, Matthew had a strong impulse to go for coffee at his favorite coffee shop, McDonald's. He took with him his textbook of Ancient Greek. Unnoticed to Matthew, the couple sitting next to him had been closely watching him. Finally, the lady spoke to Matthew. They were from England. They were on a vacation and were on their way to meet family in British Columbia. She told Matthew that she had taken Greek and wondered why he was. He explained his situation and was encouraged by this stranger from England to pursue Greek. She said that he would never be sorry. That was a powerful confirmation for Matthew. In a sense, a complete stranger from another continent helped make the decision for him.

Matthew enrolled at Associated Canadian Theological Schools, which is an affiliate of Trinity Western University. After he was accepted at Trinity, he applied for all the necessary student loans and started packing. He was both excited and fearful. He definitely was taking a step of faith. I had a farewell party for him. There was a houseful of relatives and friends who showered him with love and encouragement, which was exactly what he needed to help him cope with the uncertainties that he would have to face.

Stephanie was taking over Matthew's apartment, and she would use his furniture for as long as she needed it. The last week in July, Matthew packed his car as full as he could, stored the rest of his belongings at our house, and left for Langley, British Columbia. It was an especially tearful farewell for Stephanie. They had developed a deep love for each other. They shared many hours of conversation, confiding their hurts and joys to each other. Matthew also felt sad, but wouldn't let the tears get the best of him until he was alone.

Trust? Matthew didn't have a place to live in Langley. He didn't know one living soul there, and his student loans hadn't yet been approved. Pastor Ed gave him the name and phone number of a Church of God pastor in Surrey, which is another suburb of Vancouver. When Matthew called, the pastor and his wife offered him the opportunity to live with them until he could find an apartment. He accepted their offer with a very thankful heart. Knowing Pastor Clay would be a twofold blessing, as Matthew had some specific requirements he had to fulfil for his degree in a church, under the guidance of a pastor. Pastor Clay would become his mentor and friend.

God was faithful. After some tense days caused by a bank error, Matthew's student loans came through. A couple of guys from seminary had rented a condominium and were looking for a third person to share the rent. Matthew settled into the condo, and his classes, without any further tests of faith. He knew he was where the Lord wanted him to be.

Stephanie settled into small town life in Swift Current fairly quickly. She easily settled into her apartment and even enjoyed her job at a local department store. When Matthew left, Douglas helped Stephanie find an older car that she could drive around town and out to the farm.

Stephanie's effervescent personality had been severely damaged during her marriage by repeated rejections and personal attacks to her self-esteem. Her contagious laugh was gone. "In the rings of our thoughts and emotions, the record is there; the memories are recorded, and all are alive. And they directly and deeply affect our concepts, our feelings, our relationships. They affect the way we look at life and God, at others and ourselves." *(1)* It was very reassuring for Stephanie to know that she was loved by her family and friends. One painful step at a time, her numb emotions were coming back to life.

In Edmonton, Stephanie had developed a deep personal relationship with Jesus. He in turn gave her a special vision for her church. Talking constantly with Jesus kept her faithful to Him. Working in her church kept her disciplined to study God's word. However, Stephanie had always kept a place in her heart for Pastor Ed and she was happy to be back in his congregation.

I was involved in the women's ministry in our church. A small group of us ladies organized a spring and Christmas party. These parties started as an enjoyable night out for our church women and, in a few years, ended up as a huge party for two hundred and fifty women, or more. We changed our program and designed these gatherings to present the gospel to the non-churched women from our community. We wanted to present a warm, non-threatening atmosphere that would glorify God. Because Stephanie has a creative talent second to none, we asked her to be the coordinator in charge of all the decorations. Her imagination soared, and she created the very atmosphere we were looking for.

Despite attempts to thwart their meeting, Stephanie and Anthony were dating and becoming good friends. Some dates were a threesome; most ending in a trip to the Dairy Queen. Sharing ice cream can melt any heart. Four-year-old Adam and Stephanie were slowly building a friendship. Unfortunately, while Stephanie and Anthony were trying to build their relationship, others were trying to destroy it.

Adam's grandma was the principal caregiver during his mom's illness and after her death. That arrangement wasn't Anthony's first choice, but he was trying to cope with his grief as well as having to be the breadwinner. He had to work. She took over the role as mother for Adam, and Anthony was too overwhelmed to argue. It was just easier to let her take over and look after everything. Later, when Anthony had recovered emotionally, he wanted to take back his role of principal caregiver. She would only let that happen under her supervision, especially now that Anthony was seeing a DIVORCED woman.

That winter, Adam's grandparents house-sat for some snowbirds. Their house was directly behind Anthony's. From time to time, Stephanie went to Anthony's house and made supper for him and Adam. She objected to Stephanie's presence in Anthony's house and told Stephanie that she didn't have to go over to his house anymore; she would look after them now. Anthony asked Stephanie to continue her visits to his house, which she did. Adam's grandma finally decided that if, against her wishes, Stephanie and Anthony should marry, she needed to get acquainted with Stephanie. She invited Stephanie out for coffee, and wanted to know all about her past, for Adam's sake. Stephanie was very upset and assured her in no uncertain terms that she would not be sharing her life story. Her past was her own.

Stephanie's friends were quizzed for information. My friends were asked about me and my life. One friend was asked if we were a close family. "No," was the reply. I wondered how anybody could really know for sure how close we were, unless they walked in our shoes. Stephanie was defamed to anybody that would listen. Some of my friends were encouraged to betray me with private information about my life, as well as Stephanie's. It's hard to let go!

When everything that was tried, failed to break up Stephanie and Anthony, others were very willing to take up the cause. They were desperate to find out why Stephanie's marriage had failed. A last ditch effort was put into motion. A call was made to Stephanie's pastor in Edmonton. A friend of Adam's grandma gave him some story about Adam losing his mom and asked if the circumstances of Stephanie's marriage and breakup would affect her ability to raise Adam. Would he please fill her in?

This chapter is about trust. Do you trust your pastor with your story? Unfortunately, not all pastors are trustworthy. He broke a personal trust and gave her every detail of Stephanie's marriage; their problems and their breakup. However, the nightmare didn't end there. Stephanie's story was shared with many people, leaving both of us reeling in disbelief. At every opportunity, this same individual revealed to Stephanie, and to others, how much she, herself, meant to Anthony, and how much a part of his life she was. To make matters worse, untrue stories were spread about Stephanie.

Stephanie was again retreating into her shell of hurt and rejection. God seemed so far away. She was really broken and she really needed Him, but it seemed like He wasn't there. Did He even care what happened to her? Why were people allowed to get away with all the awful things they were doing? How could she trust another living soul? Could a friendship destroyed ever be restored?

Stephanie wept in my arms many times. I was angry at everyone who had betrayed Stephanie and me, and I was very unforgiving. I put my own feelings of bitterness on hold so I could help Stephanie navigate the hell that she was being put through. Somehow I had to find the strength to encourage her and try to build her up emotionally.

She wept when she asked me why these people were trying to destroy her. What had she ever done to them? It was so unfair! I agreed with her, but I still had to try and help her keep her eyes on Jesus. I told her that Jesus hadn't done anything wrong either, but He had to endure the cross. Job hadn't done anything wrong, yet he was sitting in the ashes, in pain. His friends betrayed him too. She agreed, but she still couldn't understand how Christians could be so hurtful to each other.

I assured her that Jesus was taking onto Himself everyevery one of her feelings. He was weeping, too. She did understand that Jesus saw the whole mess from the beginning to the end and that He would show His mighty power to work things out, in His own time and in His own way. Stephanie's part would be the hardest; when the injustice continued, she would have to trust Jesus for her every breath.

My thoughts were this, "You can do what you want to me. You can say what you want to me. But hurt my kids, and I won't be gentle." When Matthew's heart was being attacked by rejection, I prayed for vengeance on his attacker. When Stephanie's heart was being pierced by malicious manipulators, I prayed for vengeance on her attackers. Hurt, anger, and unforgiveness were my allies. But in the midst of all the turmoil, God, in the quietness of my prayer closet, gave me two words. Love and Trust.

Did I love Him? Yes! Did I trust Him with my life? Yes! But I must be honest, I didn't think He was doing such a good job with the lives of my kids; but I didn't fully understand the power of God. In an effort to grasp His greatness, I wrote a short poem:

God Is...
Perfect Creator, Maker of man,
Masses He molded, to fit in His Plan.
Fragrance in flowers, feathers for birds,
All this He made with a few simple words.
Sunshine by day, moon and stars for the night,
Darkness He conquered, for He is The Light.
Rain, then the rainbow, His promise to all,
In valleys of sorrow, He hears my heart's call.

Justice and love, and a joy that I feel,
Peace everlasting, and power to heal.
Merciful Father, Giver of life,
He calms my soul, in the midst of my strife.
He's faithful to carry me through each dark test,
After the teaching, He gives me sweet rest.

It wasn't enough. I still didn't grasp His power. When I read, "To whom will you compare me? Or who is my equal? says the Holy One," *Isaiah 40:25 (NIV)* I slowly began to realize that God is God. He is "Holy and Blameless." He can do anything He wants. He is not accountable to me. He can and will allow whatever trials are necessary to teach me trust. All I have to do is take a step of faith and give everything to Him, my husband, my kids, my friends and me. He became real!

"Sometimes our view of God is determined by our relationship with our father or some other authority figure. If we have been brought up in a very strict, harsh home, for example, then we are likely to see God primarily as a judge. Truly believing that God is love is key to any response we have to Him." *(2)*

Learning how to totally love and trust God was like a roller coaster ride for me. There were many ups and downs, and turns. But I knew that putting my trust in Jesus was the only hope I had of finishing the ride. When the ride was over, He was in control. I even learned how to enjoy the ride.

My trust in God was high on the roller coaster ride after Matthew emerged from the twelve step program as a diamond and heeded to the call of God on his life. My trust in God was in the climbing position on the ride after one couple that had hurt Stephanie moved to another province; half of Stephanie's problems were gone. The ride to trusting God in my home life was always up and down.

One of the low parts continued to be concerning my responsibility of playing the organ in church every Sunday. That was a thorn in Douglas' side. I had to defend myself, my church, and my God, every time I needed to go to a practice. It caused our marriage to leave the track of the ride, and almost break up as it hit the ground. Somehow, through God's intervention, I finally got through to Douglas that the talent I had was totally God-given; it was one of the ministries He wanted me to participate in.

I reached the highest point on my roller coaster ride after Douglas returned from a Promise Keepers convention that was held in Denver, Colorado. He came home a changed person. He was again the loving, thoughtful man I had fallen in love with. I was important to him and he seemed to enjoy being around me. In a practical way, he showed his love by buying a brand new fifth-wheel travel trailer, so that we could go on vacation with our friends.

I reciprocated by throwing Douglas a surprise fiftieth birthday party. He was totally oblivious to the plans I made. I hid the large birthday cake, and all the other food for lunch, in the fridge. I covered what I could with other food and kept him out of the fridge. My biggest problem, however, was trying to keep him home after supper. He picked that night to go check the crops. (It looked like a bumper crop.) I knew by the clock that friends would soon be arriving, so I stalled our departure by spending an extra long time in the washroom. He knocked on the door, and called, "Let's go," and went outside. Next, I picked up the phone and pretended to be talking to someone. He came back in the house, and gave me one of "those looks" that told me I was almost on the verge of being in trouble. I shrugged my shoulders as if to say, "I can't help it if someone wants to talk to me!" When he came in, again, I hung up the phone and said, "Okay, I'll just go get the camera so we can take pictures of the crop." I silently thanked the Lord when two of our neighbours arrived. He seemed pleased and invited them in. Every few minutes, friends arrived bearing gifts and cards until the house was filled with twenty-eight people. He was extremely surprised that I pulled the party off without him suspecting anything. When everyone was gone, he gave me a hug and thanked me for making his fiftieth so special. He had a wonderful evening.

Against my wishes, Douglas wanted to set his son-in-law up in a business that involved hauling freight. He was so anxious to impress Rick that he neglected to take enough time to do all the necessary investigation of profitability. He spent a lot of money on a three-ton utility truck, and he spent a lot more changing and repairing it to make it road worthy. Douglas supplied the fuel, tires, license, insurance, and so on. Rick was supposed to start paying the money back with monthly payments as soon as he could. Unfortunately, that never happened. The business never grew and Douglas ended up totally supporting them for some months. He felt obligated to do that, as Vanessa was expecting their first child and there wasn't an abundance of money on hand.

In late September, Taylor was born. Douglas was a Grandpa, and he was proud! We made a quick trip to Saskatoon so that Grandpa could hold his grandson. This little bundle of joy had almost black hair. He had tiny little fingers, tiny little soft ears, and a nose as tiny as a button. Vanessa hoped that Taylor would have blue eyes like his grandpa Douglas. He never opened them while we were there, so we couldn't check the color. He was content to sleep. Vanessa insisted that I hold Taylor. She said, "Grandmas get to hold their grandsons too." I was pleased, and thanked her for letting me be a part of her happiness. We weren't sure who he looked like, but we thought he favored Rick's side of the family. Only time would tell!

The Lord blessed me with two new friends. Verna is a lady I worked with a few years before. She and I worked in the same department at one of the local department stores; actually, she was my supervisor. She just recently started attending our church, so I was happy to befriend her. The other friend, Sonya, was one of the pianists who accompanied me when I played the organ. Many times after worship team practice we shared some of our hearts' desires together.

At Christmas I received a gift from each of them. I thanked them, and told them they really shouldn't have done that; I hadn't given them a gift. But they assured me that they did it because they wanted to, not to get a gift in return.

Verna's gift was a beautiful hand-painted box displaying the name - *The Cottage Garden Collection.* Inside were three hand-painted books: a diary, a notebook, and an address book. Most beautiful of all was the elegant, hand-painted ivory pen.

Sonya's gift was a book called *Reflections from a Mother's Heart.* The book was divided into twelve months, with many questions to answer in each month. Every question was either about my life or my likes and dislikes. Tears filled my eyes as I read the note she put in the book. She wrote that she loved and appreciated me. She thanked me for lifting her spirits when she was sad, and she thanked me for my gentleness and understanding. She continued by telling me to be honest when I answered the questions, even if I had to shed a few tears. Only my children would read the answers.

As soon as I had some spare time, I took the pen that I had received from Verna and started answering questions. I skipped a lot of pages because the questions were too personal, and many didn't apply to my life. My life had not been that tame. After a few days, I closed the book - unfinished. I concluded that these two wonderful gifts were symbols, and maybe, after all these years, God wanted me to write "the book." I excitedly composed five or six paragraphs; then it was all over. I wasn't ready to face my life.

The greatest part about learning to trust the Lord was that He never let me down. He gave me enough strength to go through each day. I could share my innermost secrets with Him and He wouldn't betray me. When I gave Him first place in my heart, He blessed me with His presence. Some days I knew He was right there. I could reach out and touch Him. He was all around me. He was just in front, and right behind; to my left, and to my right. Below me, above me, and definitely in my heart. I could give Him the groanings of my soul, and He would intercede and take my deepest hurts and my desperate longings to God Himself and leave them there at His feet.

CHAPTER TEN

Out of the Ashes:

Restoration through Jesus

"Job was still sitting in a pile of rubble, naked, covered in sores, and it was in those circumstances that he learned to praise God." *(1)*

A lot of my life was spent sitting in the ash pile, in pain. I must have enjoyed it, because I sat there long enough for my hair to turn the color of ashes. I worked hard at life for my salt and pepper colored hair - and my pain. When the Lord showed me that I needed to rise above life's circumstances, I knew that I had to find a way out of the ash pile, sores and all.

Spring is a time for growth, and Stephanie was the rosebud that was wanting to burst forth into full bloom. Anne was her leader in the same twelve-step program that Matthew had taken. It would be a growing time for both Stephanie and me. Stephanie pulled away from me for a time while she dealt with the hurts brought into her life because of my self-serving lifestyle. When confronted with it, I felt like a mud duck. I had to face the cold, stark realities of what a lifetime of sin can do to a family, but it did hurt to have her pull away from me and move toward my sister. Being rejected by Douglas was a way of life, but with Stephanie it was more than I could bear. I felt very sad and remorseful. What if I had lived my life differently? But wondering, "What if?" didn't get me out of the ash pile of hurt.

I told God, "You don't know what I'm going through! You aren't suffering my pain!" (I let the devil control my thought life and I became very discouraged.) "Life isn't fair! Look at all the injustices Douglas gets away with. He's so nice to other people, and he treats me so badly. We go to see his kids all the time, and I only get to go see Matthew once in a blue moon. He's always gone. When I had pneumonia, he didn't even stay home long enough to see if I would live. He shows affection to other people with hugs and kisses, and he doesn't even see me. He doesn't keep his promises and he blames me for everything. Now Stephanie is upset with me. Life is so hard! I am so unloved, so unwanted! Bless My Poor Broken Heart!"

The Lord gently nudged me back to reality when He showed me His scars. Jesus was rejected and betrayed, yet He suffered in silence before His accusers. He felt His pain, my pain, all of mankind's pain - as He hung there, alone, on the cross. Pastor Owen, our Minister of Discipleship and Evangelism, put it very clearly, "Life is life, but God is still God. Don't confuse God with life." I had to ask God to forgive my attitude of self-pity, take myself off the throne, and put Jesus on it. I would have to learn how to make Him the foundation of my soul.

The Lord's gentle nudge was exactly what I needed to start me on the long journey to restoration. He would stay right beside me while I was being remade. I wouldn't change overnight; it would be one brick at a time! I would learn to accept the fact that pain is a part of life. My friend Evelyn put it this way after she learned she had cancer. "People say, 'Why me, Lord?' I say, 'Why not me, Lord?' Who am I to think I should be exempt from pain. This too shall pass!" I would learn that even if things around me didn't change, my attitude would have to. As Pastor Ed put it, "You need to understand self for what it is; death leading to hell."

At just the right moment in time, Anne gave me a book called, *The Nevertheless Principle*. Restoration would be possible "... my Bible search bore out what I suspected. Nevertheless was no ordinary lifestyle. It was a supernatural way to live, no matter what life dished out - a power and a dimension that seemed to be reserved mainly for the desperate. I qualified! Further, meditating on these scriptures, I saw that thoughts beginning with what-if never came from God, but from the enemy, the fear monster. Was it possible that he could be destroyed by one powerful, God-given word turned into a lifestyle? ... God is not a God of what if but the God of nevertheless." *(2)*

"The Nevertheless Principle traces the journey from despair and hopelessness to peace and joy. To reach Nevertheless Living, one must travel the dreaded road of fear and deep depression. There is no other route and no shortcut. The secret of arriving at the much desired goal is to keep moving along when there no longer seems to be any purpose in moving. The rewards of Nevertheless Living are so intense that it is worth whatever the cost. For strangely, it is people who have been terribly hurt, even devastated, who seem to enter most readily into Nevertheless Living ... One cannot arrive at Nevertheless Living by being smart or strong or determined, by fighting or by will power. The paradox is that you get there by simply giving up and entering a stage of trust that staggers the imagination." *(3)*

This new way of living brought healing to my soul and it showed me that God is big enough and strong enough to look after my marriage, and my kids, and big enough to restore my broken friendships. "Nevertheless Living" would help me to change one wrong attitude at a time. As Joyce Meyers, a retreat speaker and Bible teacher, puts it, "You can be pitiful or powerful." Here is what I learned:
(1) Instead of getting hurt feelings when Douglas withheld his love and affection from me, "...

I realized that something comes to replace romantic love. You really learn to love someone on days when you can't think of a thing you like about them, but you know you are committed to them ... whatever." *(4)*

(2) Instead of getting upset because Douglas was always gone somewhere, fishing, hunting, out for coffee with the guys, or just gone again - I had to be thankful that he wasn't sitting in the bar somewhere getting drunk.

(3) Instead of getting upset when Douglas said "no" to 'most everything I wanted to do, I could go by myself, ask a friend to go with me, or find something constructive to do at home.

(4) Instead of feeling like a worm when Douglas made some degrading remark toward me, I chose not to believe him, and besides, Jesus loves me flaws and all!

(5) Instead of picking a fight, or holding a grudge when my feelings got hurt, I learned to accept my part in the problem and make changes in the way I handled them.

(6) Instead of trying to make Douglas see how unfair and hurtful his attitude was toward Matthew, I had to give it to Jesus. He is the only one who can fix it. I am still learning how to not let the hurt I feel for Matthew destroy our life together.

(7) Probably the hardest thing for me to do was, and still is, to forgive those who hurt and betrayed me and my kids and forgive those who gossiped about us. I read somewhere that "forgiveness is as if it never happened." I had to learn how to turn hate into love, and forget. "Anyone who hates his Christian brother is really a murderer at heart; and you know that no one wanting to murder has eternal life within." *1 John 3:15 (TLB)*

I finally got it! I found the secret that would give me peace in my soul!

EVENTHOUGH: I am unloved, and unwanted. I am alone, or ignored. I am refused, and rejected. I am verbally dishonoured and degraded with words. I am not avenged, or treated fairly. I am betrayed by actions and words.

NEVERTHELESS ... (No matter what) I can be happy and content, in spite of my circumstances, as long as I stay close enough to Jesus to hear Him breathe!

I answered a Spiritual Gifts Questionnaire at Bible study, and discovered that one of my gifts was prayer. Everyone in the church who learned they had the gift of prayer was asked if they would participate in a monthly schedule to pray for our pastors, church leaders, the unsaved, and other special needs of the church family. The group was called the "Abrahams." Saying yes was the smartest thing I ever did in my entire life. It disciplined me to pray and lead me into a deeper relationship with Jesus. The Abrahams were asked to fast and pray the first Wednesday of every month, which I did. I prayed regularly and I enjoyed it. It wasn't a last resort anymore. When I prayed, "Make me like you," He started pruning away at my bad attitudes and it was painful.

I had always followed the A-C-T-S method of prayer - adoration, confession, thankfulness and supplication, but I learned that there is so much more to prayer. God created us to worship and praise Him. He wants us to fellowship with Him, not just talk to Him. He wants us to lift up our hands to Him in worship, and sing to Him in praise. "Delight yourself in the Lord, and He will give you the desires of your heart." *Psalm 37:4 (NIV)* To delight means to take great pleasure and joy in something. What a great pleasure it is to be able to get face to face with our Creator, see His beauty and feel His Spirit. I was falling in love with Jesus all over again and, in return, He gave me peace and contentment that penetrated deep into my soul.

After two years of dating, Stephanie and Anthony said their vows before God and our immediate families. Lorraine, Harry and Anne's daughter and close friend to Stephanie, was the Matron of Honor. Lorraine and her husband Kevin's back yard was the setting for the "garden wedding." The white wrought-iron tables and chairs enhanced the beauty of the luscious green grass and trees. The Lord completed the scenery by sending down His radiant beams of summer sunshine. Matthew was given the honor of escorting his sister down the aisle, and Pastor Ed performed the ceremony. After Stephanie and Anthony spoke their vows of love to each other, Stephanie and Adam ended the ceremony with some special vows also.

The relationship between Stephanie and me wasn't completely healed by her special day, so it was a little stressful for Douglas and me. We were happy for her, but we felt more like guests than parents. It was a wonderful, yet hurtful, day. In my heart I knew the Lord would answer my prayers and give us back our special love for each other.

Adam, our newest grandson, stayed with his grandma and grandpa while Stephanie and Anthony were on their honeymoon. The events following that week would only be the beginning of many hurts directed at Stephanie. The first thing Adam said to Stephanie when he got home was, "You're not my mom. My mom was special. I don't have to call you Mom and I don't have to listen to you!" Stephanie had worked very hard to build a friendship with Adam, and it took exactly one week to destroy it. Stephanie needed moral support from her husband, but quickly found out that she was living is a similar situation to what she grew up in.

It was indirectly pointed out to Stephanie that most of the furniture had been bought for Anthony and not for her. Stephanie said they could have it back. On visits to the house, when pictures were taken, Stephanie was excluded from them. Anthony continued to receive son-in-law cards with handwritten messages of undying love for him and Adam. Stephanie felt that she was not accepted as part of Anthony and Adam's family, and never would be. Some of our friends were pumped for information inquiring as to how Stephanie treated Adam and, when asked, Adam freely shared with his grandparents, details of his life at home.

When visiting rights were restricted because of boundary issues, the threat of legal action erupted. When Stephanie and Anthony had coffee with Adam's grandma, at her request, they felt that they were asked leading questions in an attempt to capture proof, on tape, that access to Adam had been denied to them.

It was too much for Stephanie to bear alone, so when I received a phone call from my broken-hearted daughter, and she cried, "Mom, I need you! Please come!" I knew our love and friendship would be restored. I would be there for her. I would help her in any way I could, and I would never betray her again. I would fight in her army.

The circumstances were hard on Adam too. He was a little boy who wanted a mom, yet many other times only wanted his dad, and his grandparents. He didn't know where his loyalties should be, he was being pulled in all directions. He favors his mom in looks; dark brown hair and eyes. He has fine features and probably will not be short like his dad. He was scheduled to start kindergarten at the same school his dad taught in. It would be good for Adam to be with other kids his own age.

Autumn is always a particularly stressful time on the farm. We have such a short period of time to get the crop into the granaries. Imagine, if you would, your salary for the entire year, lying out in the field, and for various reasons, you can't have it. If we haven't already lost the crop to hail, there is always the possibility of machinery breakdowns or early snowfall. Maintaining a household of harmony at harvest time can be a real challenge.

I always had a love-hate relationship with harvest time. After watching the plants grow from tiny seeds into large green plants, full of many kernels of wheat (or whatever we had seeded), into magnificent, golden colored fields ripe for the harvest, we felt a sense of accomplishment that we never achieved as wage earners.

I loved the purring sound of the combine engine as it drove around the field to pick up the swaths, but I hated the sound of silence after it broke down, leaving the swaths lying there - waiting. I loved having extra people around to feed and visit with. I especially loved the big, golden harvest moon. Sometimes it was so big that it looked like it was just lying at the end of the field, and all I had to do was take a step and I'd be walking on it.

I hated the total breakdown of communication between Douglas and me. Over the years I learned that if I didn't ask questions, I wouldn't get yelled at; he would tell me what I needed to know. But it was always the dreaded hand signals that did me in. I could see Douglas in the combine or the grain truck; arms flying, lips moving, but I couldn't hear him, and I couldn't understand what he wanted me to do. Whatever I thought he was saying or pointing at was usually wrong. For many years I got frustrated and cried lots. Finally I got wise, and just shrugged my shoulders if I couldn't get it. He either shook his head and I knew, without a doubt that he was thinking, "What a dumb woman," or he slowed his actions down to a speed where I could understand him. Sometimes he did it himself because I never did "get it." I hated the fact that we always had to be in such a rush. There was no time to really enjoy the beauty of the leaves changing colors or appreciate the taste of fresh garden produce. Nobody took time to stop and smell the roses. Oh, the joys of being a farmer's wife!

Always after harvest came hunting. I didn't mind it when Douglas hunted around our area, because he was always home at night. I hated it when he went up to Northern Saskatchewan, though, because I would have to be alone. It always seemed like I was a little girl again, and some big, bad man was going to come into the house and hurt me. It wasn't too bad when the kids were still home, but after they moved away I always found a place to stay while he was gone.

One morning in my prayer closet, I realized how pathetic I was; in my forties and afraid to be alone. I would have to learn how to handle my emotions and face my fear head-on. For a while, before Douglas left, I lay awake after he fell asleep and listened to the sounds of our house. Every house has its own sounds: the furnace just before it starts, the cracking sounds of the house as it settles on its foundation, and the wind on the shingles and window panes. All of that helped, but I knew that I would still be afraid.

I found two verses in my Bible that I read over and over. "Now you don't need to be afraid of the dark anymore, nor fear the dangers of the day." "For he orders his angels to protect you wherever you go." *Psalm 91:5, 11 (TLB)* So by the time Douglas went hunting, I was actually able to turn the light off in my bedroom when I went to sleep. I still had to pull the covers up around my head and carry on a very one-sided conversation with Jesus, but by the time Douglas got back I had my fears almost conquered.

One morning in early November I received a disturbing call from Lorraine. Her dad had had a heart attack, and after being stabilized in the Swift Current hospital, he was transferred to a Regina hospital by ambulance. The next day he was scheduled for an angiogram, and possibly an angioplasty. Harry had been my friend and best buddy almost forever. I was devastated. I was so afraid that he was going to die, and what made it worse was the fact that he wasn't a Christian.

I was in my prayer closet, crying and praying for Harry's life to be spared, when I saw a picture in my mind. Two very large hands were under the operating table, holding Harry up. The doctors and nurses surrounding him wore green masks and gowns when they did the surgery. When one of the doctors said, "We're all fixed up," I knew everything would be all right.

Moments later the phone rang. Anne was calling from Regina and she was very happy. She told me she had had the privilege of leading Harry to the Lord. He would have to have open heart surgery, but they were both trusting God with his life. I told her about my vision and that I believed Harry would be fine. I don't know if it helped her, but I knew in my heart that my friend would still be around for me to lean on. Harry had a quintuple bypass, but he lived. God is good!

When I prayed, on my face before God, "Lord I want to see You," He overwhelmed me with His presence, His peace, and His power. He picked me up out of the ash pile and dusted me off. He healed my sores, and restored my brokenness to beauty. He gave me a promise, "... Fear not, for I have redeemed you; I have summoned you by name; you are mine. When you pass through the waters, I will be with you; and when you pass through the rivers, they will not sweep over you. When you walk through the fire, you will not be burned; the flames will not set you ablaze. For I am the Lord, your God, the Holy One of Isreal, your Saviour; ..." *Isaiah 43:1b-3a (NIV)*

CHAPTER ELEVEN

Alone With God:

Here I am Lord, use me

San Diego in February is a wonderful place to be. Douglas and I hadn't gone south for a few years, so wanting to see Alice was a high priority on my wish list. Douglas wouldn't go, but said I could. At first I was upset with him because he said "No" to me again, but gradually a plan formulated in my mind. Harry could use some rest and relaxation - maybe they would go with me. After consulting with his doctor, Harry, Anne, and I were able to visit with our sister, and work on a suntan as well.

Douglas had been trying to sell some of his land, so while we were gone, he did, and rented out the rest to the buyer and his family. My house was included in the deal. We would schedule an auction sale to sell the machinery. I could only imagine what the rest of the year had in store for me; my life was definitely going to change.

Life would also change for Matthew. He would be graduating from Seminary in April with a Masters Degree in Religious Education. I was very proud of him. We were invited to the ceremony, but as the story goes, we couldn't go because Douglas scheduled the auction sale for the same day. Matthew was hurt and so was I. He said he understood, but I could hear the
disappointment in his voice. He said, "Maybe you and Dad can come and visit this summer. I've got lots of room for you to stay here." I prayed, "Please Lord, let something good happen to him to replace the sorrow."

God is good! Pastor Clay, Matthew's mentor, was retiring. The church board of directors asked Matthew to be their new pastor. The congregation was small, but the experience would help him in the future. He accepted their request. The condo Matthew was living in was sold, but the Lord provided him with a furnished apartment. The rent was twice as much as he had been paying, but Matthew believed the Lord would provide. The Lord further blessed Matthew by giving him the opportunity to lead a man in his congregation to the Lord.

Summer turned out to be a season of surprises. Stephanie and Anthony announced that "they were pregnant." Douglas told me that we would be going to visit Matthew for a few days in July. We had never been to his place in the two years he was there. When we got back, we would look for a house to move into Swift Current. The biggest surprise of all! While we were on vacation, we went golfing. Neither one of us had touched a club in many years. We were rusty, but we had a great time. We finally found something we liked to do - together!

When we got back from holidays we found a house we both liked, bought it, hired a mover to move it to Swift Current, and excitedly made renovation plans. When the house was finally settled on its new foundation, Douglas decided against the inside renovations he had promised, but we would still add on a large entry way, and a two car garage. We would have to do the renovations at a later date. He had broken his promise to me, and I was upset.

God has a sense of humor, and I know He chuckled when Jeffrey, my nephew (our contractor), said major renovations needed to be done to add on the entry way. Something about the door not being able to close! Jeffrey suggested we do all the renovations before we moved in. So Douglas had to keep his promise after all. Three months later, the house was remodeled, the painting done, and the carpets laid. Moving day would be January 6th, 1998.

The Holy Spirit helps us to dream dreams and see visions. He reveals to us what God wants to do for us, and through us, and He reveals to us what God wants us to do for Him. He helps us understand God's truths as written in the Bible and Christian literature. He shows us the Father, and He uses His power to communicate with our spirit.

You could also say, the Holy Spirit is "The Hound of Heaven." He certainly was at work in me. Over a period of about a year, in many different ways, He convicted me to write a book. My argument was that I didn't have enough education to use anything more than three letter words; and then there was sentence structure. Maybe I should take a creative writing course? That idea didn't appeal to me at all. "Oh, well. I just won't write. Besides, I have nothing important to say."

The Holy Spirit, in His unique way, gave me more affirmative replies than I wanted to hear. Our pastors happened to be preaching a series called, "Listening to God's Heart." Pastor Owen was talking about Moses finding excuses to not lead his people out of Egypt. He concluded, "God goes before you. If you're in His will, He will do it for you." Pastor Ed, continuing the series, said in two different sermons, "You can do anything if God is with you," and "Do what ministry God wants you to do. He will help you, and be there for you." Joyce Meyers, the retreat speaker said, "He (God) has qualified you because He has anointed you." Then I read, "God will not look you over for medals, degrees or diplomas, but for scars." *(1)* All right, already, I hear you! How could I argue with all that? But I did.

My next line of defense was fear. I pleaded, "Why should I write my story? My friends will think that I'm an awful person for revealing all my deep dark secrets, my personality shortfalls, my marriage and my childrens' problems. People will talk about me, and say that I shouldn't have revealed all that about my friends and family." I agreed with my arguments and declined, yet again.

I read, "God is not the author of all events, but He is the Master of all events. This means that nothing has ever happened to you that God cannot and will not use for good if you will surrender it into His hands and allow Him to work." *(2)* Followed by, "Now what I am commanding you today is not too difficult for you or beyond your reach." *Deuteronomy 30:11 (NIV)* I was starting to get the picture and told myself that if my friends judged me, they really weren't my friends anyway. A true friend would love me, no matter what! I had a brief moment of comfort when I believed that if He appointed me to write a book, He would be there to help me write it.

My next step was to bargain with God. "If you give me some very specific signs, than I'll know for sure it's Your will; I need definite confirmation from You." I don't know if God likes to bargain, but He used many different people, in many different situations to clearly show me that I needed to be obedient.

One morning while Douglas and I were on our way to town to work on our house, it was quiet except for the radio. I wasn't really listening, as I was deep in thought. I came to a sense of awareness just in time to hear the announcer say, "You should write a book." I thought that it was strange that he should say that at just that particular moment in time. For months on end, it seemed like every time I participated in a conversation, somebody would say to me, "You should write a book" or, "Why don't you write a book?"

Signs of affirmation continued. I wrote a poem, and read it in church one Sunday morning. The next day a friend called and told me how good the poem was, and I should try to get it published. While renovating our house, if I asked Jeffrey any questions concerning a certain thing he was doing, or if I asked him how his weekend was or whatever, he would reply,

"Are you writing for Seinfeld, or are you writing a book?" or "Go get your pen and paper so you can write everything down." On and on the affirmations came, but I was still dragging my feet.

I prayed, "Lord, just give me one more sign, then I'll know for sure that you want me to do this!" Silence! I began to have serious doubts. All the things that were said were just a coincidence! I'm only hearing what I want to hear! Maybe I should try to write a book? I'm sure the Lord just got tired of giving me signs. I mean, how many times does He have to explain it to me?

Maybe writing about my life would forever cast away the demons of my past, and mend my broken heart. My future is now shorter than my past, so maybe it is time to open my heart and try to help others. Maybe God can use my hurts and how I dealt with them to manifest His love to others.

Procrastination was the final defense before obedience. I tried to explain to God that there were people who lived in extremely more painful situations than I . My story was insignificant in comparison to some of the horrific events some people have to live through. He assured me He was aware of that, but He had called me to write, and I was to be oedient to Him. In other words, don't put it off one minute longer - just do it!

So there I was in my prayer closet, remembering His words, "Do you trust me?" I finally said, "Okay Lord, if You give me the words, and stay so close to me that I can hear you breathe, I'll do it!" He broke His silence!

A friend I hadn't seen all summer told me that while they were on holiday, she had a dream about me. I was standing in front of some women, speaking to them. She couldn't remember what I said, but that what I said was very interesting and helpful to them. I told her that was just what I needed to hear. The Lord, yet again, showed me what He wanted me to do.

Finally, Matthew called me and said that he remembered something that happened many years ago while he was still in Bible School at Camrose. He took a summer class and, when it was completed, I volunteered to type his assignment for him. I had an old manual typewriter, and I plunked away at it for many hours. He remembered that, when he walked by my office door, he had a very strong sense of knowing that this is what Mom could do. He said it looked so natural for me to be sitting there for hours, at my desk, typing.

Things started to take shape. Over the past twenty-some years, whenever a good or bad thing happened to me or my kids, I wrote it down on whatever was handy. Some notes were even scribbled on napkins. I threw the notes into some file folders and forgot about them. Once I had the chapters numbered and named, I couldn't believe how all the information fit into the right chapters. God's plan for me had truly started when I saw those two chubby little birds sitting on a bare branch.

I had one more obstacle to hurdle. I was definitely not a typist. My typewriter came over on the "Mayflower" and I didn't have a computer. Now what? The Lord had recently brought a new friend into my life. Her name is Bonnie. While we were working on a project together, I shared with her that I was going to write a book. She was excited for me, and arranged for us to have lunch in the near future. I didn't know why I told her about the book, so on the day we met, I prayed for God to show me what her part was. I shared with her all the many signs the Lord had given me. When she offered to type the manuscript on her computer, we both had
tears in our eyes. God is so good! He gave me a new friend who would be a very important part of my life. I believe she

was an answer to prayer. I also believe the Lord will bless her for her faithfulness.

For a brief moment of time I was proud of myself. I was going to write a book! God chose me to write a book! I knew I wanted to share with others how I learned to be content in any circumstance, and I wanted to glorify God and tell of the patience and mercy He shows toward His creation. But I wanted to tell all my friends about it too. I knew He didn't want me to put it on the front page of the newspaper, but why couldn't I tell my friends? Most of my friends encouraged me, but pride came crashing down around me when I told, "just one more friend!" When she laughed, I was crushed. The Lord gently nudged me to stop talking about it and just do it. Besides, how could I be proud of something I hadn't even started yet?

Lastly, I needed to convince Douglas! On one of our trips to see his kids in Saskatoon, I took the opportunity to tell him what I was going to do. We would be in the car for over two hours, so he couldn't go anywhere; he had to listen. I told him about all the signs the Lord had given me, about my vision so long ago, and about my friend's dream. I cried happy tears as I was talking to him, and I soon realized that he was wiping his eyes too. My soul was so blessed, it was overflowing. Douglas was skeptical at first, but after Pete gave me some words of encouragement, Douglas became very supportive, and has let me spend many, many, hours in my office, writing.

As I near completion of this manuscript, I still tell the Lord that I can't do this. I still plead for His help, and beg Him not to leave my side. As I look at the manuscript, and it gets thicker and thicker, I shake my head and say, "Thank you, Lord, but I still can't believe I had all those words in me."

"Here is God ... all powerful ... all wise ... all loving ... and we act as if whatever He wants for us would be the worst thing that could ever happen. Oh, we don't usually admit it to each other ... but listen to our conversations. Do we consider God's will exciting, adventuresome, fulfilling? Something to be actively, joyously sought? Or worse than taking castor oil?

Think of it! Whatever we present to God, He actually has a will for it, a plan for it. His is a will we can trust. It's a will that ensures us of fulfillment. It's a will that fulfills God's purposes through us." *(3)*

CHAPTER TWELVE

Fill Up With Jesus:

Empty is defeat - full is victory

I decided to sit down for a few minutes while I waited for the laundry to finish. I chose the old chocolate brown glider rocker and footstool. As I started to rock, I glanced at the stairs. My eyes followed them to the top. How many times had I gone up and down those stairs? I sat as if in a trance, not even blinking. I thought about my life on the farm over the past twenty-one years; I tried to remember the good times. At that moment, I honestly couldn't remember many happy times; lots of hurts and heartaches.

I remembered the times I came down here to the rumpus room and knelt at my downstairs prayer closet, in the dark, and cried and prayed. I remembered the times I had been so frightened by the thunder storms that I slept on my prayer closet and covered my head until the storm passed.

Tears welled up inside me as I glanced at the organ. How many times had the tears run down my cheeks as I practiced? How many times had a particular song touched my heart and I played it over and over, until I had worshipped so much my body was tired?

The buzzer sounded on the dryer and I took one last glance - so many memories! The silence was broken by the ringing of the telephone. The movers would be here at 9:00 a.m. tomorrow morning.

My state of mind was becoming very melancholy, almost depressed. I could easily have let my sadness overcome me. I managed to get a grip on my emotions; I wasn't going to let anything ruin my last day on the farm.

243

I walked to the end of the lane to get the mail. I had walked this path a million times over the years. I inhaled the clean air deep into my lungs; it smelled wonderful. The sun shone so brightly; my soul cheered up a little. The fresh, white, fluffy layer of snow sparkled like diamonds. The temperature was cold enough for the snow to make a crisp, crackling sound under my feet. It couldn't be more perfect! Our old cat must have enjoyed the air, too, as he walked along beside me, or should I say, under my feet.

As I was doing the supper dishes, I studied the outline of the pine trees in the back yard. After tomorrow I would never see those wonderful trees again. They were a very dark green now, but in the spring they changed to a beautiful bright color. Later, because of the miracle of new growth, the brown tips that developed would break forth into soft, light green pine needles.

By the time darkness arrived, my packing was almost complete. Tomorrow my life would change. I would need to keep busy in the morning while the movers emptied my home. How would I feel when the house was empty and the movers had my entire life on their truck?

Moving day! I rushed to get all the last-minute stuff packed. In a few minutes the movers would be here. As I sat on my upstairs prayer closet, waiting, tears that had been bottled up inside surfaced into a steady stream. The more I looked around the house, the more I cried. I was about to lose it when the movers arrived. As they backed into the driveway, I couldn't contain myself any longer; I went into the bathroom and wept. "Please Lord, help me through this day."

The movers worked quietly, in almost a rhythmical manner. The rooms were emptying fast. Douglas suggested I go to town, as there was no need for me to be there any longer. My emotions went into overdrive, and I suddenly found all kinds of last-minute things to do. Finally I let my emotions take control. I rushed into Douglas' arms and wept. He held me for a few minutes, then pushed me away. I thought, "Oh sure, he's not even here for me in this!" As I glanced at him, I could see why. He was fighting back tears of his own. At that moment I realized that his life was going to change also. He had memories here too.

As I drove out of the yard, I took one last glance. I could picture Douglas and me planting the second row of pine trees. They had grown from eight-inch seedlings into strong, sturdy fifteen-foot giants. They grew up along with the kids. Now I had to say good-bye.

My truck was packed to the roof with clothes, bedding, bags filled with odds and ends, and of course the coffee pot, coffee and cups. When I arrived at our new home, I couldn't get out of the truck. I was too overwhelmed! I was frozen in my seat. I prayed, "Well Lord, here I am at the beginning of a new journey. Use me where you need me. I will be obedient."

The rest of the day passed quickly. We managed to unpack most of the boxes. It almost looked like home, but it felt strange not to have a second floor on the house. As soon as I got the beds made, we would crawl in; it had been a long, emotional day.

I had purchased some new lamps for the bedroom, and was looking for them all day. I wanted them set up for bedtime, but they were nowhere to be found. I was very frustrated! I remembered putting the bag that they were in on the steps in the garage. Douglas would pack them into my truck for me. I remembered that he had thrown some boxes into the burning barrel before I left, and lit it. I was positive that he had burnt up my new lamps. I was not happy! Douglas said he didn't burn them! I said he must have, or they'd be here! Our fuses were fairly short, and a small explosion occured. He assured me that there were more lamps in the store, all I had to do was go buy them. I retorted, "That's not the point. I had lamps, now they are gone. Why on earth wouldn't you look in the boxes before you threw them in the fire?"

I had thrown the bedding in the closet so it would be out of the way. As I pulled the bedding from the closet, I spotted a large box. There they were! My two, beautiful brass lamps, unopened, unscorched! Have you ever eaten crow? It doesn't taste very good! My apology was accepted, but not without, "I told you I never touched your lamps!"

Brooks Anthony: eight pounds, nine ounces. Our beautiful little blue-eyed, red-haired grandson. I tearfully praised the Lord for making such a perfect little boy. I prayed that he would grow up to be sensitive to the Holy Spirit, and that he would be a man of God. I was grateful to God that Stephanie had a relatively short labor, and I thanked the Lord for giving us a little person to love. I had so much love to give.

It was hard to leave our newest little grandbaby, but a Florida vacation with Pete and Gail sounded wonderful too. We took in all the tourist attractions and had a terrific time exploring Orlando and area. My favorite was the Kennedy Space Centre. We walked in an exact replica of a space shuttle, and as we walked under the huge orange-colored fuel tank, I shivered as I remembered the sight of the Challenger blowing up, and I remembered exactly where I was.

In the IMAX Theatre, we watched the tremendous flame as the shuttle blasted off; the noise was deafening. Then we were aboard - climbing, climbing, until finally we were miles above the earth, in orbit. The silence was overwhelming. There are no words to explain the beauty of the earth from the heavens. I thought, "This is what God sees!" We earthlings aren't even visible to the naked eye from outer space, yet God sees our every move. There is no other being on earth, or above the earth, that is capable of creating such a magnificent sight.

Shortly after we recuperated from our vacation, seeding time was upon us. Farming from town would be a challenge. The land we were renting was too far away to drive home every night, so we pulled our fifth-wheel travel trailer onto the empty yard and took up residence.

While Douglas was seeding I had to be available to do all sorts of tasks, so I decided it would be the perfect time to start writing. Sitting in the quietness of the trailer, or absorbing the warm sun in the truck as I waited for my next job, the vision I had twenty years earlier was finally becoming a reality. The words that I thought I didn't have flowed from my eversharp pencil faster than I could write. So the task began! God is so faithful!

I wrote until the end of June, and then I put my pencil down for July and August because it was going to be a busy summer. In July we were going camping for a week with friends, then on to Saskatoon for Mitch's wedding.

Mitch was marrying Rick's sister, Amanda. Mitch was handsome in his black tuxedo. Amanda, a blue-eyed blonde, was beautiful in her gown of white. It was a wonderful, hot, sunshiny day. The ceremony went well, the pictures went well. Our mistake was staying around to visit at the reception. Events took place, and Douglas said things to me that I wasn't able to deal with for many months. Only through God's bountiful mercy am I able to forgive.

Matthew decided to take one more year of seminary to complete his second Masters Degree of Arts in Christian Studies. The Lord blessed Matthew's faithfulness to Him for all those many years by having the congregation where he was pastor give him a scholarship for his tuition and expenses. I am trusting the Lord for a church for him to pastor when his education is complete. God has not let Matthew down in the past, and I have enough faith to believe that He will provide.

Things were out of sorts between Douglas and me since the wedding, so when he opted out of Brooks' baby dedication at the church to be in a fishing derby, I was not very happy! Stephanie took it better than I did. She felt that if she didn't expect anything from Douglas, she wouldn't be disappointed when he let her down. Finally I decided that if Douglas wanted to miss out on such a precious moment, he was the loser!

The big event of my summer was going to be the Mueller family reunion in Medicine Hat. The highlight would be going back to our family ranch in the Cypress Hills. Our roots!

The family events prior to visiting the ranch were a mixed bag of happiness and sadness. Alice came from San Diego. Sharon and Shirl were there, along with the rest of my brothers and sisters, and many of my nieces and nephews. I felt sadness because Douglas and I hadn't resolved our problem, and our relationship was strained. I felt sadness because of some unresolved issues between one of my sister's children and one of mine. But God is merciful, and I believe healing will come, because Christians are commanded to forgive each other.

The Cypress Hills of Alberta - where it all began - would be the place where all the hurts of the past would end for some of my sisters and brothers. It was a time for good and bad memories, as family members shared hurts and happy times.

After some of the bad memories were shared, Sharon said, "It's a wonder that all you guys didn't have brain damage!" We laughed, and replied, "We did." The brain damage was real, but
it wasn't physical, it was emotional. I believe, because of Mom's prayers that were left unanswered before the throne, that day we were able to face the demons of the Mueller family's past.

The beauty of the Cypress Hills hadn't changed. The luscious green pine trees stood stately, as before. The leaves of the birch trees still fluttered as the wind tickled their leaves. Where the cattle once roamed freely, there stood an oil well rig. Dad lost again; he had had the mineral rights to the ranch. Where stooks stood before, huge round bales now lay, row upon straight row. As far as the eye could see, flat pastures displayed their beautiful colors - yellow sweet clover, mauve alfalfa. It looked like we were on top of a very flat world. I wondered how such a beautiful sight could be home to such abuse.

The yard! Most of the buildings were gone, but wouldn't you know it, the old chicken coop was still there! I was almost waiting for that old turkey gobbler to chase me. The gas house where Snuggles and I rode our horses off into the sunset was gone too. The summer kitchen, where my little tea kettle whistled at prayer time was caved in. Only the wall with the cupboards was recognizable. The big house was basically intact, but the white paint had been replaced by the grey-brown rustic color of many years' neglect. When I was little the house looked so huge! Now I wondered how all of us people could have lived in such a small area. The root cellar door was off, but I was still afraid to go down there. My emotions were too overwhelming, and I had to cry. As I walked in every room in the house, the child in me thought of the happy times, the adult in me re-lived the fears. I could feel Mom's presence in the house and, at that moment, I missed her very much.

Under a pile of junk, one of my great nieces found three cutouts of girls taken from an old catalogue, and one doll cutout. They were in excellent condition, the colors had barely faded. I couldn't contain myself any longer - I cried uncontrollably, and I needed to be held. Douglas didn't come along to the ranch because he said there was nothing there for him. I was there, and I needed him. I can't honestly say which one of my sisters held me, but one of them did, until I got my emotions under control. I clung to my little cutouts like they were a part of my soul. Before I left the house, I tore a tiny piece of wallpaper off the wall in the room where the milk separator had been. As I left the old house I knew I would be able to forget all the bad things, because in my hand, and now in my photo album, were pieces of my memories. As I left the yard for probably the last time, I felt sad. Such beauty, yet such pain.

I had forgotten about the amazing rock formation that stood guard at the top of the hill before we drove down into the yard. It was the shape of an anvil, but it wasn't a solid piece of rock. It was many millions of tiny rocks that seemed to be molded and pasted together with clear colored glue. It was two or three times taller than us and wider than a couple of vehicles standing side by side. As the three generations of Muellers and their families climbed up on top and stood together arm in arm, and at the foot of the rock for pictures, I drank in the beauty, I inhaled the smell of hay, and absorbed the quiet of the countryside. I knew Mom was smiling down on us as we released the ghosts of the past.

After our visit to the ranch, it took me a while to put my life back into perspective. But with much prayer and a willingness to be obedient to the Lord, I am learning, yet again, that no matter what happens around me or what hurts are directed at me or my kids, I will not lose my peace and contentment as long as I stay in a close, intimate, relationship with Jesus. He will not leave me! He will love me, and He will do what is best for me!

Each of our three grandsons are special, but I believe that our newest grandbaby, although he was given to Stephanie and Anthony as a symbol of their love for each other, was also given as a gift to Douglas and me. Brooks has brought healing to our home. Grandpa loves to play with him - make funny faces, and funny noises, and when Brooks tries to imitate him,

Grandpa laughs so hard his body shakes. There is always a big production number to get kisses when Brooks plays hard to get. My heart bursts with love when his little arms reach up for Grandma to pick him up or cuddle him. He makes Douglas and me laugh, and he unites us in a special bond.

In my lifetime I have been defeated, and I have been victorious. I have lost some battles, but won the war. I have learned many truths, and I have learned that God's word, God's truths, are absolute!

Defeat has many faces, many masks. Sometimes we appear to be victorious, but inside the war rages on, because, "... our struggle is not against flesh and blood, but against the rulers, against the authorities, against the powers of this dark world and against the spiritual forces of evil in the heavenly realms." *Ephesians 6:12 (NIV)*

I was defeated when I took the Lord off the throne and put myself on it. My needs and my kids' needs had to be first. Victory came when I fell in love with Jesus again and inched my way into a closer relationship with Him. I gave Him His throne back.

I was defeated when my spirit was crushed and I shut down emotionally, or when I felt rejected and unloved. Victory came when I remembered Jesus and the cross. "We despised him and rejected him - a man of sorrows, acquainted with bitterest grief. We turned our backs on him and looked the other way when he went by." *Isaiah 53:3 (TLB)* And victory was mine when I understood that Jesus took the cross for me because He knew I couldn't survive the punishment I deserved. He loves me so much that He didn't want me to be destroyed.

I was defeated when I didn't admit my mistakes, and I have made many in my life. "A man who refuses to admit his mistakes can never be succesful. But if he confesses and forsakes them, he gets another chance." *Proverbs 28:13 (TLB)* Victory came when I asked Jesus to forgive me. He picked me up and gave me the courage to start over. He was beside me to support me. When I couldn't walk, He carried me. My kids and I had to suffer the consequences of my mistakes - my sins. We carry the scars, but victory over sin is ours through Jesus.

I am defeated if I say hurtful things to others, or if I let words spoken against me destroy me. Words can never be taken back. They will forever be on file in our memory banks.

I am defeated when anger turns to revenge. Revenge is sin.

I am defeated when my attitude is wrong; when I sit in the ash pile and feel sorry for myself. Poor me! When my negative thoughts rule my mind, or when I grumble and complain.

Victory is mine when I learn how to control my tongue. Put a bridle on it, so to speak. When I listen to other peoples' hurts, and I encourage rather than destroy. "Therefore encourage one other and build each other up .." *1 Thessalonians 5:11 (NIV)*

Victory is mine when I rebuke the spirit of anger and replace it with peace and contentment. "Peace I leave with you; my peace I give to you; I do not give to you as the world gives. Do not let your hearts be troubled, and do not be afraid." *John 14:27 (NIV)* And I am victorious when I give up my plans to get back at somebody that hurt me or my kids, and let God handle it. "For we know Him who said, VENGEANCE IS MINE, I WILL REPAY. And again, THE LORD WILL JUDGE HIS PEOPLE." *Hebrews 10:30 (NAS)*

Victory is mine when I talk about the positive things in my life. When I look for good in people and situations. When I work for the Lord at home or in church, even if it is a menial task. All things done for the Lord out of love is a ministry, and God will bless me for doing it.

I am defeated when I am bitter and unforgiving. Unforgiveness is sin, and sin hinders answered prayer.

Unforgiveness that turns to bitterness will poison my soul and destroy me, my marriage, my family, my friendships, and most of all my intimacy with Jesus.

Victory comes when I forgive before I am asked to forgive, or harder yet, forget it ever happened. When I forgive my husband who promised to love and honor me, but betrayed me, and caused me pain. When I forgive the child that lashed out at me, and family members who ignore me, and when I don't hold a grudge against a friend who unwisely spoke against me.

I am defeated when I am like the peacock - proud and puffed up, displaying my beautiful tail feathers. "The Lord detests all the proud of heart. Be sure of this: They will not go unpunished." *Proverbs 16:5 (NIV)* If I ask for praise, then I don't have the opportunity to be honored by others.

I am victorious when my spirit is quiet and gentle before the Lord; humble and sensitive to the Holy Spirit's leading. I don't need to blow my own horn, all I need is for the Lord to be proud of me. When my spirit is "up close and personal" with His Spirit, there is no room for pride.

I am defeated when my soul is filled with loneliness and despair, or when I feel empty inside. I am defeated when I become a victim of my heartache, or when I withdraw into my own little world of aloneness, where I can meditate on my sadness - stuck in the agony of defeat.

I am victorious when I make a choice to stop sitting around feeling sorry for myself, and go out into my world and show love and compassion to someone else who is worse off than I am. If I am drowning, I can give Jesus the life-line. He will pull me out. Instead of wanting to run away and hide from the world, I can hide in Jesus. He will breathe His spirit into me and fill me with His presence. "We are pressed on every side by troubles, but not crushed and broken.

We are perplexed because we don't know why things happen as they do, but we don't give up and quit. We are hunted down, but God never abandons us. We get knocked down, but we get up again and keep going." *2 Corinthians 4:8-9 (TLB)*

I am defeated when I am so overcome with fear that I am paralyzed. My body can be hurt or I can be killed, but if the Lord takes His hand off my life, I am finished! I fear God in the sense that if I am not living for Him, He has the power to send me to hell. But I am not afraid of Him, because He is my loving Father who wants to do good things for me. "Charm and grace are deceptive, and beauty is vain [because it is not lasting], but a woman who reverently and worshipfully fears the Lord, she shall be praised." *Proverbs 31:30 (TAB)*

I am defeated when I am rebellious, stubborn, and disobedient. When I say, "Leave me alone, I can do it by myself," or "I'm going to do it my way," I don't let the Lord do it "His way." I mess things up that the Lord has already fixed, and I make it harder for Him to fix things that are broken because I tried to fix them and did it wrong. Not only does He have to repair the damage I did, He has to start all over again on the correct plan. His plan! "For rebellion is as bad as witchcraft, and stubborness is as bad as worshipping idols" *1 Samuel 15:23 (TLB)*

I am victorious when I submit to God's plan and purpose for my life, and I say, "Yes Lord - okay Lord - I'll write the book." When I ask Him what I should do for Him today, instead of saying, "This is my day to do as I please." If I keep falling in love with Jesus, it will be easy to do what He asks, because when I love somebody I want to please them. "For God is at work within you, helping you want to obey Him, and then helping you do what He wants." *Philippians 2:13 (TLB)*

Load your weapons with God's ammunition. The war is serious, but you can win the battle with confidence, because you have Jesus as your Commander and Chief.

I will win the battle through prayer: In my prayer closet, on my face before God my Maker, I will tell Him my deepest, darkest secrets. I will make the "desires of my heart" known to Him. By name, I will ask Him to save my lost loved ones. I will talk to Him when I am sad and when I am happy. I will fast and pray when the answer seems impossible - because fasting is powerful. I will ask for wisdom in decision-making, for victory over the devil, and power to overcome hurt and anger, so that I can forgive my enemies. I will share my joys with Him, and I will pray for the needs of other Christians.

Lastly, when the answer to my prayer request doesn't come as soon as I would like it to, I won't give up. As the angel said to Daniel, "Don't be frightened, Daniel, for your request has been heard in Heaven and was answered the very first day you began to fast before the Lord and pray for understanding; that very day I was sent here to meet you. But for twenty-one days the mighty Evil Spirit who over rules the kingdom of Persia blocked my way. Then Michael, one of the top officers of the heavenly army, came to help me, so that I was able to break through these spirit rulers of Persia." *Daniel 10:12-13 (TLB)* There is an old saying, "If I don't pray for a day, I know it. If I don't pray for two days, my family knows it. If I don't pray for a week, the whole world knows it."

I win the battle with praise and worship: I will tell Jesus I love Him. I will worshipfully sing praises to Him. I will lift my hands in awe of Him, and I will worship Him while I play the organ - His gift to me. I will honor Him by reading His word, and I will glorify Him by trying to be like Him. I will honor Him by telling others how much He loves them. Praise and worship will break the bondage of doubt, and give me victory through faith in His power.

I will win the battle when I am thankful: I will thank Him for everything: my life, breath, and salvation. I will thank Him for holding me when my arms are empty. I will thank

Him for healing my broken, bleeding heart. I will recognize the blessings He has given me, and thank Him. I will thank Him for what He has planned for me. Best of all, I will thank Him for the Cross. "At all times and for everything giving thanks in the name of our Lord Jesus Christ to God the Father." *Ephesians 5:20 (TAB)* I will even be thankful for the pain of discipline. "No discipline seems pleasant at the time, but painful. Later on, however, it produces a harvest of righteousness and peace for those who have been trained by it." *Hebrews 12:11 (NIV)*

I will win the battle when I am given wisdom and discernment; when I am silent, I can become wise by listening. When I ask Him to give me insight into a situation, He gives me knowledge to gather information about the problem, study it, and find the best solution. I will be able to understand peoples' motives and actions because of what I have learned through my experiences. "If you want to know what God wants you to do, ask Him, and He will gladly tell you, for He is always ready to give a bountiful supply of wisdom to all who ask Him; He will not resent it." *James 1:5 (TLB)*

When I can't stand on my own I will lean on Him. When I can't see Him, I have to believe that He is there. When my heart is breaking, He lets me have my cry, then He lifts my head, wipes away my tears, gently puts me back on my feet, and lovingly gives me a "nudge" to carry on. I will hang on to my sanity through trusting Him. I will trust Him to walk me through the valley. I endure because I am totally and completely dependent on Him. "Consider it all joy my brethren, when you encounter various trials knowing that the testing of your faith produces endurance." *James 1:2-3 (NAS)*

If I am a Christian, the Holy Spirit lives in me. So if I repeat a lie to someone, betray a confidence, or if I cause another human being to have a heartache, because the Holy Spirit is living in me, I am grieving Him. When someone does the same to me, they are hurting not only me, but the Holy Spirit in me. "A perfect God now lives inside very imperfect human beings. And because He respects our freedom, the Spirit in effect 'subjects Himself' to your behaviour. The New Testament tells of a Spirit we can lie to, or grieve, or quench. And when we choose wrongfully, we quite literally subject God to that wrong choice." *(1)* What a horrible thing to do to such a Holy Being!

"A cheerful heart is good medicine, but a crushed spirit dries up the bones." *Proverbs 17:22 (NIV)* A spirit will dry up if it has to see Jesus' hand in everything that happens. Life happens! Just believe His hand is there. There might not be a personal spiritual message in everything. There might not be a definite sign from God, positively showing the correct direction to take. Remember, "... Christ is all, and in all." *Colossians 3:11e (NAS)* Try hard not to sin, but when it happens, ask for forgiveness, and start over. Worrying about what to do for Jesus or others will wear a spirit down. God wants us to ask Him. He will lovingly give the answer. God is in control! Believe it! Then forget about it! He can and will look after us. As Pastor Ed says, "Don't be so heavenly minded that you are no earthly good." In other words, lighten up. Christians are allowed to have fun.

How big is God? Is He big enough to tear down the walls we put up to protect our hearts from pain? Is He big enough to restore a broken friendship? Is He big enough to "wait patiently in line," while we look for fulfillment in material things? Is God big enough to turn the other cheek when we blame Him for personal tragedies? And is He big enough to forgive us, and love us, no matter what? My God is! He defeated the devil on the Cross, and He lives victoriously in Heaven.

It amazes me how many Christian men treat their wives badly, and how many men and women wear masks to cover it up. Out in public all is well, but at home they live in hell! If the relationship you are in is hurting you and your children, don't let it kill your spirit, give it to Jesus. He can and will fix it, if you let Him do it His way. Wait patiently if it takes a while, and be willing to change if He asks you to.

In a bad marriage, it is easy to say, "I can't take it anymore, I've had it, it's over, I'm 'outa' here." Don't leave! There are consequences! Being a single parent, living below the poverty line is not fun. Will divorce solve the problems or will it add to them? And what about the kids? If a re-marriage takes place, will they be hurt by being rejected by a step-parent? And where will you rate in a re-marriage? Second - fourth - tenth? You can learn to live in a bad marriage, if you remember that when bad things happen to you, "nevertheless" you can live in peace and contentment if you stay in a right relationship with Jesus.

To make a marriage happier, there are many ways to do it. Talk to your pastor, or go to a marriage counselor. Men can go to a Promise Keepers group where they will teach the right way to treat a wife and family. Join a Christian support group that deals with the same type of problems as yours. Then there is Alcoholics Anonymous and Al-Anon.

Make time for your spouse. Go out on a date, just the two of you. Say love words to each other; do something special for each other. Together, take time for the kids. Do things with them. Take them fishing or go to a movie. Don't play favorites between your children; somebody will get hurt. Don't abuse their precious bodies and spirits. You will scar them for life. Love them equally - each one is a special and unique gift from God.

Some days writing this book was emotionally overwhelming. I wept for the little girl who was raped. I grieved for her lost childhood, and I cried for the lonely, frightened girl who was afraid of the dark. I relived the agony of tragedy, and I wept when I remembered infidelity and betrayal. But I am real! Sometimes I still feel betrayed. Sometimes I still struggle with feelings of rejection. Sometimes I still struggle with unforgiveness. Sometimes I still get angry when an injustice is not avenged, especially when it affects my kids. Sometimes I still act like the mother bear who will do anything to protect her cubs. But I will be victorious! I will overcome! I will keep fighting for peace and contentment. I live by faith. I believe things will change, and I will be happy until they do. As Pastor Shane, our Minister of Christian Education said, "Without a battle, there can be no victory."

I want to finish with the final scene of a Billy Graham movie that I saw many years ago. Picture it! A huge, thriving twentieth-century city, complete with skyscrapers, businesses, malls, and homes. There are thousands of cars on the freeways, hurrying to get home. People are standing in line to board buses or trains! People are everywhere! Hustle and bustle! Horns are honking! People are laughing and talking, kids are playing!

To the left of the city, high on a hill. There - there was Jesus, hanging on a cross. His head was bent forward, but I knew He was still alive because every once in a while, I saw His lips move. He was battered and bruised, and He was bleeding. He wasn't wearing the latest fashions, and Nike runners. His feet and hands were adorned with nails and blood. His back was bare and bleeding from being whipped. Drops of blood dripped from under the "latest head apparel" - a crown of thorns!

As I looked at Him, all the chaos and clamour of the city was drowned out by the deafening silence of Jesus suffering for me. He took my pain, my sin, so that I can live. He loves me that much!

The movie ended there, but the story didn't end when He died. That day - He won the war for me when He took the keys to death and hell, and rose victoriously to defeat sin. Thank you, Jesus: You saved my life!

NOTES

Chapter 5 - I Hear You Lord:

1. Carolyn Huffman, <u>Bloom Where You Are</u>. (Santa Ana, California: Vision House
    Publishers, 1977). p. 12-13

Chapter 8 - Sink or Swim?

1. Carolyn Huffman, <u>Bloom Where You Are</u>. (Santa Ana, California: Vision House
    Publishers, 1977). p. 24

2. David A Seamands, <u>Healing for Damaged Emotions</u>. (Wheaton, Illinois: Victor Books,
    A division of SP Publications, Inc., 1981). p. 99

Chapter 9 - "Yet Shall I Trust In Him"

1. David A. Seamands, <u>Healing for Damaged Emotions</u>. (Wheaton, Illinois: Victor Books,
    A division of SP Publications, Inc., 1981). p. 12

2. Cynthia Heald, <u>Becoming a Woman of Excellence</u>. (Colorado Springs, Colorado:
    NAVPRESS, A Ministry of the Navigators, 1992). p. 21

Chapter 10 - Out of the Ashes:

1. Philip Yancey, <u>Disappointment With God</u>. (Grand Rapids, Michigan: Zondervan Publishing
    House, A Division of Harper Collins, 1988). p. 240

2. Marion Bond West, <u>The Nevertheless Principle</u>. (Old Tappan, New Jersey: Chosen Books,
    Fleming H. Revell Company, 1986). p. 11

3. Ibid., p. 17

4. Ibid., p. 63

Chapter 11 - Alone With God:

1. Marion Bond West, <u>The Nevertheless Principle</u>. (Old Tappan, New Jersey: Chosen Books,
    Fleming H. Revell Company, 1986). p. 119

2. David A. Seamands, <u>Healing for Damaged Emotions</u>. (Wheaton, Illinois: Victor Books,
    A Division of SP Publications, Inc., 1981). p. 139

3. Gilliland Glaphré, <u>Talking With God. A Womans Workshop on Prayer</u>. (Grand Rapids,
    Michigan: Zondervan Publishing House, Lamplighter Books, 1985). p. 64-65

Chapter 12 - Fill Up With Jesus:

1. Philip Yancey, <u>Disappointment With God</u>. [Grand Rapids, Michigan: Zondervan Publishing
House, A Division of Harper Collins, 1988). p. 141

The Living Bible, Paraphrased, [Wheaton, Illinois: Tyndale House Publishers, 1971].

New International Version Bible, [Grand Rapids, Michigan: Zondervan Publishing
House, 1984].

New American Standard Bible, Reference Edition, [Chicago, Illinois: Moody Press, 1984].

The Amplified Bible, [Grand Rapids, Michigan: The Zondervan Corporation and the
Lockman Foundation, 1987].